Between
Good
& Evil

Between Good & Evil

Curse of the Windsor Witch's Daughter

By Beth M. Caruso

Between Good & Evil: Curse of the Windsor Witch's Daughter

Cover Art by Sue Tait Porcaro
https://susantaitporcaro.com

Book Cover Design & Typography by Patrick Schreiber

Editor: Christina Carmon

By Beth M Caruso

Published by Lady Slipper Press, Windsor, Connecticut

ISBN 13: 978-1-7333738-3-8

Library of Congress Control Number: 2023915106

First Edition Date: March, 2024

To Joe Caruso, Will Endres, Bill Harris, Lori Truly, and Mary Hotaling, those influential ones lost to us on Earth while writing and publishing one of the three books in the Connecticut Witch Trials Trilogy. And to those ancestors, blood or adopted, who held me close, protected me, guided me, and divulged their secrets, wrapping me in a huge warm hug, I thank you for always being there from the depths of my existence, the place where we are ONE.

Prologue:

Windsor, Connecticut, 1642: The Three Ravens

Female figures hunched over the little plot of vegetables and corn. Muted-colored skirts caressed the Earth's floor as the hands of mothers and their little daughters plucked out weeds intent on invading their modest agricultural experiment. The three sisters of corn, beans, and squash had grown in harmony for centuries with the encouragement of Native women in the Connecticut River Valley. The English women wanted to emulate them in the unseen and remote little garden space far from the disapproving glances and comments of most men in their community.

At the confluence of a stream and the Rivulet, the women relied on a small Native field that had been abandoned to fulfill their undertaking. Indulging his sister Rhody, and his cousin Alice, John Tinker and his servants had burned the space of all brush and had readied it for them in the spring.

Rhody and her daughters, Hannah and Anna, along with Alice and her daughter, Alissa, carefully tended their hidden crop almost daily. But Rhody and Alice's farming trial in a location surrounded by woods and water was not only that; it was an excuse to be in their retreat away from the Puritan rules and regulations not known in their childhoods — a place where remembering the carefree days of their youth happened and the joy of old passions never died.

Alissa was the youngest of the girls. Her chubby toddler hands worked like oven mitts as she tried clumsily to mimic her older cousins whose long slender fingers pulled and tugged deftly to clear the ground of spreading weeds.

"Look Mama" she said, rising as she opened her palm revealing more dirt than unwanted plants. Alice, her mother, hugged her tightly and kissed her on the forehead.

"You're doing so well, my love! Soon you'll be as fast as your cousins!" she beamed, taking in every detail of her precious daughter's round face. The others smiled in unison.

They continued to work throughout the morning as Rhody hummed English tunes from the old country. Rhody was musically gifted and discovered those talents as a child in New Windsor, England. She'd learned to play the lute and had enjoyed harmonizing and playing songs with her sisters. In the days of her youth, her family appreciated the beauty of music and embraced song and dance. But after becoming a widow and following her sisters' husbands' embrace of the godly people in the colonies, she and her girls had been forced to leave her finely crafted musical instruments and cherished ballads behind. However, one can only fight against their true nature for so long. Soon she and her cousin, Alice, escaped in as many ways they could from the suffocating, dull routine of their imposed religiosity.

"Mommy, sing about the three ravens for us," begged Hannah.

"Ah, The Three Ravens!" Rhody laughed.

"'Tis a favorite among these girls, is it not?" Alice asked in a chuckle.

Nearly every day, Rhody's girls asked their mother to sing the ballad of the valiant knight and his loyal hawks and hounds. They knew the refrain by heart and taught little Alissa too.

Rhody and Alice straightened their bodies, no longer bending over the fields. While Alice began to sway with Alissa in tow, Rhody enchanted them with her beautiful voice.

> *"There were three ravens sat on a tree."*

> *"Down a down hey down hey down."* Everyone joined in until Rhody continued the verse.

> *"They were as black as they might be,*
> *With a down.*
> *Then one of them said to his mate:*
> *Where shall we our breakfast take?"*

"With a down derry derry derry down down." The girls loved their part singing the gibberish words.

"Down in yonder greenfield."

"Down a down hey down hey down." The girls belted out the nonsense words in their hidden garden next to the river. Alice grabbed their hands to form a dancing circle and Alissa giggled with glee.

"There lies a knight slain under his shield;
    With a down.
    His hounds they lie down at his feet,
    So well they do their master keep."

"With a down derry derry derry down down." They danced slowly around the circle, feeling free and joyful.

"His hawks they fly so eagerly,
    Down a down hey down hey down.
    There is no fowl dare him come nigh
    With a down."

"But down there comes a fallow doe,
    As great with young as she might go."

"With a down derry derry derry down down."

"She lifted up his bloody head,
    Down a down hey down, hey down.
    And kissed his wounds that were so red.
    With a down.
    She got him up upon her back
    And carried him to an earthen lake."

"With a down derry derry derry down down."

"She buried him before the prime,
    Down a down hey down hey down.
    She was dead herself ere evensong time.
    With a down.
    Now God send to every gentleman.

Such hounds, such hawks and such a loved one,"

"*With a down, derry derry derry down down,*" everyone sang the refrain together.

The emotional melody lingered in the air peacefully until suddenly, a clap of thunder in the distance ended their soulful reverie and diverted their attention to the moody weather. Crooking her head and noticing the dark clouds moving in swiftly from the west, Alice motioned to the others to gather their belongings and prepare to leave. The sun was still shining, but blue skies were beginning to acquiesce to the bleakness filling the horizon in heavy gray hues.

Alice clasped little Alissa's hand tightly. Rhody's girls were in the lead still humming the Three Ravens tune and singing the silly words of the refrain on the path toward home. Alissa kept singing too even as darkness encircled them and the first raindrops fell. Once they were close to the village, Rhody called for their attention.

"Hush. You mustn't now," Rhody commanded, bringing a finger to her lips.

"Aye, Mama," It was not lost on the girls as to why they must listen to her closely and do what she said.

The light drizzle changed to a steady rain the rest of the day and the entirety of the next night. The vines of beans grew around the stalks of corn and the squash took over the spaces on the ground between the small earthen hills. The three sisters soaked in the rain and grew as they had for centuries with the right love and care.

As for Alice and Rhody, they longed to bring their girls into the sweet sunshine and sing again in the garden overlooking the river with the laughing waters below, framed by the fragrant wildflower-filled banks.

Chapter 1

Windsor, Connecticut, October, 1651: Militia Day

I remembered being happy as a child in a distant past; the sun shining on me over a clear blue sky. Then, it all went black in an instant — like someone fainting in darkness, falling until they hit the cold, hard ground. From that moment, I was perplexed, a fragment of my former self, unable to distinguish between what had really happened when my mother was hanged to death as a witch and the hellish nightmares of my own creation.

In my younger years, I made peace with having little recollection about the majority of my early childhood. Only faint yet cheerful memories of my mother and friends on Backer Row lingered. They were nothing more than small rays of light escaping from brooding clouds reflecting a life before the "dark time" as my Aunt Rhody called it — a time when death, loss and suspicion permeated the core of our lives.

I blocked my own pain unknowingly. Aunt Rhody created a soft, thick fabric around that encasement of the past, a cushioning so the darkness would seldom enter into my life or her own. She looked forward in life and insulated me from anyone or anything that might rekindle the spark of memory. Aunt Rhody was my fierce protectress and with her my life was busy and full. In her household, I remained immersed in chores and family activities; my thoughts occupied mostly with the present and not the past.

On the rare occasion I was curious and wanted to remember something more about my mother, Alice, Aunt Rhody smiled kindly and responded with a simple sweet answer and then moved on quickly to another conversation. The unsaid message was that it was better to remember tiny moments fondly rather than to veer toward what was unspeakable and hellish. We kept to ourselves on Backer Row, except for the few town activities that pulled us away.

Indeed, Aunt Rhody must have feared that if we dwelled on the pain of the past, the guilt and bitterness it might invoke would destroy us both. Aunt Rhody's approach was also practical for she was not completely safe from harm or suspicion caused by her association with my mother. It was better for both of us to survive by forgetting. Yet, the act of forgetting my mother, pushing her below the surface, could never be permanent. Her life force was in me and my connection to her would only allow it for the first years I lived with Aunt Rhody — until that fateful, tragic day on the green.

October 3, 1651, was a festive day, a militia day, when the men in town practiced their military drills. Aunt Rhody tidied up our cottage and fussed that her boys, John and Thomas, wore their best. She sat me down to comb my long hair until it shined and smoothed her own dark hair in her cap until it looked perfect. She'd done her girls' hair on multiple occasions, but today it was just me.

"In old England this wasn't the sort of day that I'd be excited about," said Aunt Rhody, now in her finest yet simple clothes, a matching salmon-colored skirt and waistcoat. "But being forbidden to celebrate Christmas or any other holiday that has any merriment associated with it, I'll make good cheer for whatever is allowed."

I knew the real reason Aunt Rhody was happy. She was getting to see her love, Walter Hoyt, practicing his manly obligations on the green. Her husband John Taylor was presumed dead. He'd been on that fateful ship that left from New Haven en route to England in January of 1646 which had been lost at sea. She was obligated to wait seven years before she could marry another since there was no absolute proof of her husband's death. Vulnerable as a single mother, the former neighbor of "the witch", she waited anxiously for marriage to Walter, the simple farmer to whom she had given her heart.

"Is that the truth, Aunt Rhody? Is it the militia or a certain man in the militia that makes the day worth celebrating?" I teased, knowing full well that she would understand my meaning.

Walter was our neighbor on Backer Row and had been very helpful to us all after John Taylor passed away. He had also bought my father John Young's property, my old home, immediately next door. Walter had also lost his spouse and was the sole caretaker for his children. A natural attraction had developed betwixt Rhody and Walter as a result. But they could only be friendly and discrete about their increasing pull toward each other because of Rhody's required mourning period.

She placed bread, cheese and a pie in a woven basket lined with linen cloth to take with us to the town green.

"Ah, ye know me too well my dear Alissa," she said, her eyes laughingly penetrating my own. "Come now, let's not miss any of the activities." She hurried about, ushering the boys and I toward the door.

Aunt Rhody had suffered tremendous loss even without the tragedy of my mother weighing upon her. Two dead husbands and both her daughters deceased and gone to the afterlife — Anna before the dark family time, and Hannah the year after. It pleased me to see her joyous again.

The day was glorious. Red maples turned to crimson, berries of a deep red-blood hue adorned shrubbery lining the woods and the wind gently escorted dancing leaves downward to the ground. Fallow fields were empty except for wandering flocks of birds and some haystacks. The sky was bright and blue, hardly an ominous sign in the sky except for a strange, sinister cloud that I likened to the Devil's profile. How ridiculous that I should think of such a thing on a fine day, I chastised myself.

Aunt Rhody and I followed her boys, giddy with excitement, up the hill of the simple dirt road to the green and the sound of a beating drum. Aunt Rhody also had Walter's children in tow. She had promised to watch them while Walter did his military exercises on the green. The beat of the drum became louder, and the cadence increased to signal the time was near. Most of the Windsor community was out in their best vestments to cheer on the militia practicing their drills and showing off their military prowess on the green on the opposite side of the meeting house.

The women from each household of Windsor greeted each other warmly as they added their contribution of food to share: sweets and savories such as puddings and fruit and minced meat pies. We put our quince pie on a table next to the meeting house in line with other baking pie tins, their contents wafting aromas of cinnamon, rosemary and sage. The local tavern carried barrels of beer to the spot generously shaded by a towering chestnut — one barrel of mild beer for children and women and stronger ones for the men to quench their thirst and give them strength for their military exercises.

We found a place to watch the drills under the canopy of a great elm tree whose branches swayed slowly with the influence of a whimsical breeze. Onlookers cheered and gossiped as the men called out their formations and drums intensified the atmosphere. Young women looking on and young men in formation hoped to be noticed by a possible love interest and match from across the green. Rhody admired Walter there, handsome and commanding, a sturdy farmer who was transparent and frank in all his dealings. It would be hard for her to wait another two years before she was free to marry again. Mother once said absence in love always made the heart yearn more and fortified a relationship when it was finally allowed to come to full flower. I hoped that was true for my dear aunt.

As we sat peacefully on our blanket observing the green, we were jolted when an unexpected single shot fired into the air. Aunt Rhody and I looked first at each other and then at the green. She grabbed my arm in alarm, panicking as a man tumbled to the ground near Walter.

"Father! Where is he?" screamed Walter's children before the gun smoke had cleared.

Rhody grabbed them close to her skirt and squinted to scan the green where the perfect formation devolved quickly into chaos.

"Your father stands. He does not look hurt. Do not fret my dears. We shall see. Give him time there. He must help the other men because someone else is injured."

She tried to maintain her composure, but her voice was shaky, cracking towards the end. Walter had been so close to the bullet that the man who fell, touched Walter's boots on his way to the Earth. My heart raced so much that it seemed as if it would burst out of my chest.

At first there was panic among the militia members, unsure of where the gunfire came from. Seconds later, it was confirmed that the body that had collapsed so suddenly was that of fifty-eight-year-old Henry Stiles. He'd slumped over and was bleeding profusely from his belly. His eyes were fixed wide open and his face was as pale as a phantom. His expression was one of shock as he grasped his stomach trying to shield himself from what had already happened. I see the dark image now as if the clock of time had stopped and the world was frozen for a few seconds. I can also see that one dark cloud that reminded me of the Devil's profile.

In a quick moment, the joy of being able to celebrate something, anything at all, in a community that allowed little merriment, vanished into confusion and fear and an overbearing heaviness covered us all. Whispers about Satan snaked through the crowd.

Several of Goodman Stiles' fellow militia members came to his aid. But a good portion of the crowd also ran toward him until the men in charge had to shout, "Stay back!"

"God bless, Goodman Stiles! May the Lord help him now in his time of need," cried Aunt Rhody, still trying to shield Walter's children. "Alissa don't look. You must not look." She managed to hold my hand tightly and continued to stare at Walter so that she could be certain he was not also injured.

Alas, I couldn't stop looking. The incident was already forged in my head, and I longed to know what was going to happen next. It absorbed me as it did everyone else who could not look away, fear implanted on our faces.

Thomas Allyn, the nineteen-year-old accidental perpetrator looked dazed, abandoned, and confused. Perhaps, he'd had a few too many mugs of beer to bolster his strength before the drill. But maybe, he'd wanted to impress the young woman of his desires. Just seconds earlier, he'd been grinning and paying amorous attention to Abigail Warham, the daughter of Windsor's minister. Possibly, her waving gesture had thrown the young man into heart-spinning elation, and he'd become cocky, wanting to show off his military skills even more. Amid his courtship display, he mishandled his firearm which fatefully went off and injured the older bachelor, Henry Stiles.

Several men surrounded Henry's body and carried him to the home of Goodman Filer, the closest one on the green to the killing. Poor Henry was covered in blood but was still alive, breathing only shallowly and moaning in pain when they transported him there. The minister, John Warham, also joined the men inside. I assumed it was to pray for Henry Stiles' soul. We waited nervously on the edge of the green with others in anticipation of his death. Goodman Stiles was destroyed by the stray bullet so quickly that the master of the house opened his door and reported him dead mere minutes later.

"Henry Stiles, respected founder of our settlement, carpenter and farmer, is dead. He lost a lot of blood from his injury and there is nothing anyone could do."

Reverend Warham was at Goodman Filer's side and added his assessment. "It is the will of God," he said. His expression was sullen as he pronounced every syllable of every word precisely and slowly to convey the full impact of the tragedy.

The gory trail of blood from the green to the residence left testament to the seriousness and the finality of what took place. People whispered as they looked at the only evidence left on the ground, still shocked by what had happened.

"Go home everyone. Pray for the soul of Henry Stiles. We will meet in the meeting house tomorrow at noon and then walk to the burying ground with his body. Search your souls for your own sins as you pray for him and ponder why Satan had his influence today." He shook his head and then ushered his family, including a distraught Abigail, back to their home for what I imagined was a contemplation of good and evil and prolonged Bible readings to make sense of Windsor's tragic day. Reverend Warham seemed like he had already come to the conclusion that Satan was involved. Did he mean that God had let the Devil have his way to punish us for our sins?

As people started to slowly drift from the green in a fog of confusion, I called for Aunt Rhody's attention.

"Aunt Rhody, there on the other side of the green," I whispered.

She looked up to see Mathew Allyn wringing his hands, walking toward his son who stood alone. The father of Thomas Allyn was one of the wealthiest and haughtiest men in town.

She looked at me knowingly, an unspoken warning.

"I wonder how he'll handle this situation," she grimaced, fully aware that the Allyn family got their way by whatever means necessary, usually through court cases that they could afford to lose but their victims could not.

"Best ye keep your eyes down, Alissa. Hide yourself from his possible glare. Do not give the horrid man any ideas," she commanded.

Aunt Rhody had advised me numerous times to stay as far away from him as possible. My cousins, the Tinkers, didn't tell me why but were certain that he had influenced my mother's witchcraft accusation. Accordingly, I disappeared, made myself small, or better yet, silent when he was nearby, careful not to attract any unwanted attention.

But Mr. Allyn was far too absorbed in what his son had just done that day to pay attention to me or anyone else. He paced and he pointed, obviously upset by the misfortune and blame that would be placed at the feet of his son.

Even Aunt Rhody had a hard time following her own advice and had to bear witness as Matthew Allyn pulled his son Thomas to the far side of the green and started yelling at him. Their words weren't perceptible among the mumbling and movement of Windsor's town folk, but clearly Thomas could only stare blankly back at the spot where the tragedy had just taken place. Thomas' brother John, also in the militia joined them. Soon the constable approached the small group. I couldn't hear what they said but he was gesturing for Thomas to go with him. They soon disappeared from view.

"Come Alissa. Come boys. Elizabeth and John, you too. There is no need to wait for your father. He's still in the house with the other men attending to Henry Stiles' body. He will be busy for a little while longer," Aunt Rhody said as she rounded them up and clasped their hands tightly.

"We must go and make our somber reflections of what happened here today. I dread what will happen next," she said, clearly shaken.

That night two images came to my thoughts and haunted me. The first was dark moving water, foam on its edge. It conveyed a deep sadness and the eerie echo of my mother calling for me as she cried. Then, an image of my old neighbor and cousin Pricilla. She'd perished during the dark family time with almost all of her siblings and all I could see was her face frozen in shock, too afraid to even scream. I was terrified and wished for the images to never return.

Chapter 2

Windsor, Connecticut, 1651: A Funeral & A Charge

Reverend Warham, pursing his lips into a perpetual grimace, looked haggard. I sensed that his uprightness hid the curtain of struggle deep within his soul. He stretched his aging hand toward the crowd that had gathered outside after his sermon and bade them to follow him into the burying ground. The air was already cool but the soil not yet frozen. Several men lowered the simple wooden box that held Henry Stiles' body into the freshly dug grave.

The atmosphere was silent and morose as the whole town paid their last respects to Henry Stiles. An underlying and unspoken current was terror at the idea that the Devil had slithered his way past the faithful of Windsor to torment the populace again. No one had forgotten the witch scare of 1647, just four years before. He had to have slipped in under an innocent cover of something or someone seemingly simple.

"The Devil is capable of fooling people, but God will always shed light. There will be more to uncover," the minister warned as we Windsor folk nodded with trepidation on our benches in the meeting house.

Thomas Allyn was not placed under arrest. His well-to-do father had assured the magistrates that his son would appear in court at the next special session to answer for Henry's death. Instead, Thomas Allyn was in the procession to the burying ground surrounded by his brothers and father. They looked aloof and untouched in an obvious attempt to avoid eye contact with others in town. If they pretended to be separated from Henry's death while making their obligatory attendance at the burial, perhaps Thomas could have avoided the deep indelible feeling of responsibility. But for Thomas, the moments must have been surreal, suspended in that one awful sliver of time when a gunshot forced Henry's life into the dark abyss. Not knowing what personal consequences would follow, I imagined his dreams for a relationship with the minster's daughter, Abigail, were fully extinguished too.

The minutes passed slowly and purposely as the congregation lined up to pay their last respects to Henry Stiles' soul. Reverend Warham stood on the other side of the crowd as the mass huddled forward near Henry's grave. Confusion on their faces bore witness to a life cut short by inexplicable violence.

The minister thundered into the silent throng, "Here we lye to rest our dear brother Henry Stiles departed from this life in a way that brings us all unimaginable sorrow. While we grieve and beg for answers from our Lord, we know that he has alerted us to our own evil ways through Henry's tragic death. We must be mindful to be kinder and more generous to each other, to live as He hath demanded us to do. The Dark One will not have his way in the end! We rebuke Satan and all his evil deeds. And we ask the Lord to have mercy on Henry's soul." With his last pronouncement he knelt to the ground, grabbed a fistful of dirt and threw it over Henry's coffin. The finality of Henry's life made clearer with each passing community member throwing their own handful of dirt over his coffin.

The gravity of the situation was etched on Reverend Warham's face and he sighed as he walked away. Was he thinking of all the lost souls he had yet to save? Why else would God agree to such a tragedy? His sermons gave testament to his reasoning for weeks afterward.

The dread of a future discovery of another possible witch was palpable and I could not be comfortable in my own skin. It was unsettling to see Aunt Rhody and Walter send each other concerned glances and then rest their gazes on me. I knew they were afraid for me, the daughter of a convicted witch just coming into her own womanhood — the perfect target for blame if something else went wrong. But I tried to stay calm with all my might. The town administrators and leaders still had to do their diligent inquiries and most of our neighbors thought that Thomas Allyn would be judged in a jury trial. I hoped it ended there.

That night I was anxious to sink into my stuffed feather mattress and hide under my coverlet and wool blanket as I tried to sleep. I couldn't stop thinking of my mother or the whereabouts of her soul. I was tormented to imagine her in the pits of hellfire, suffering for the bewitchments I had been told that she crafted for Satan's pleasure. But that image made no sense. It never matched the loving mother I knew to exist. I had to stop thinking about it before it drove me mad. Eventually, the grace of slumber enfolded me and I saw my mother again. She was not in the depths of hellfire but in a place where she was almost lifeless, shocked and alone, a type of void where nothing happened and never would. It was a relief to see her salvaged from the flames of eternal damnation, but her loneliness left me with impenetrable sadness and unexplainable guilt. It covered my waking hours like a heavy wet wool blanket and intensified after Henry's death.

Were it not for the soothing presence of Aunt Rhody and her clear direction to the daily tasks at hand, I'm not sure how I would have muddled through on my own. As long as I could keep moving forward with each chore, going through the list with focus in the safe space of her home, I hoped that eventually the heaviness would pass. Rhody made a point to sing the old songs of England from her childhood "before life was so strict and so severe," she explained. One about three ravens helped to calm me the most. Echoes of the refrain "Down a down, derry, derry, derry, down, down" still float into my thoughts of those times.

Depending on the season, Aunt Rhody brought in bouquets of flowers, branches of pine and winter berries or even bunches of colorful leaves to make our little home even sweeter. And if we had time, she'd make sure to cheer me up with the shared cooking of our favorite puddings, pie, or bread. Anything to make up for the guilt she also felt at not being able to defend my mother. But it wasn't just guilt as the reason she did so many kind things for me. She loved me too and I knew she wanted me to have a better life.

We continued on past Henry Stiles' death by embracing daily life until solid news of a trial broke out in December of 1651. The Windsor community learned that the court in Hartford had appointed a jury to do a grand inquest into Henry's murder. Rhody and I didn't go to the trial, but we did read the jury findings that were posted on the meeting house door.

"This jury finds that the piece that was in the hands of Thomas Allyn was the cause of death. Furthermore, we find that thou Thomas Allyn did suddenly, negligently, carelessly cock thy piece, and carry the piece just behind thy neighbor, to the great dishonor of God, breach of peace, and loss of a member of this commonwealth."

According to the announcement, Thomas Allyn freely admitted to causing the death of Henry Stiles by "sinful neglect and careless carriage of his piece". The magistrates called the crime "homicide by misadventure." The jury demanded that Thomas pay a hefty fee of twenty pounds and his father, Matthew Allyn, had to submit a bond to ensure his son's intention for reformed behavior. Thomas was not allowed to carry a weapon for the length of a year.

The whole issue seemed to be resolved in a way that emphasized Thomas Allyn's guilt by charging him with the accidental murder of Henry Stiles rather than preoccupation with occult forces of the supernatural. We all breathed a sigh of relief for a time, but I wondered how many realized that the trauma and crime of Henry's death had not been neatly put to bed. Too many rumors of Satan having his way swirled about. How long could they be ignored?

I became aware of the more complicated outcomes that most people expected when discussing the Allyn family later that week. Rhody and Walter met at the fence between their properties. Walter stood firmly in his leather boots on the property my father, John Young, had sold him before he left town. After he'd taken over my parents' old house, he fixed the busted-in door and revived my mother's garden, all while he waited for his beloved with the patience of a man in love.

"A poor family's child would have already been in jail for the same crime," stated Walter as a matter of fact. He'd come over to see Rhody and let her know about the latest news after the trial. Leaning against a fence post, he stayed on his side of the fence almost as a mere formality of helpful neighborliness and the obligated separateness he and Rhody had to continue to endure.

The increased spark in his gentle blue eyes as he spoke to Rhody was markedly stronger under her delighted gaze. She looked at him longingly. Still more time to wait. Their courtship could not officially begin until another two years had passed. Seven years to wait in total to make sure her previous husband was in all probability dead.

She'd loved her previous husband John Taylor with a full heart. She told me that at first, the long nights getting used to living without him seemed endless. If not for her family and their support, it would have seemed impossible to go on. But as any mother with children knows, she had to move on, for their sakes. Deep in her heart she knew John Taylor had perished at the bottom of the cold sea. She'd confided as much in me. It was no comfort to her that the villagers thought they saw the phantom of his ship on the shores of New Haven one stormy night the following summer.

Answering Walter, Rhody walked close to him touching the same fence post.

"Indeed Walter. Mr. Allyn controls the purses and therefore the power in this town. He won't stand for this even though his son received the lightest sentence possible for taking another man's life. The courts may do what they will to keep the illusion of justice, but I personally know too well what Mr. Allyn is capable of. Any smear against his child will unleash a venom in the man that few can fully comprehend. And any tarnish to his or his family's reputation he will rub away by any means available until he and his family members shine at the top of the heap of humanity like shiny coins which he holds over everyone else like threats," she stated, looking wearily toward the house. At that moment, she saw me in the yard.

"Alissa, please leave us alone to talk of serious matters," she commanded, gesturing for me to go inside. "The boys may need your help with their chores."

Normally, she did not care if I was privy to her insights or her gossip so I knew it was about Mr. Allyn's connection to my family, the horrible things he had done to my own mother, and Rhody's unstated fear that he could go after me as the daughter of a condemned witch. I vaguely floated through life knowing there was an underlying story, one that would rattle me, perhaps fill me with fear. I remembered very little from that time period in my life and found comfort in my ignorance of it. I dutifully followed her direction, went inside, checked on her boys and tried to busy myself with a little spinning and some darning to guide my thoughts elsewhere.

"I suppose time will be the judge of Matthew Allyn's intentions for his son's future," I said aloud to my surprise as I fed the spinning wheel. The outcome weighed on me. Would the wealthy merchant really shift the blame for his son's behavior? How would that even be possible? And who would be the target of his maliciousness?

Chapter 3

Windsor, Connecticut, 1652-54: Lydia Gilbert

"Mind your tongue, Lydia Gilbert. Wait for your turn with modesty," the miller scowled.

Lydia was indignant that the miller had placed several "important men" ahead of her and her husband in the queue. He was taking names and lining up the recent harvests that were to be ground in Reverend Warham's mill.

"Please Lydia, let the old coots do as they will. They've already got a target on both of us. We've invested too much in the Stiles property as is. We'll lose everything if they chase us out of town now," whispered Thomas Gilbert Jr., furrowing his bushy brows.

Aunt Rhody and I were right behind them in the line. I tried to avert my eyes so they wouldn't feel that I was watching them. Rhody did the same and tried to engage me in simple conversation. We had already heard the rumors that the Gilberts were starting to regret settling in Windsor. It was a tight community, a God-fearing community, and if one didn't fit in from the beginning, they probably never would. Honestly, Lydia's chances of being accepted into Windsor were nil with her penchant for mischief and her and her husband's reputations preceding them to Windsor. The fine piece of land they procured could never substitute for an embrace into the fold of their new town — something they would never receive.

Lydia glared at her husband sourly against the backdrop of the continuously turning grinding stones. Sacks of oats and corn lined up to be crushed next. Lydia did her best to maintain her composure, but her anger was palpable and could have replaced the energy of the flowing water moving the grinding stones.

"Alissa, I've been told the harvests this year are even more bountiful than the previous year. God is bestowing His goodness upon us." I noticed Aunt Rhody feigning increased piousness when powerful men were near us. I think it was her way of protecting me and letting them know that I was being raised as a godly woman, the taint of being the daughter of a witch no l onger noticeable.

Lydia turned and displayed a deep knowing smile as if to say, "I understand you. You don't fool me in the least. Aye, I'm a former convict, but you're the daughter of a witch no matter how you or your kin try to hide it,". But she never said it, and in all honesty, it might have only been my imagination thinking that her coy expression conveyed such an uncharitable sentiment.

In any case, it was uncomfortable with her peering deep into my soul with that mischievous grin, almost a smirk. Lydia was young and brash. She usually spoke her mind and not just at the mill, much to the chagrin of her husband who wanted to start anew in Windsor. It was common knowledge that she and her husband Thomas and been sent to the House of Corrections for several months after stealing from a prominent man in Hartford. Also serving with them was George Gibbs and James Hallett. People also knew that she was a part of the Bliss family of Hartford, the stepdaughter of Margaret Bliss whose husband Thomas had moved them to Hartford from Braintree. Once widowed, Margaret moved her family to Springfield. Lydia no longer had a father to protect her should she get into trouble once more.

Lydia and Thomas had married after serving their term in the House of Corrections and settled in Windsor after buying the property of Francis Stiles at a bargain price. Francis' brother Henry Stiles had once lived across the lane south of the ferry road. But in his aging years and now alone, he needed the help of a hard-working woman for his domestic needs. It was because of that situation that he became a boarder of the Gilberts. Thomas

Gilbert promised Francis that he and his wife would help take care of his brother like he was their own. The bargain price for their property may have implied that they were obligated to do as much. As a result, Henry received his meals from them, having no desire to cook or clean for himself. Consequently, Lydia also washed his clothes, changed his bedding and did her best to take care of him when he took ill. His lack of appreciation made her less willing to attend to him and infused her manner with bitterness.

"Your family is not one of the chosen ones in this town either, are they?" Lydia uttered with a frown. I didn't know what to say and remained silent until Aunt Rhody rushed to my rescue.

"Goody Gilbert, 'Tis nice to see you here today. I trust that you are starting to get used to this place. Over time, we will all start to merge into a new people regardless of our English origins. We wish you well and hope that Windsor allows your family to be fruitful in both accomplishments and children," she stated a bit nervously for it was really a dishonest judgement of the way things were.

Lydia stared at her and then at me. She was a tall young woman and appeared even more so as she wryly placed her hands upon her hips in amusement.

"We shall see, Goody Taylor. 'Tis only been fertile for growing pumpkins so far. But time will tell, won't it?" she nudged her husband's arm and chuckled or rather cackled as Aunt Rhody would say.

Even her laugh was boisterous and crossed the lines of accepted femininity. But she couldn't help it if she had a booming, coarse voice and carried herself with an air of confidence. Rather than making her fearful or subdued, the House of Corrections had boosted her confidence. She didn't seem to be afraid of anything. I suppose she realized that if she had the strength to withstand a couple years under the severe punishment of staying in the House of Corrections, she could overcome anything. It was easy to see how any man lacking in his own confidence could feel even smaller in her presence.

The men folk didn't like that. They wanted total control over women, over their slaves, over the Indians, even over the vast wilderness. For her own sake, I hoped Lydia was careful. She already drew unwanted attention from others because of her past, her childlessness, and her untamed nature. I knew the men who controlled everything in town didn't care if Lydia or her husband were treated unjustly at the mill or elsewhere. They would stand up for their own and not for her.

Henry Stiles' family had valuated his estate within a relatively short time after his death. His brothers had done an inventory of his property and assessed his assets and his debts. They'd settled his accounts and sold off several parcels of Henry's property including the one just south of the ferry road. His will seemed in order. The inventory he once owned consisted of carpentry tools, weapons of a musket and two swords, and the produce of his farm: six loads of hay, ninety bushels of corn, and two hundred pumpkins. He also owned half a canoe, money and plenty of wampum to trade with the local Natives or Windsor town folk.

The only strange part of the account to some people was that Henry Stiles was deeply indebted to Thomas and Lydia Gilbert, the young couple engaged to help take care of him while he was alive. The new public knowledge of these debts corresponded to the time that the gossip about the young couple increased in earnest. Matthew Allyn seemed quite happy to fan the flames of suspicion.

As the rumors continued to circulate, almost everyone came up with reasons that might explain Henry Stiles' death. I witnessed it for myself during one of the days at the meeting house. Needing some time by myself between sermons, I walked toward the back of the building and around a corner to sit next to a tree. There, I overheard a young group of servant girls talking about the tragic event. The chief gossip was named Hester and she reported to her friends within my earshot that Mr. Allyn had been going around to all of Henry Stiles' neighbors asking if they knew anything about someone who might have wished him ill will.

Matthew Allyn wasn't satisfied with the explanation that his son Thomas was to blame for Henry's death. Thomas would never be able to marry the beloved Windsor minister's daughter if his conviction stood as it was, his reputation too soiled, his soul too dirty. So, his father, with only one intention, the cleaning of his family's reputation, went full force to discover if someone else might be to blame. Rhody was convinced he would invent and fabricate supposed facts until another person emerged as the true culprit responsible for Henry's death.

It wasn't clear to me at the time what method he might employ to do this. I was still naïve. Aunt Rhody had kept things from me to protect me and spare me further pain. What was certain was that I was to stay away from him.

The servants continued gossiping at the back of the meeting house, hoping to catch just a few more cherished minutes of time with their companions. I continued hiding behind the tree to hear more. The servant girls buffered themselves from others by pulling their caps a little lower as they spoke.

"So, Master Allyn was up the road by the ferry trying to dig up some dirt, was he?" asked Prudence, another servant in the neighborhood.

"Aye," affirmed Hester. "Like I told ye, he was asking around about anybody who had a grudge to bear against Henry Stiles. He said there was reason to think that evil was afoot, and we should all be on guard against it just as the Reverend Warham always warns us."

"What else did he say?" continued Prudence, fully enjoying the gossip, a respite from the mundaneness of her life.

"He asked me and the other servants to tell him if we'd ever seen anyone arguing with Henry or saying wicked things about him before his death. Aye, he said we should go straight to him and let him know," said Hester with pride to share new knowledge about the goings on of the town.

"Well, what kind of evil was he implying?" another young girl named Debra asked innocently. "Isn't he the father of the man that killed Henry Stiles in the first place? What do you suppose he's up to?"

"I imagine he's trying to understand how such a horrible situation could ruin the lives of both his son and Goodman Stiles. Some say that Mr. Allyn thinks his son wasn't at fault, but rather thinks the Devil is lurking about. There are two main kinds of evil that have shown up here in recent years and that's witchcraft and Indian attacks," Hester said with authority and looked quickly beyond the clapboard wall of the meeting house.

"Leaves only witchcraft in this case," Prudence said, shaking her head.

"Aye, I shudder to think about it!" stressed Debra.

"As do I!" agreed Prudence.

"I overheard my master saying that Goodman Stiles' brothers recently settled his will. They stayed with Master Wolcott. I remember seeing Master Allyn go in to speak with them. They all seemed quite upset after he left," Hester added, soaking in the shocked reactions of her companions.

Just then, the meeting house bell tolled for us to come in again. I was startled but quietly slipped away before running to find Aunt Rhody. A number of addled thoughts ran around my head, and I wished I hadn't been prying. Aunt Rhody knew something was amiss and stared at me quizzingly as I took my place on the bench beside her again.

At home, Aunt Rhody tried to prod me to tell her why I seemed upset, but it soon became clear to her. Other neighbors had already arrived to tell her the news. Katherine Gibbs, a kind widow who lived up the lane of Backer Row had remained friendly with us and appeared at the threshold. She was older and tired from having to raise her children by herself after her husband died. But that was many years ago. I didn't even remember him. And her children were mostly grown. George Gibbs who had been in the House of corrections with Lydia and Thomas was her distant nephew, so she knew the Gilbert couple better than most.

"Word spread after congregating in the meeting house today that Matthew Allyn was poking his head around the households near the ferry trying to find damning evidence against anybody that might have had a grudge against Henry Stiles," Goody Gibbs said.

I shook my head and finally said something.

"'Tis true. I heard some servant girls saying he's visited them and also Mr. Wolcott's where Goodman Stiles' brothers had stayed when they came to town," I said.

"You did know? No wonder you seemed troubled at the meeting house. I can only imagine the type of hornet's nest that horrible man is trying to disturb now," Aunt Rhody stated, obviously despising him.

"Can't be good," said Goody Gibbs, clicking her tongue. "You watch this little one and keep her close," she advised Aunt Rhody, gesturing to me.

"You need not worry there. I'd protect her to the ends of the Earth. We all owe it to her mother," she responded strongly.

"What do you mean, Aunt Rhody?" I asked, sensing something horrible, yet not really knowing.

"At least some of us will carry guilt to our dying day that we couldn't do more to save your mother. I know we haven't talked much about it. But you're old enough now," she said reaching her hand out to gently take my own.

"Aye, you're fast becoming a young woman. We wouldn't want the wrong that befell your mother to ever come your way," stated Goody Gibbs genuinely. "I suppose that's the gist of what you need to know. That we're here for you and we intend to keep you safe away from the fray of whatever chaos Master Allyn creates with his manipulations."

"I know he'll do just about anything to take away the black mark of his son," said Aunt Rhody, looking deeply into the fire.

Goody Gibbs came to me and squeezed my shoulders.

"Don't worry, my dear," she said. "I haven't heard about him snooping around here asking questions. But I'll be sure to let you both know if I do hear anything."

I must have glanced at her like a terrified doe about to be taken down by a hunter.

"There, there now. You haven't done anything wrong. And we'd both fight for you. Throw your worries in the fire."

Aunt Rhody and I watched Goody Gibbs walk out of the house and up Backer Row to the last home lot at the very end where she lived. She and Aunt Rhody had gotten closer over the years through the bond of widowhood as well as single motherhood. After most of the Tinker family left, Aunt

Rhody got to know her better and took her advice about how to survive in the world as she patiently waited to be with Walter.

It seemed as if everyone had an opinion about the large debt that had been owed to the Gilberts. Some undisclosed people in town were busy at work weaving an ominous story because of it. As for me, I was both terrified and distant. But I dared not get caught up in what felt like a snare. Luckily, my curiosity and fear about them was no match for my increasing interest in a young man named Simon Beamon.

Chapter 4

Windsor, Connecticut, 1654: Reunion

Normally I would not have been near the dock, but Aunt Rhody had wanted to go with Walter to Hartford to find some dyed linen and wool for her marriage celebration. She and Walter had just posted their marriage banns on the meeting house door for the first time, and they hoped to be married in the following month. Our shallop was to leave for Hartford shortly. Rhody said the opportunity to go to Hartford to see something new on such a pleasant spring day would do me good.

A hand-hewn canoe pulled up to the dock laden with goods from the north.

"Alissa? Alissa? Is that REALLY you?" a voice boomed from the water.

Aunt Rhody was surprised to hear an unfamiliar voice talking to me and looked on with curiosity.

I squinted and looked down to see. I held Aunt Rhody's arm.

"That's Simon Beamon. Uncle John's friend and Mr. Pynchon's assistant," I whispered. She finally remembered and nodded.

"Aye, he works for Springfield's leader. I remember," she said.

Simon was boyish with straight sandy brown hair and navigated the river currents so skillfully he might as well have been a shad fish. His satchel was full of papers for the leaders of Windsor and Hartford from Mr. Pynchon. The leather bag was always kept dry in his capable care. He'd been coming around for a long time to Windsor from Springfield doing errands for his boss, Mr. Pynchon.

I smiled shyly. "Aye, Simon. 'Tis I, the little girl you used to tease so mischievously."

He grinned. "Aye. I was guilty of that, but I needed you to laugh then so I was only helping your uncle to get a smile out of ye, it wasn't so bad, was it?"

"No. Well, I suppose it wasn't," I grinned.

"I was hoping that I would see you here in Windsor. I heard you were here but never had the good fortune to see you again…until today." He smiled.

"She's become quite the young woman now, almost unrecognizable for the child she once was," Aunt Rhody said, beaming as proud as if I were her own daughter.

I'd met Simon Beamon when I was a little girl through my Uncle John. The two had formed a bond through the many times they'd met when assisting two colonial leaders, their patrons and employers. Both Uncle John and Simon were easy to get along with and tried to make life a little merrier if they could. Uncle John Tinker, assistant to John Winthrop the Younger for many years, was well acquainted with Simon Beamon, his counterpart and an assistant to the Springfield colonial leader, Mr. Pynchon. They had those roles in common and spent many hours together when their employers met to discuss colonial affairs and share experiences.

After my mother was murdered, the town authorities in Windsor decided that I needed to be with godly church people to save my soul. They placed me into the care of Elder and Mrs. Hoskins who read their Bible nightly and followed its instructions to every sacred word. I hated them with every fiber in my being. They weren't kind to me. Rather, they treated me as capricious and as the spawn of evil. They'd lie to me and tell me how horrible my mother had been and that it was her own fault that she would burn in hell for all eternity. They compelled me to do an endless list of chores with a smile on my face and gratitude in my heart for being saved. They frowned and harassed me when I refused to nod and agree about my mother's supposed pact with

Satan. As the scripture told them, they did not spare a rod in their unsuccessful attempts to force me to concur with their opinion.

When the couple decided to move to Springfield, I was forced to go with them. My only saving grace was that Uncle John had traveled there with Mr. Winthrop and petitioned that I should go to live with his sister, Rhody, to be with family again. His requests were repeatedly refused until one day the Hoskins couple decided to return to England. It was only then that I was allowed to be disconnected from their severe discipline and strict upbringing of me.

Until then, the only respite from darkness in the Hoskins home before their move to Springfield was Uncle John. His proposed visits to me were granted at the urging of Mr. Pynchon and Mr. Winthrop. I was allowed to go with Uncle John into the environment of the Pynchon mansion. The Hoskins' were assured that I would not slip into anything untoward or distasteful at the Springfield leader's home and workspace. It was there that Simon and Uncle John would work together to make me smile and give levity to my day. It was no surprise to me that my spirit immediately lightened to see Simon again.

Aunt Rhody told me later how obviously smitten he was to see me as a grown young woman. So, when Simon Beamon told us that he was dropping off a few things briefly in Windsor but intended to go to Hartford, Aunt Rhody suggested that it would be acceptable for me to ride with him in his canoe. They'd be right near us in the bigger shallop.

"Well, you could even load your canoe onto the shallop," Walter suggested. I took note of Aunt Rhody's discreet side jab of her future husband. She was clearly giving liberties to Simon to get to know me better as the young woman I had become.

"Alissa would love to ride in the canoe with you," she said. "It will be a fun adventure for her, and we will be right next to both of you. No need to pay for a shallop when you have your own way to travel the Big River to Hartford," she said, grinning.

She raised her eyebrows at me in question to make sure it was something I wanted to do. I nodded in agreement, both giddy and shy. Rhody had enough brazen enthusiasm for the both of us.

I'd loved to be around Simon as a little girl. In such dark times, he'd made me feel normal again, made me feel special and loved. I was truly happy and excited when it was time to step into the canoe with him and learn more about who he was. There was ample room in the small vessel to stretch my legs since he'd dropped off most of the goods to the ferryman near the dock and bade him send the papers from Pynchon to the town magistrates. He laid a small sack on my seat to make it more comfortable and gave me instructions about how to sit and where to put my weight as we navigated the local waters.

I was glad that it was a calm day. It was just warm enough that the feel of the sun on my skin was a gift. I sat like a princess in Simon's canoe that day as he called from the back of it to look at the marvelous birds I'd never paid attention to before. Gray broad-winged birds, dipping their long beaks into the water to fish, greeted us around almost every bend in the river. There were tufted ducks with their babies who filed quickly after each other, towering willow trees, and vast expanses of agricultural lands coming into maturity with a light green hue. Simon pointed out anything that might interest me like the giant woodpeckers that fed from massive trunks of old trees and hawks with wing spans that were wide and majestic.

Dear Aunt Rhody, she was never far and waved to me from her watchful perch on the shallop every so often.

The weather was mild and quiet, enough that Simon and I could talk to each other easily. We bantered about almost anything with ease which was unusual for me: Uncle John, life in Springfield, life in Windsor, Aunt Rhody getting married, and the natural world that we saw. It was an endless and easy discussion. I'd been afraid of everything since my mother died. He made me forget all of that.

Simon angled the canoe toward the shore and scooped up some little white flowers floating there. Sweet little poplar flowers. "For you, Alissa," he presented one to me. I blushed.

"Look Alissa, over there," he pointed. On a dead log were numerous painted turtles basking in the sun. As we approached, they quickly slipped into the water to avoid our gaze.

"All kinds of little families out enjoying the day!" he laughed. I joined him feeling engulfed in the vibrant life around us.

As he talked about the animal families we passed and the schools of fish we could see surrounding our boat, I dared even wonder if our time together might be the beginning of something else. He had always been kind-hearted toward me but this time he seemed even more interested in my well-being.

The time passed way too quickly as we reached the docks along the Big River in Hartford. Aunt Rhody and the others had just pulled in with their vessel. Her eyes were bright and beaming as she came up to me holding her hand to help me step out of the canoe.

"Did you enjoy yourself?" she teased. She was very happy at the unexpected development of Simon showing up. I knew how much she worried about my future and had been actively assessing all the suitable young bachelors in Windsor with whom she might arrange a match. No one ever seemed appropriate to her to be my suitor. By the cheerfulness in her voice and her approving glances toward Simon, I could tell she thought he was different.

She and Walter were going to sell their properties shortly after their marriage and go to Norfolk to live near her sister Mary's family. So much tragedy had happened in Windsor. It was important to both Walter and Rhody that they get a new start in a new place. I was always welcome to come with her when she moved, but she also knew that the time for me to make my own way in the world was fast approaching.

"Thank you for taking our girl on such a pleasant ride down the river," Aunt Rhody said as Simon pulled up the canoe from the edge of the riverbank. "We have some shopping to do now as does Walter, but it would be so nice if you could join us at the tavern for a meal later."

"Please join us," reiterated Walter. "I hear Mr. Ford's wife is a marvelous cook and we'd love to treat you to a hot meal," he emphasized.

Simon grinned. "I'd be quite pleased to join ye there at the ordinary a little later on. It shouldn't take me too long to drop off supplies and convey John Pynchon's communications from Springfield. I'm not sure how long I'll need to be in Hartford after I meet with some of the leaders. But 'tis for certain, meeting at the tavern to share a meal would make this day even better than it already is." He winked at me and then took off his hat, giving a gentle bow to both Aunt Rhody and Walter.

"We'll meet again in the afternoon. See you soon," he smiled and walked back towards the canoe for the rest of his supplies.

"Someone is cheerful! It seems to me that that young man has a bigger bounce in his step now than he did just a few short hours ago, Alissa. I wonder if it has anything to do with you," Aunt Rhody mused.

As we walked up the hill from the Big River up to Meeting House Square, I barely took note of the new scenes around me. Hartford was similar to Windsor with the same clapboard English homes, an occasional brick structure mixed in, and the little meeting house stood prominently on the green. But Hartford's vantage point along the Big River up on a hill looking down and closer to the Sound, even if by just a little, gave it a clear advantage over Windsor. Hartford had the distinction as a place of heightened trade and the seat of colonial business. Accordingly, the town house was a little more elaborate and the docks more concentrated and bustling than in Windsor. It was the central hub of Connecticut Colony. It made sense that Aunt Rhody wanted to come here to find some of the goods she needed.

The rest of the day, Aunt Rhody and I looked for some fine fabric that she could use to make herself a special dress in which to be wed. Extravagance was frowned upon, but Aunt Rhody would never forget her luxurious childhood and fit in little pleasures where she could. She found some fine linen dyed in a gentle pastel blue color, recently imported from England, at White's dry good shop. We even managed to find some contraband lace that could enhance her cuffs and skirts for the special day. The beautiful materials hadn't made their way upriver to Windsor so I was glad for her that she could find exactly what she wanted in Hartford. We also scoured the small businesses there for rare spices that we could use to cook a small feast for Walter and Rhody's celebration.

Around two in the afternoon, we all met at Mr. Ford's tavern. Its shadow had disappeared from the green now in full sun. It was one of the largest buildings in Hartford with several fireplaces and meeting rooms and was often the site of governmental meetings and hearings. Aside from the meeting house nestled in the center of the town green just across the road, the tavern was the hub of Hartford's intellectual activity. The tavern had been so successful that fine chestnut paneling was added to the walls. The smell of freshly brewed beer and stews of local fish engulfed the senses and greeted each visitor as they made their way through the door. We meandered through small groups of men, sometimes with their families, until we found space on a wooden bench pulled up to a large oak table.

For the first time I learned things about Simon I never knew, things a little girl wouldn't care about: that he was from a humble town not known for much, that his father had taught him to be a cobbler by trade, and that his impetus for starting a life in the colonies was to learn to be a young entrepreneur. He also told us more about the little things in this world that brought him contentment like paddling swiftly, mastering tribal languages better than most, his admiration for the Pynchons, his occasional boredom working at the company store, his pride in making fine quality leather boots for his employer, and his love of being a messenger. After our meal we toasted to our families and wished happiness for Walter and Rhody in the next chapter of their lives.

"I should only hope to be so happy one day," he stated. "When you find a good woman and you feel comfort and kinship with her, there can't be much better in life," he said.

"Aye. We've gone through our many sorrows, but with Rhody, I'm ready to take life on again," said Walter.

"As am I, Walter. We have waited a long time to be with each other. I'm not quite sure how I would have survived these past few years without you as my neighbor. I'm grateful to John Young for selling his property to you. You've made me feel safe and secure when I thought that wouldn't be possible. You're a blessing, dear Walter," she caressed his cheek lightly.

We raised our glasses and continued with our merriment until finally we heard the bell ring for the last shallop of the day. Simon had to stay in Hartford to finish John Pynchon's business, but he promised he would stop and visit us again in Windsor before returning home. That night my head was filled with seeing Simon's broad shoulders as he paddled the canoe downriver and pointing to nature's pearls on our route to Hartford that day. No nightmares for once. Just bliss.

Chapter 5

Windsor, Connecticut, 1654: A Marriage and an Arrest

Aunt Rhody remarried to Walter Hoyt only three weeks after one of the most wonderful days of my life. Simon started showing up often and was invited to come for the celebration.

On a fine hot day in early summer, Rhody and Walter came together in a simple ceremony at Rhody's home. A small group of friendly neighbors and some of Walter's family joined us. I had helped set up a wooden table in the yard with a little feast of bread, butter, several kinds of fish, and herbs. The local magistrate asked them each if they were in agreement to bind themselves together legally according to the marriage contract. Their banns had gone unopposed, and Mr. Warham had read a passage of the Bible of Rhody's choosing with their announcement. Aunt Rhody was a stunning bride and I was very happy for her. She had gone through so much loss in Windsor and deserved happiness.

As they settled into a household together, they continued to make plans to move near Aunt Mary in southern Connecticut, in the town of Norwalk. Walter had already bought land there the previous year with the help of Mary's husband and went there from time to time to oversee the building of their new home.

Aunt Rhody and Walter also had their first baby together, Zerubabbel. I had the honor to be at his birth and support Aunt Rhody through her trial of labor. It wasn't too much of a trial though. As if purposefully making his mother's life easier, he simply slipped out without too much fuss. We called him baby Zub, a little cherub that sweetened all of our lives the following cold winter.

Some changes are blessings. Little Zub was one of the biggest ones. I could sense that I was on the verge of major change too and Aunt Rhody wanted to prepare me for it. She encouraged me to take care of baby Zub so I could learn how to be a mother. Aside from feeding him in his early months, I did as much for him as Aunt Rhody would let me. It was an intense time of learning about how to care for children and run a household. For months, life hummed along in this way with the exception of Simon's occasional visits.

Simon had recently taken to visiting Windsor more often than usual on trade errands for his boss and colony leader William Pynchon when the weather would allow it. He'd stop by and visit Aunt Rhody's with the pretense of finding out how Uncle John was doing and if she had heard from him. He'd bring me little gifts, even a pair of shoes that he'd cobbled together. Quickly, he asked Aunt Rhody if he could court me. She was pleased and always left us alone to get acquainted better. I was a good ten years younger than him, but he didn't seem to mind. I was lost in daydreams about him, his good nature and boyish laugh. Unfortunately, life turned sour on other fronts.

In opposition to my increased happiness, rumors continued to circulate about Lydia Gilbert. At first, it was just simple gossip such as I'd heard from the servant girls behind the meeting house. The fact that Henry Stiles owed the Gilberts a debt became widely known. From there, arguments between Henry and the Gilberts were dissected, embellished, reinvented and rehashed until the final story was probably not even close to its original.

Indeed, the Allyns seemed intent on drumming up another witch hunt. Any time Walter saw them in town at the tavern, the mill, outside the meeting house or elsewhere, they were talking about the injustice done to Thomas and the need to find the real culprit for Henry's murder. I feared for Lydia because of her proximity to Goodman Stiles before he died. Everyone also knew she had a hot temper and a no-nonsense manner. This personal disposition made her an easy target for men who needed one. Walter recounted details so that we could stay ahead of whatever storm was coming.

After months of pushing and poking around, the Allyns were able to pressure the Gilberts' neighbors to recount that Lydia Gilbert was angry with Henry Stiles. They said Lydia was angry because in reality, it was she who had not been paid. As the woman in the Gilbert couple, she was the one obligated to sew, wash, and mend Henry's clothes, cook his meals, and clean his room. Her husband Thomas had agreed to this arrangement with the Stiles family, yet it was she who did most if not all of the work for Henry's upkeep and well-being, a man who had never once treated her with respect or gratitude according to her neighbors.

They said they knew these details because Lydia complained frequently about Henry, saying he was lewd at times and crass in his language towards her. According to those living nearby, Lydia had made fun of the bachelor by talking with others to release some of her anger towards him. Some neighbors said that they had even witnessed the fights between them become physical.

The Allyns already knew that Lydia was brash and strong in her way of being about the world, qualities acceptable in a man but not approved of in a woman. Aunt Rhody surmised that the Allyn family knew if they rooted around enough in the mud and squalor of negative relationships, something would reveal itself that could be used to their advantage. It was obvious they hoped it was a way to transform Windsorites' views about Henry Stiles' death. They seemed desperate to shift the blame from one of their own to someone else. Matthew Allyn's increased visits to the neighborhood near the ferry, far from his own home at the other end of town, seemed to reflect this. It became clear to Aunt Rhody that Lydia made a sensible culprit for Allyn's desire to change the course of destiny and he was indeed the reason for the rumors about Lydia.

As the gossip swirled about and took their grip on the populace the more times it was repeated, Aunt Rhody became increasingly alarmed that Lydia was in real trouble and by an association of a past condemned witch, we might be as well. Aunt Rhody had been very careful not to mingle too much with the rest of the town folk with few exceptions and had been on her guard for both my sake and her own. I sensed it was torture for her to think about my mother's circumstances, even more than for me, because she remembered everything that had happened whereas I had few memories. The child in me had blocked them out and refused to come to terms with them except for the nightmares that creeped in sometimes.

The rumors against Lydia Gilbert had become sensational. Our family had no choice but to discuss leaving Windsor. Lydia was no longer a person in the eyes of many Windsorites. She'd become a character in a woodcut depicting witches. The uproar was untenable, and I could no longer hide with Aunt Rhody on Backer Row.

On a day when the boys were busy in the fields and Elizabeth, Walter's daughter, was playing with Zub, Aunt Rhody requested that I spend time with her to talk about important matters.

"Today, you and I will focus our attention on harvesting much of the garden. Dear niece, there is much we need to talk about," she said. "Come. Let us enjoy the feel of the sun after the days of rain."

"Alissa, the time is coming where you will need to make a decision. All of us must leave Windsor very soon. I'm afraid what comes next will be a repeat of the treachery and horrors experienced by your dear mother. I'm thankful that Simon has come into your life again."

"Aye, Aunt Rhody, he makes me happy. I look forward to seeing him with each visit.

"I'm so relieved." She put some onions into her basket and looked directly into my eyes. "I hate to discuss this with you Alissa, but time is critical now. I fear deep in my bones that panic followed by more tragedy will happen again. Walter has recently told me of more sinister rumors darkening the name of Lydia Gilbert. They are more treacherous than ever. People are starting to call her a witch, saying it was she who was responsible for Henry Stiles' death by bewitching the gun that killed him," she said.

"That's absurd. I don't recall Lydia even being near the green that day. You don't think she could really do that do you?" I asked.

"It seems bizarre to me too, Alissa. And it is most likely the handiwork of the Allyn family. I told you they would try and find a way to rid Thomas of his guilt for Henry Stiles's murder. You will need to leave here in case this becomes an even larger panic than it has already been stoked to be. It is the only way that I can truly know that you will be safe."

She continued with concern. "Walter and I have decided that by the end of the year we will go to join Mary and Mathias Sension in Norwalk. Our new home is almost ready and awaits us." She sighed. "Before Simon came into your life again, I had always thought that you would come with us but now…" she looked down at the garden.

I was torn between two people — one who had loved me as a mother and the other one who I was starting to love and could see the possibility of having a family with — Simon Beamon. I didn't want to be separated from Aunt Rhody. In addition to Aunt Rhody being a second mother to me, I was a surrogate daughter to her. But now my world was changing with Simon in it. I knew our time together would end soon.

"I understand, Aunt Rhody. We have meant much to each other. It brings me great sorrow to think of ever being separated from you. But I am a young woman now and I also hope my courtship with Simon will continue," I acknowledged.

"The Lord will guide you, Alissa, but I must be frank. If the witch panic engulfs all of Windsor again and spreads beyond the malicious tongues against Lydia, I fear for your life because the blood of your mother runs through your veins. I have done all I can to protect you here, but I'm not so sure I can help either one of us now. I pray for Lydia that the foreboding talk and the vicious slanders against her name will dissipate." She looked at me with sorrow. "I cannot convince myself that it will."

I stared at the home I once shared with my parents next door from the garden. Even though it was close, I could never bring myself to go there. It represented another time, a happy time with my mother that ended abruptly in cruelty and tragedy and the estrangement from my father, a man who had failed to protect and love his family sufficiently.

Aunt Rhody put a gentle hand on my shoulder.

"Alissa, we shall see. Let us pray for clear direction for you. But promise me, you will leave with us if your relationship with Simon does not progress further. I could try to find you a position as a servant in a home in Windsor, but I'm afraid they could not protect you. We could do the same in Springfield, but if for any reason it did not work out with Simon, I would be worried that you would feel abandoned there. You are still slightly young, but not too young for marriage. My sister Anne married Thomas Thornton at fifteen. There is no reason why you could not do the same. I like Simon, Alissa. I have a good feeling about him," she assured me. "I do think it will work out," she squeezed my hand and smiled lovingly.

My footing in the town of Windsor now seemed as precarious as walking on cracked ice. They wanted me to be prepared for anything and assured me, it was possible to bring me to Norwalk to be with them and Aunt Mary should the need arise.

One day in early fall, it all came to a head. Aunt Rhody and I were on the town green, trading produce and buying goods at the open market when we saw her. Lydia Gilbert was in the back of a wagon, hair disheveled and screaming. They'd placed irons over her wrists. The hay from the cart that the authorities placed her in had started to cling to her clothes. Everyone at the market paused what they were doing and stared.

The cart stopped near the green and authorities pulled her out of it roughly by the chains she was attached to.

"I'm no witch! I AM NOT A WITCH! You'd love to see me hang wouldn't ye? But you'll have the wrath of God at your back if ye hurt me. I'm not a witch I say. NOT A WITCH!" She snarled as they brought her to the small jail nearby.

"Aye, then tell it to the magistrates tomorrow," the jailer heckled as he grabbed the chains again, pushing her into the simple jail near the town house. Her face was red and defiant as she tried to protect herself in the only way she knew how. Her husband Thomas was not with her. She was utterly alone in a crowd of people who stared at her humiliation, doing nothing to help her gain her dignity back.

Aunt Rhody already had tears streaming down her face. She wiped her face quickly hoping no one had seen her cry. Even that simple act of compassion could be a clue for someone of a witch-hunting nature that she was on the wrong side of "good and evil".

"Come Alissa, quickly please," she commanded softly so no one else would hear. We finished our last transaction for eggs in haste and she led me away while the others were still captured with the spectacle of Lydia's imprisonment. Aunt Rhody's grip on my arm was hard. I could feel through it how scared and desperate she was at that moment.

"No good will come of this," she shook her head as she bounded for home with me in tow. The first action she took when we got home was to take out her parchment paper and briefly write a letter to my Uncle John Tinker with the news. Aunt Rhody requested his help to come and protect me. Walter might not be enough. A well-connected man willing to defend us was the best protection she could think of short of moving out of town as quickly as possible. Walter dutifully found a messenger he could trust and sent the message on to Uncle John. Aunt Rhody was grateful for her marriage bond to Walter. She felt safer because of it. I knew most of her worries were for me.

"Uncle John will come. I know he will, dear Alissa," Aunt Rhody said trying to comfort me. There was nothing to do but wait for his response and be very quiet in our little corner of town. The angry, riled up mobs directing their anger towards Lydia were no match for us.

Chapter 6

Windsor, Connecticut, September – December, 1654: Witch Trial

Lydia Gilbert remained in her jail cell in Windsor for only a few days. The leaders in town met with her, the Allyns, and Lydia's neighbors to accumulate testimonies and determine guilt. I didn't witness any of it. Aunt Rhody forbade me to go for my own protection. Nor did I wish to see Lydia slandered in a way that would make her culpable for a murder she did not commit or maligned as a witch. Even so, we heard about her from our one friendly neighbor, Goody Gibbs and Walter's brother Nicolas.

It had not gone well for Lydia. Several of her neighbors testified against her saying that she complained frequently about Henry Stiles, precisely how difficult he was to care for and how demanding and demeaning he was towards her. But they also took note of Lydia's quarrelsome nature and openly speculated that she and Henry's relationship was fraught with rancor and bitterness because of her attitude. If Lydia had ever thought that she had friends in her neighborhood, she was sorely mistaken, for they slowly betrayed her, one by one, perhaps only to save their own reputations. They were fully aware that Matthew Allyn looked on menacingly hoping to clear his son Thomas's name. Some would even say later on that the Allyn family had paid them handsome sums to malign their former neighbor. The exact truth of the matter was hard to extract.

Lydia's own husband sat disturbed yet mute as he heard the testimony. What could he do to protect his wife without incurring the wrath of those that wanted her held responsible for Henry's death? He patiently waited for Lydia's kin to come and others who promised to act on her behalf. After just one day of compiling testimony, town leaders indicted her on the charge of witchcraft. She was transported to Hartford for her trial before any character witness could arrive in her defense.

True to his dutiful nature, John Tinker heeded the call quickly and came to Windsor to be with his sister, Rhody, and me. His hatred of some people in Windsor, those who were responsible for my mother's death, and his vow to never come back, was overcome by his love of family only.

By then, he was living in Lancaster, in Massachusetts Colony, and working more frequently for Winthrop the Younger. On his way to Connecticut Colony, he stopped in Springfield to visit John Pynchon whose father, William, had recently been ousted from New England for his radical religious views. Pynchon's son, John, then became the new leader of the town after his father, a broken man, returned to England in sorrow to live out the rest of his days. In Springfield, Uncle John met with Simon and other Pynchon associates to catch up on news and to find out the details of the latest witch scare in Windsor.

When Uncle John rapped on Aunt Rhody's door, I was surprised yet pleased to see that he was accompanied by Simon Beamon.

"You came!" cried Rhody hugging her brother. "And you're here as well Simon! What a blessing for all of us!" She turned to me and smiled.

"I'm not about to lose any more family members to witch hunts," Uncle John whispered and assured her. "And Simon is here to give his regards to all of you before leaving for Hartford in the morning."

"Aye. We've gotten word about Lydia's trial. I'm here to help Lydia Gilbert's family be there to defend her. Her stepmother Margaret Bliss pleaded for me to act as a representative for our Springfield leader. She thought I could vouch for their family and the good things the Blisses have done in our town. Mr. Pynchon agreed. We just traveled with the family and escorted them to the

Gilbert home lot near the ferry crossing," Simon said, removing his overcoat and taking the beer that Aunt Rhody offered him.

"I've known the family a long time," he continued. "We fear that those thinking Lydia a witch might have been misled by believing the slander against her own sister Mary by another town resident a couple years ago. 'Twas Molly Percy, Hugh Percy's wretched wife who accused her as such."

"What? You say that Lydia's sister was accused of witchcraft in Springfield?" asked Walter in disbelief.

"Aye. Mr. Pynchon held court and determined it was nothing more than cruel words against a woman wallowing in grief. Hugh Percy's wife had done a similar thing before to another woman. Lydia's sister, Mary Bliss Parsons, wife of Joseph Parsons, was devastated after she lost her second child, a son, and would sneak out to the boggy land next to the river at night, roaming amongst the reeds in her shift. Some said they saw her cavorting with another woman. But I can't say that I know that to be true. Joseph, her husband, was so concerned that he locked her in at night, making her sleep in the cellar that had a door with a lock. He feared what might become of her at night alone away from the house. But Mary could always figure out where he placed the key, hid it, and went on visiting the swamp all the same. The grief had caused her to do strange things."

"Oh, the poor woman! Some women take it very hard when they've lost a child. 'Tis not an easy experience," Aunt Rhody said with sympathy to everyone now seated at the table in front of the hearth. "Your mother had once lost a child, Alissa, and was so grief-stricken, she'd do just about anything to have another one. 'Twas not meant to be," she sighed.

I was starting to see why Lydia, simply for having a bad reputation already because of her crime years before and her strong personality, could easily be viewed with suspicion if neighbors and other town folk heard misinformed gossip about her sister, once accused of witchcraft also.

"Mary, Lydia's sister was a victim of bewitchment not the cause of it. She was so affected by Hugh and his wife that she dropped onto the floor in the meeting house and had fits before God when Hugh's wife walked in. Other women were equally distraught that day. In the end, it was Hugh Percy and his wife Molly who were sent to Boston, to be tried for witchcraft."

We were silent, taking it all in. It was not easy for me to sit in my place on the bench unaffected by it. When Aunt Rhody mentioned earlier that my mother had lost a child, something very familiar in me opened up, a deep feeling of grief and disquiet. I tried to maintain my focus and willed myself to be still.

Uncle John and Simon together seemed to know a lot about Lydia's case and had also stopped at the tavern to hear what people were saying. Uncle John became the storyteller once more as he explained what was going on there in a similar way to what I'd remembered as a little girl. Only this time, it wasn't a fun story and it filled me with dread. He grimaced to tell it as did Simon who filled in the important details.

"Just days ago, I suspect the same time that Rhody wrote her letter to me, Thomas Gilbert galloped with his horse to see Lydia's kin, the Bliss family. Thomas let them know of the great trouble that his wife was in. He had hoped they could help with a strategy to save her life," Uncle John said.

"Margaret Bliss, his mother-in-law, was forlorn when he recounted their troubles in Windsor and the sight of her panicked and agitated son-in-law, Thomas, gave her little hope for her stepdaughter's survival" he continued.

"Margaret was a witness to the witch panic in Springfield with Hugh and Molly Percy and has observed with everyone else up and down the Big River how people are becoming more fearful of witchcraft with each case," Simon added.

"Our trip into the tavern has sadly confirmed just how much of a grip the lies against Lydia have taken hold. I'm sure Allyn has done his manipulations behind closed doors to make the conclusion to this story — one that fits his desires," stressed Uncle John.

"Is there any chance for Lydia's release Uncle John?" I asked meekly.

"Simon will try his best to clear her name," he said, not able to offer more hope.

"You know, I don't like telling you any of this. But you need to know exactly what's happening. Rhody, I don't want any of this to affect you or Alissa, but you weren't confident in your letter. Considering that, the best we can do is properly assess the situation as it changes and as we find out more information," he reasoned.

Walter shook his head in agreement, "We'll be out of the town of Windsor in an instant if they expand the accusations of witchcraft. If they dare touch a hair on my Rhody's head or give her so much as an odd glare, we're gone. I've known most of these people my whole life. Most are good, but when they fear a demon is about, they'll act on it before they give a reason. Tell us, John, you said that the Bliss daughter Mary was pulled into the witch drama. Did the town folk of Springfield believe she was a witch too and did she suffer for it?" he asked. "It seems to me that there was talk of it reaching Windsor a couple years ago. Do ye think folk here might conclude that since her sister was called a witch, she might be one?" he added.

As Uncle John paused and weighed how to give the best answer to both questions, I noted that Aunt Rhody was holding onto Walter and not letting go. She looked nervous and would glance my way every so often with concern etched on her face.

Simon answered for him. "As I said before. It's possible people here have come to that conclusion, but I think most in Springfield realized that she wasn't a witch after Pynchon set them straight despite her peculiar behavior. The real witch accusations there were laid at the feet of mostly Hugh Percy but also his wife Molly who also admitted to being a witch."

I felt worse as I sat at the table. I couldn't do it anymore. I stood up. "I must take my leave. Please excuse me for I feel rather unwell," I said.

"Of course, my dear. All this talk is distressing. We should speak of other things now. Let me help you." Aunt Rhody held my waist and accompanied me to my bed in the other room. She poured some water and soaked a cloth, wiping my forehead with it.

"Try not to worry, Alissa. John, Walter, and I will do everything in our power to keep you safe. I know Simon will do the same."

She kissed me on the forehead and tucked me in tenderly as if I were a young child.

"Try to sleep now, dear niece." She blew out the candles and headed back to her guests.

Aunt Rhody had been such a comfort to me that I surprised myself by sleeping deeply all night. By the time I awoke, Uncle John had already ridden off with Simon to Hartford to take care of business and be there the next day at the court in case Simon or the other witnesses for Lydia needed anything. They weren't sure how many days they would be gone but promised the day of the verdict, they'd ride back even under cloak of darkness if need be.

I promised Aunt Rhody that I would fetch the extra lard Goody Gibbs agreed to sell to her. As I went down the road to get to the other part of Backer Row, my eyes locked with a new servant of the Clarks, a neighboring family. Her name was Patience. I'd met her once before. She'd been released from another family in Springfield to finish her service to the Clarks. But she looked at me strangely that morning. She was hitting a small rug against a rock to clean it and paused when I came close.

"Alissa, did I see Simon Beamon leave your house? People say he's been courting you. Be careful Alissa. I know about your mother, and I know Simon Beamon's history in testifying against other witches. What if he decides you're a witch?" she teased.

"What do you mean by this?" I snapped, taken by surprise.

"Well, he might turn on you if you do something he doesn't like. You know he hasn't always stood up for witches. He had a couple of devilish run-ins with Hugh Percy and did what he could to see that Hugh went to trial for witchcraft."

She'd stopped her work because torturing me in such a way seemed much more fun, I was sure. Just then, Mr. Clark came to the door and spoke to her in a stern voice.

"Patience, come inside now. You will finish your other chores. Good day, Alissa," he said and darted back inside. With her chastisement, Patience lost a little of her exuberance to trouble me.

"Just remember that I warned you," she whispered before grabbing the rug off the rock to obey her new master's warning.

When I returned home, I told Aunt Rhody about the incident.

"What a horrible thing to say to you!" Aunt Rhody cried. She was also upset and tried her best the rest of the day to reassure me that Simon was trustworthy.

"Alissa, I can see he is different than that. With God as my witness, I can never believe that he would turn against you in that way. He is enthralled by you. In fact, I have a mind to think he loves you! Please think of this no more," she commanded lovingly.

For the rest of the time of Lydia's trial, as we waited for the verdict, Aunt Rhody came up with new projects for us to do to occupy our thoughts. There were new mince pie recipes to experiment with and a cloth that had to be delicately embroidered, extra cleaning in corners that had long been neglected, and anything else she could think of to stay busy and away from the suspicious eyes of the rest of the town. And little Zub helped, though he always left a trail of havoc in his curiosity.

If the subject of Lydia came up, Aunt Rhody gently changed it and talked about things far removed from the events that weighed heavily upon us. She requested of her boys that they not talk about Lydia or the trial in her house, at least not until a verdict was certain. She decided that if we were called to a special sermon in the meeting house, she would send the boys there but say she was feeling so poorly that she needed me to stay home to take care of her. She would do anything she could to protect me even if it meant accepting the sins of lying and bucking the wishes of the minister.

Chapter 7

Windsor, Connecticut, November 1654: Condemnation and a Proposal

On November 28, 1654, the special court in Hartford convened bringing Lydia Gilbert to trial for the murder of Henry Stiles. Led by Matthew Allyn, many people in the town of Windsor had been looking for three years for someone to blame for Stiles' death. They finally found "her" they told themselves. I'm sure that Allyn's spiteful tongue and manipulation had convinced them. Brazen Lydia, unrestrained Lydia, criminal and sister of a "witch". She was the perfect suspect as the real killer of Henry Stiles through acts of witchcraft.

We waited patiently to hear the results of the trial, but everyone knew including me in a horribly visceral way that Lydia's life had already been sentenced to death by hanging. I realized there was no hope if you were considered a witch.

Eventually, Uncle John and Simon entered the house shortly after the sun had set. Their faces were sullen, and they spoke not a word to each other or to us. They both took off their hats, Uncle John bringing his to his chest and Simon, staring at nothing, let his hang from his dangling arm. They looked unsteady as they navigated their way into the dimly lit hall. We didn't have to ask what had happened to Lydia. We knew. They'd given us all the clues we needed to know that Lydia, like my mother, had just been sentenced to death for consorting with the Devil.

"They've done it again — condemned another woman to her death but this time for a crime another man committed," Uncle John said in disbelief. "These are not easy times to live in."

"Lydia's stepmother collapsed on the meeting house floor when she heard the verdict. Her sister Mary would have been no help had she been there. Her anxiety would have gotten the best of her. It is right she stayed home. Lydia's husband stood silent and stunned staring at the remains of what was once his proud wife now shaken and sobbing after she heard the verdict," Simon added.

I went to Aunt Rhody and held her hand as we listened in anguish to everything Simon and Uncle John were saying.

It was difficult to hear the words and even harder to fathom what had happened behind the closed doors where men of privilege met together and decided the fates of those they saw as their weaker counterparts and helpmates.

"Of course, Thomas Allyn walked away with a clean reputation when the court declared that he was not responsible for Henry Stile's death. They said they were bound to consider the new evidence. He was innocent they said, merely caught in the wrong place and the wrong time, while Lydia practiced witchcraft and her revenge on behalf of Satan," he scoffed. "That smug father of his got what he wanted in the end. Matthew Allyn asked to address the court after the verdict. First, he congratulated them in making the right decision, holding his head high, not a single care for Lydia's family or the fact that his meddling had probably caused her death sentence, he asked right then and there for his fines back,"

"Fines? The nerve!" screamed Aunt Rhody.

"Aye, the fines he paid to the court three years ago when it ruled that Thomas Allyn was responsible for Henry Stiles' death. The bastard got it all back. Every sixpence. Now weigh that against another young woman's life! Isn't her life worth more than that?"

I had never seen my Uncle John so angry.

"I must take my leave for a few minutes out in the yard under the clear sky with some fresh air. I'm sorry," he hung his head and moved out the door into yard.

"'Tis distressing to be sure," said Simon. "They're going to hang her out by way of the cow pasture high on a hill tomorrow morning."

"To be an example of what befalls witches," Aunt Rhody mumbled. She was also distressed and held me around the waist.

Simon continued, "Her stepmother wants to say goodbye but is afraid she won't be able to live with what she sees. Her husband said he'll be there to see her one last time and give her strength. Such a horrible conclusion to a terrible murder. It's understandable your uncle is taking it this way" said Simon as he looked at me.

"'Tis true there may be witches at times but this was clearly a manipulation to shift the blame for a horrible death from one person to another. I'm going to go check on John," he said and walked outside.

"We must leave Windsor soon," said Aunt Rhody to her husband. "Alissa, you must go with us or go to live with your Uncle John. I am certain that staying in Windsor is not an option for you now. I've protected you child but cannot anymore if you stay here."

She saw me tearing up and hugged me. "You are rightly troubled child. But don't worry. We will figure out a solution together, I promise," she said.

I must have looked very pale at that moment, so pale that Aunt Rhody ushered me to my bed. I was very confused. I thought I loved Simon and didn't want our courtship to end. At the same time, I wondered if he could ever turn on me as the daughter of someone convicted as a witch just as he had testified against Hugh Percy. Most of my doubt dissipated again with Aunt Rhody's assurances and his defense of Lydia but Patience had planted enough of a seed of doubt that I couldn't be sure that he would ever love me because of my mother's supposed crime. I wanted to ask him why he thought the Hugh Percy and his wife were witches and why he spoke against them. I wondered what had happened with Hugh in Springfield but at the time, I couldn't bear to ask. I was not ready to find out.

I tossed and turned until finally I sobbed myself to sleep. It was a time of great uncertainty when an answer to my future was needed urgently.

Later that night, I stirred about in my bedding, finally waking in a cold sweat. I'd had another unpleasant nightmare. I was standing on the edge of a stand of massive rocks overlooking a body of water when I heard the desperate call of my mother for help. I couldn't see her clearly, but I had the sense that she was under the water, forced down swiftly into the current by an event so forceful that she had no chance of avoiding it. As in all my other nightmares, I couldn't reach her.

I was upset and needed some air, so I crept in silence towards the door. I thought everyone had gone to sleep. I was mistaken for when I pulled the latch to go outside, Uncle John and Simon were talking over a small bonfire in the distance. As I tiptoed closer toward them, I started to hear my uncle's words. He was talking about me. I hid behind the thick trunk of a tree, compelled to hear what he wouldn't say in front of me.

Simon had a stick and was intently looking at the fire while poking it. Small sparks flew and the fire rekindled and lighted up their faces more clearly. Uncle John had a mug of beer he held as he spoke to Simon.

"I fear trouble for Alissa. She was very young when her mother died, but Lydia's sentencing must stir up powerful memories for her. Even more critical is the question, who will they turn on next? That's what worries me the most. If you love our dear Alissa, I beg you to ask for her hand in marriage sooner rather than later," he said catching Simon's attention and his eye.

My hair stood up on my arms and I'd been more focused than I could ever recall. I knew the next few moments might change my life forever. I clung to the rippled yet comforting bark of the oak tree for my support. Did he love me? Did he not? I did not want him to feel pressured or obligated to marry me! I think I was holding my breath so as not to miss a single word of their conversation.

Simon swallowed hard. It was the moment of truth. He croaked slightly with his first words, but then they became clear, "John Tinker, with all my heart, I do declare that I love Alissa and I have every intention of marrying her if she will have me. I've only waited because she is not yet the marriage age of most young women. In reality, I would have proposed to her the day of our reunion, after we traveled the Big River to Hartford. I knew I wished her to be my wife and the mother of my children from that day forward."

John Tinker put down his mug, and patted Simon's shoulder. When he was done, he grinned in approval.

"I hear your words with great happiness, Simon. Aye, Alissa is still somewhat young, but not too young for marriage. I've known others to marry at fifteen including my own sister. I am very pleased," he extended his hand to shake Simon's as a symbol of an agreement and pact.

I let out a deep breath of relief from behind the oak tree and relaxed so much than I accidentally tripped and made a noise alerting them to my presence.

They both turned. "Hey! Who is that over there?" said Uncle John calling to the presence near the oak tree.

I got up and brushed off my shift with my hands. "It is I, Alissa," I stepped forward sheepishly. "I couldn't sleep and thought I'd relieve myself in the night and get some fresh air. The moon is so beautiful and the sky clear," I explained and smiled as I walked to join them.

"Alissa," he beamed. "Come here. Did you hear our conversation?" he asked with a probing grin.

"Aye, I did," I admitted, unable to stop smiling.

"Well, there's no use in waiting another minute then," Simon said. He came close to me and grabbed my hand.

"Dear Alissa, before God and your uncle, I humbly ask that you share my life with me in marriage. I love you, Alissa. What say you?" He looked deeply into my eyes.

My heart had gone from grief to joy and the two most important men in my life were there.

"Alissa, I can vouch for Simon that he is a good man. And I am certain that he will do right by you as your husband, but the decision is yours and yours alone. You can think on it if you need to, child," he assured me.

I didn't need to think about it though. I also knew from the first few times that Simon and I had spent time together in Windsor that he would be the father of my children. I was worried about what would become of our relationship if I left for Norwalk with Aunt Rhody and her family. Now that he had confirmed he loved me too, there was no way that I could leave him.

"This answer is AYE, Simon. I will be happy to be your wife and share a life with you! I love you too," I said clearly.

Uncle John hugged the both of us. "Your Aunt Rhody's going to be a little jealous that she wasn't here to witness this. She's loved you and raised you as if you were her own daughter all these years," Uncle John said.

"I know. We will tell her first thing in the morning! Thank you, Uncle John!" I hugged him again. It felt so good to be cherished, cared for, and loved. I felt at peace in that moment even though the world as it was in Windsor was exploding with fear.

Chapter 8

Windsor, Connecticut, December 1654: Fertility

The first time we went to the meeting house after Lydia's conviction, the authorities placed the verdict with her sentence on the meeting house door.

"Lydea Gilburt thou are here indited by that name of Lydea Gilburt that not having the feare of God before thy Eyes thou hast of late years or still dust give Entertainment of Sathan the great Enemy of God and mankind and by his helpe hast killed the Body of Henry Styles besides other witchcrafts for which according to the law of god and the Established Law of this commonwealth thou Deservest to Dye. Ye party above mentioned is found guilty of witchcraft by the Jury."

Lydia had already been hanged, but it didn't stop the worshipping faithful from slowly reading the conviction aloud if they could for the benefit of others who had no reading skills. I observed their faces. Some didn't care and were gleeful the witch was gone. Others were quiet and subdued, probably afraid to say anything lest it be taken in the wrong way.

Windsor's congregation walked to their benches in slower, somber steps anticipating the lashing from the pulpit that they would receive. Aunt Rhody knew we had to go and be a part of it or people would talk. So, we did what we were obligated to do.

I bowed my head throughout Reverend Warham's sermon. When I couldn't bear to listen to his suffocating words in the meeting house any further, I thought of Simon and the love and approval bestowed upon us by my Aunt

Rhody and my Uncle John. I thought how curious it was that my life seemed to be in the middle of both good and evil — in between the devilishness of hunting and killing innocent women as witches and the blessing of a strong love between family members and a wonderful man who I would marry very soon.

That day at the meeting house in his sermon, Reverend Warham laid blame for the recent town tragedies on the doorsteps of every townsperson who, in his words, had "strayed from paths of virtue, overvaluing secular interests while ignoring spiritual ones". He talked a lot about the sins of "tippling in alehouses, nightwalking, and engaging one another in repeated controversy."

I believe he truly did feel that way. However, it was interesting to note that less than four years later, Thomas Allyn, of a redeemed reputation, married this minister's daughter, Abigail. Simon had heard they had started courting once the controversy had dissipated.

That was our last appearance at the meeting house in Windsor. The rest of my time there was easy and filled with family in preparation for our big moves and my marriage contract. I was glad that Reverend Warham's sermon may have helped to put a pause on further thoughts of witchcraft accusations, for I didn't hear another thing about Lydia's misfortune again, nor did we hear of any other accusations unfolding. Neither did we seek out those possible conversations in the tavern or elsewhere. We kept to ourselves and prepared for our imminent moves.

Aunt Rhody was relieved and jubilant after Simon and I told her about our engagement the following day. She thanked Uncle John for his help profusely and hugged us both many times.   Walter too was pleased. They were excited to start their new life together. Hence, Aunt Rhody and I packed our belongings with care and prepared for my marriage day with great joy.

Sometimes, even the most joyous things in life can be bittersweet. I'd catch Aunt Rhody tearing up at times.

"I will miss you so much dear niece. You have been like another daughter to me. It has not been easy since the deaths of both Hannah and Anna."

I nodded and started to tear up as well for they both were my cousins and my friends. We had all hung out in a pack. My mother teased that we were the she-wolves of Backer Row — a description that Priscilla and Anne's father, Thomas Thornton, scoffed at. He didn't like his daughters to be referred to as such. Now they are all dead, laid to rest in the burying ground: Priscilla and Anne Thornton along with their two brothers Thomas and Samuel, our other cousin, Sarah Sension, my Aunt Mary's girl who died with the great sickness, and Rhody's girls, Hannah and Anna Hobbs Taylor. Rhody's girls died at other times and from other causes. It was sad to think about all that loss. I was the only survivor in my close group of cousin friends who played together on Backer Row.

"Of course, you understand," she said, tucking a stray strand of brown, chestnut hair gently back into its place underneath my cap.

"Aunt Rhody, before we go, can we see their final resting place one last time in the burying ground?"

"Yes, child. We will do just that," she said, cheering up.

Simon and I married in Windsor on December 16, 1654, only two and a half weeks after Lydia's formal conviction and the tenth month of the Julian year. We had a very small ceremony on Backer Row with Aunt Rhody and Walter, their children, Uncle John, Walter's brother and Goody Gibbs down the lane. Aunt Rhody helped me get ready for the wonderful day.

Several hours before our guests arrived, she led me to my old home next door that had been bought by Walter. I wondered if she'd brought me there, so that my mother could be there with us in spirit. I'd hadn't gone in since her death and paused. I remembered John Young as he left the home forever. He saw me in the yard and told me," "Well, I'm off to Stratford now. Ye take care."

"Rhody has put your mother's things into a box if you want them one day. I'd best be going," he said, tipped his hat, and I never saw him again.

I was very hesitant to go into the house where my mother was taken from me, but Rhody coaxed me until I relented.

"Come now," she said inviting me into a room newly cleaned with the bedstead near the hearth, a fire blazing for warmth, "I scrubbed it well and thought only about good memories of your mother — namely, how much she loved you."

Rhody handed me a new linen shift that she'd made for this day.

"I give this to you in love, my dear niece" she said. "Put it on Alissa. It's embroidered with fine lace from the European continent in the region of Flanders. It was once a gift to your mother. Please put it on and let me see you in it."

Her stitching was exquisite and the lace beyond beautiful even though it was against local restrictions in accordance with sundry laws.

"No one will know," she winked. Aunt Rhody had also appreciated lovely things and she would always be that way.

I felt like a queen. Once I had done as requested, she asked me to lay on the bedstead for a few minutes so she could pray over me on this important day.

As I laid down, I noticed that she had gathered dried herbs. I recognized them: red clover, red raspberry, angelica, mugwort, juniper, and motherwort. She laid the fertility herbs, one by one, in a circle on my belly. "Dear God, I ask that you help Alissa to be fruitful and blessed with many children. Help her to seek union with her husband in all ways. I ask that in her fruitfulness, she will be protected and that her children will bring her peace. I thank you dear Lord," she bowed her head, placed her hands at either side of my belly, and became silent in further prayer over me.

Finally, no longer invoking her wishes to the Divine, Aunt Rhody looked at me and began to speak again, one to one, woman to woman.

"Alissa, it may bring you joy to seek union with your new husband in the marital bed, but understand that it is also the one thing that will help to protect you as a woman in this world. Hopefully, you will bear many sons as a result and their voices will protect you should your husband die before you. May you have many children to prove to your community and your church that you are a good woman. Your children will protect you in this way."

She cleared the herbs off my belly and placed them in a tiny leather pouch with a pull-string.

"Keep this with you, always. Tie it under your marriage bedstead for good luck and abundance in married life," she said.

I'd sat up by now and was intently trying to make sense of the words she spoke.

"It is not I who think these things, but it is the way of the world. I do not want to bring you sorrow. Just know your mother is with you in spirit today. I have tried to be like a mother to you and acted to protect you in her place. I know that she would give you the same advice I give you now."

She paused again to give emphasis to her most sage words.

"Pray that you may bear many children so you will never be accused of being jealous of another, so that you will be viewed as occupied with your brood, your offspring — too busy mothering and too fertile to ever be thought of as the kind of woman vulnerable to consort with the Devil out of desperation. I need not say more. May you be blessed in this way. That is my greatest wish for you in a world defined and created by the desires of men— men who seek any reason to squash our own desires as women — men who would come up with any excuse to keep power over us, even by defining us as evil to maintain domination in this world,"

She paused. "Enough. I would be labeled a heretic should anyone hear my words. Keep quiet and do not repeat them, but hold them tightly in your breast as a salve of protection throughout this life. Forgive me for openly speaking in tongues of blasphemy even if it is the truth."

She closed her eyes and cried softly. I knew she was remembering my mother.

"Remember, wear your children around you as a cloak, a cloak of both blessings and protection," she whispered, embracing me.

Even though she did not say it directly, I knew that Aunt Rhody was encouraging me, in part, to have many children to avoid the same awful fate that befell my mother, a woman with only one child, a child to survive during the great illness when many other children perished. I thought of Lydia, the young woman without child, recently hanged in Hartford. I came to the conclusion that it could be dangerous not to be fruitful in unfavorable circumstances.

With each child I carried who survived, I would be assured that I had one more layer of protection against the rumors caused by my family's tragic past and a decrease in anxiety that I might be the next to be accused of the terrible crime of witchcraft. Hopefully, Simon and I would be blessed with the sounds of children's laughter and little feet on our floorboards. I prayed as well that I would not be barren.

Rhody hugged me again. "Come," she said, "We have a few more things to do before your guests and your future husband arrive."

A couple hours later, our family, a few neighbors and the local magistrate came to watch Simon and I commit to our marriage contract.

We held hands as the magistrate asked us. "Do you agree to commit to marriage with this man?" I nodded my consent.

"And do you agree to marriage with this woman?"

"Aye" said Simon.

We had to agree to work together to be with each other and to provide for each other in the ways that were delegated to each of our sexes. Also, as part of our contract, we agreed to have children. Marriage was a big decision, but the official agreement was basic and simple. After our simple vows to honor our contract, we had a small celebration, and it was only then that I fully understood I was married. In only a few minutes, I became a grown woman about to have her own home, no longer a child watched and worried over. I smiled at Aunt Rhody understanding that I might not have come this far in my life without her. I'd probably have gone mad. I looked at her in appreciation until she caught my glance and smiled back at me. I always felt that she was happy to have me, that I took away some of the grief and sorrow she had from losing her own daughters.

"Come, everyone. Gather 'round the new married couple so we may make a toast to them!" she said. "May you always be happy and never want for anything. May the Lord bless you with many children!"

"Hoozah!" our room full of celebrants answered followed by other heartfelt wishes for Simon and me.

"Please come and eat!" Rhody uncovered the richly aromatic array of food before us.

Aunt Rhody and I had prepared a small table full of baked apples, pork and parsnip stew, and a real luxury, a gingerbread cake, for the celebration of the day.

I soaked in the time with my cousins, especially my little Zub, Walter and Rhody's child together, the sweet boy I'd helped Rhody to birth with Goody Gibbs. He was especially close to my heart and was already almost two years old. It would be difficult not to see him every day once we parted ways. But I'd also miss John and Thomas, Rhody's boys with John Taylor. They were growing into young men and the tone of John's voice had lowered an octave. They had all welcomed me into the family after losing my mother and after the authorities took me out of the care of my estranged father.

And I still felt welcome when Walter joined us and brought his son, James, and his daughter, Elizabeth, with him. Walter was such a hardworking and honest man. He transformed my old house to be full of life again with Rhody's tacit approval. His bluntness in talking about my situation helped us all for he was always optimistic and had practical solutions to any problem including my future.

Indeed, there was much to be grateful for on that wonderful day as we feasted and enjoyed each other's company.

As our time together was reaching its close, and the other wedding guests had already left, Aunt Rhody refused to let me clean up after my marriage celebration. "Leave it, Alissa. Elizabeth and I will have plenty of time for tidying up after your departure. For now, I want to take in every moment of our last remaining minutes together." Simon for his part, had gone to the barn to ready his horse for the trip back to Springfield. He wanted us to reach our new home on our wedding night.

Aunt Rhody wanted me to know that she felt more at peace to make the move to Norwalk now that I was married with Simon at my side.

"Dear Alissa, you must understand how much I will miss you. But know that you have your full life ahead of you with Simon. I don't think I could have left you here alone, but know I feel at peace to move on with Walter and the life awaiting us in southern Connecticut. Your Aunt Mary waits for us there and has for a few years. It will be good to embrace her and the rest of her family again."

"I miss Aunt Mary too," I said. "I don't remember much from the dark time, but I will never forget being in her home right after mother was taken. She rocked me to sleep that night holding me tightly on her lap and singing sweet lullabies from the old country. Aunt Rhody, you and Uncle John protected me and gave me comfort also. You made sure I could come back to Windsor away from Elder Hoskins and his wife to be with my own family. I will always be grateful to you for that and for so many other things," I stressed.

"Dear child, you have truly become like a daughter to me."

"And you as a mother to me to stand in for my own lost mother," I sighed. "It will be a bittersweet parting between us," I stated sadly. In truth, all these years I thought that it was not only love that motivated Rhody to take care of me but also guilt that she had been too afraid to stand up for my mother Alice more. I overheard her talking about it with Walter one night. I could never blame her. They'd have hanged her as a witch too and more children would have lost their mother.

"Promise me that you'll coax Simon to bring you to visit before too much time passes," she pressed.

"I hope for that," I said. "But there's no need to go to Stratford. John Young and I have nothing to do with each other. It is only your homes and the people in Norwalk that I need to see."

"I understand, Alissa," she said.

I hoped to never see John Young again. Nor did he care if I ever saw him. It was best to leave things as they were.

"Before you go, I must give you the little dowry chest that I had John Moore, the furniture maker, carve for you a few years ago in anticipation of this day. I put all your mother's things in it. Perhaps one day when you are ready, you will want to look inside."

"Perhaps," I said as Simon heaved it over his shoulder and put it in the cart that he had recently purchased for our departure. "Thank you, Aunt Rhody."

Even though it was beautiful, and my mother's belongings should have enticed me, I knew it would be a long time before I could bear to look at them. I sensed the beautiful box held secrets that I might never be courageous enough to unravel.

The rest of the family had come outside and hugged us and said their good wishes to send us off.

"I'm so proud of you Alissa," stated my Uncle John, hugging me tight. "I'm glad I could be here with you at this important time. You've been more important to me than you will ever understand. I promise we will see each other again in Springfield."

"You saved me, uncle, from a fate which I would have never recovered. I'm sure I would have gone mad without your assistance. But you've always been so much more than that. You were always here when I needed you and always brightened my days when they were the darkest. I should always be grateful to you," I kissed him on the cheek.

More tears and more hugs ensued until finally, I squeezed my little cherub, Zub, tightly. He had just started to say my name. "Bye 'Lissa," he waved as we stepped into the front seat of the cart.

"I will never forget your kindness and you will always be in my heart no matter how many miles we may be from each other. Please send my love to Aunt Mary," I called to Aunt Rhody. I had to step down again to embrace her one last time before Simon and I set off toward our new life together in Springfield.

"It's time to go, Alissa." Simon grinned and gave me his hand knowing how difficult it was to leave. "There will be very good things to come. I promise."

I took the invitation and his hand, tearfully waving goodbye as Backer Row disappeared to me forever. I checked to make sure the fertility pouch Aunt Rhody made for me was securely fastened to the pocket of my skirt. I had no idea what life would bring in Springfield, but I knew it was time to move forward. I hoped my nightmares would let me.

Chapter 9

Springfield, Massachusetts, 1654: A New Start

After the bittersweet parting with my Aunt Rhody in Windsor following our marriage celebration, Simon and I headed to Springfield led by his trusty horse. Simon would later tell me that Nutmeg was the same mare spooked by Hugh Percy. The dowry chest that Aunt Rhody prepared for me was rattling in the back of the cart. It haunted me that my mother's possessions were knocking from the inside, pleading to be seen. I wouldn't look in the decorated wooden box for years and asked Simon to store it in the attic space, concealed in an out-of-the-way place in the eaves. I couldn't dispose of it since it was Aunt Rhody's gift of beautiful craftsmanship to me and held the essence of my mother through her belongings. In truth, I hoped to forget about it, leaving it to my children who wouldn't have memories of a dark time brought to life by looking at its contents.

After the ferry crossing on the outskirts of Windsor, it was a fairly straight route to the north to find Springfield. We traversed the main street of most of the town before reaching our final destination.

"Here we are Alissa," Simon told me shortly after we turned around the corner from Main Street. It was the second little cottage on the road leading down to the upper wharf. We'd already passed the grand homes of the past minister, Mr. Moxon, and Springfield's wealthiest founders Mr. Smith, Mr. Holyoke, and Mr. Pynchon on the main street. Before that we'd passed

Robert Ashley's Alehouse across from where the Old Bay Path entered into Springfield. Next, we passed the meeting house, training field, and burying ground, all built adjacent to the Great River. I was finally home.

"I suppose it's not much, but I sincerely hope you'll be happy here with me, my lovely new bride. I'm glad you're with me and even more pleased that we're starting a life together."

I hugged Simon beaming and then dismounted from my seat on the cart with his help. I ran to the door of the cottage to push it open.

"Come here my love. You can't be going over the threshold to your new home without your husband carrying you now, can you? It's supposed to be good luck and help a couple to be fruitful," he winked. He extended his arms out to me.

"Ready? Up you go!" He laughed as he slung me over his shoulder and carried me into our home together.

Giggling, I was happy to let him do it. I felt freer and happier than I'd ever been. It surprised me just how much I felt unincumbered and lighter being away from Windsor. I'd never even realized how much I'd had to be on my guard while I was there, avoiding certain people, deferring to others, just to keep the peace and keep suspicious and malevolent eyes off of me so I'd never suffer the same fate as my mother.

It even surprised me that my melancholy at departing from my Aunt Rhody's side was replaced with excitement to have my own household, to be grown, to be independent and responsible for myself.

The little cottage wasn't much but I loved it. It was no different than most and we could add on as we had children. It was clean and simple with a full hearth and chimney made of bricks and two full rooms with a loft. It might as well have been a palace with how full my heart felt that day. It was more than enough, and it was my domicile, my domestic domain with my beloved new husband, my savior from the suspicious folk in Windsor who might have been glad to eventually name me as Lydia's accomplice had I not been whisked away following our marriage.

I smiled at Simon, glowing with pride to be his wife. I had married a man I loved, a man who was respectable, the assistant for the town leader and most importantly, a man who knew my history and wouldn't hesitate to valiantly stand up for me and protect me if the day should ever come when it was needed.

"It's perfect Simon!" I cried. "You'll see how much a woman's touches will transform this sweet little place even further."

"I have no doubt of that Alissa." He took my face into his strong hands and said, "You have no idea how much I really do believe in you, Alissa. You're always safe with me. You need never fear anything."

I melted into his embrace and inhaled his sweet smell until he pulled me away and grinned. "I haven't shown you the featherbed yet dear lady. Come with me. You might enjoy the surprise I've waiting for you there," he winked again, fully enjoying his mischievousness.

I grinned and played along.

"Shh, be patient husband. I pulled the little fertility bag of herbs from my pocket.

"What's this?" he asked.

As I dutifully fastened it to the bottom of the bed as Aunt Rhody had instructed me to do, I explained, "The fertility herbs in the little satchel, prayed over with love, is supposed to draw our future children's souls to us."

"I'm in complete agreement," he laughed and began to kiss me again, starting with my neck.

I thought I'd be nervous the first time he brought me to his bed, but as I tussled his hair and took in his deep smile, any nervousness left me. We'd already been together at Aunt Rhody's one night and practiced for our time together with the bundling board as was the custom. It made us more comfortable with each other.

We enjoyed each other for a while. Every awkwardness was laughed away as we familiarized ourselves with the body of the other. I surprised myself by how much I wanted to connect with my husband, something not taught but rather was instinctual. He showed me what pleased him and was ever so careful and gentle with me throughout the act of coming intimately together, what was required to make our marriage official before God.

"Do you think the spirit of our first child is lurking about?" he winked. He nuzzled me and smiled before closing his eyes.

"We can only pray that God will send him near," I whispered and kissed his head before curling into him and laying my head on his chest. In no time, we fell asleep in each other's arms. It was late and we had had a very long day.

The next morning, he stood up and announced our plans for the day. "We'll go visiting to the neighbors and I'll introduce you to John Pynchon."

William Pynchon, Springfield's founder, was already gone by the time of my arrival, having been forced out by the religious leaders. They said the treatise he had written back in 1640 was blasphemous and frowned upon its publication in 1650. Two years after that, he fled from the plantation that he had worked so diligently to build, afraid of persecution as a heretic. He left the town in the capable hands of his son John who had been learning from his father since the beginning of the settlement.

"I've a nice surprise for you Alissa. There's another woman next door who I think you'll be fast friends with. Someone to share chores, to share birthing babies and all those womanly things that you might be missing your mother or your Aunt Rhody for. You won't be alone in that way. And this other woman, she just lost her own mother only a mere six months ago. She'll be seeking out the same. Her husband also works for Pynchon. Aye. I've known them quite a while now."

I couldn't believe what I was hearing. How had I found such a kind and caring man? I drank in every detail of his face.

"How did you get to be such a wise man? And a caring one at that?" I asked him softly. His only answer was a slight squeeze of my hand.

Even with Simon's support, I was still a little nervous. What if I wasn't liked by this woman? What if she had heard about my family history? Would she shun me? I kept these thoughts to myself wanting to trust my husband's words and his eagerness for me to have a female companion that I could relate to.

"Would you like to meet her after we have our porridge?" asked Simon.

"Aye, my love. It would be my pleasure to make her acquaintance. What is her name and that of her husband?" I asked.

"The Millers, Sarah and Thomas, I'm sure they'll get along splendidly with you."

After I'd managed to figure out how to stoke the fire in my new hearth and made stock of the food stores, I started cooking cornmeal. I added a little butter I found in the pantry.

"Delicious," he said. "Rhody taught you well, but I've been a bachelor awhile. I'll surprise you one day with the list of meals I can cook," he smiled.

He grabbed my hand. "Come on. I can't wait for you to meet my good friends."

He led me to the property next door, the corner lot we'd passed earlier on the same side of the street when we'd first arrived. On it was the cottage up the hill similar to our own. It was almost identical to Simon's with clapboards nailed on solid wood framing surrounding a central brick chimney. The sun was rising in the east, opposite the river creating morning shadows from trees and buildings between the two. Frost covered farm fields next to the river while they slept until spring. The scene was beautiful. Another gift out of many, I told myself.

Simon knocked on the massive door with one hand and held on to me with the other. I rocked back and forth as we waited, unable to remain still.

A slightly heavyset young woman with golden curly hair and a bright beaming smile greeted us. I judged her to be no more than twenty-one, but her full figure showed that she was not in want of anything. She looked very familiar, but I couldn't place her.

"Why Simon Beamon, who do we have here? Have you taken yourself a wife?" she peered at me kindly. Soon her husband Thomas Miller was at the door as well.

Simon responded. "Indeed, I have. This is my new wife, Alissa Beamon, the daughter of John Young of Windsor."

"What good news! Come into the house and drink some ale with us. Let's toast to your new marriage," said Thomas. As we entered the humble home,

I caught a glimpse of two children sleeping in a cradle under quilts that looked brand new.

Sarah motioned for Simon and me to sit at the rough wooden table in front of the hearth. As soon as Sarah caught a better glimpse of me in the fire's glow, she knew that she recognized me too.

"Wait a minute. I know you, Alissa. And I recognized your father's name. You might not remember me because I'm probably just a few years older than you and slightly plumper than I used to be. I do know you though. Aye. Indeed, I do!"

I sunk into the chair knowing that the notoriety of my family would always put me in a position to be judged. Whereas I'd just been feeling free in my new home an hour earlier, reality had set in. Sarah must have sensed my thoughts with my change of expression.

"Oh no. I don't mean it that way. You needn't be worried about any judgements from me. I'm from Windsor too. I know what you've gone through," she said kindly.

Of course, that's where she was from. I had never been anywhere other than Windsor except for Springfield.

"You wouldn't have known me by the name Sarah Miller at that time. I was Sarah Marshfield, the daughter of Mercy Marshfield and the disgraced Samuel Marshfield. My father left us with his bad investments and his overwhelming debts. His poor decisions and then not taking responsibility for them when he fled brought great shame upon my mother and his children including me. We moved to Springfield to make a new start about a year after you lost your mother. They looked down upon us in Windsor. My mother couldn't be there anymore."

My perceptions changed in an instant. With her confession I felt more comfortable and on equal footing with Sarah. Her family had suffered humiliation and loss as well. I was familiar with her family's story and my Uncle John Tinker had acted as attorney to recoup some of the investments made by his clients in Sarah's father's unsuccessful enterprises.

"So, you see, you need not be embarrassed. I really won't judge you for the damage to your mother's reputation and the cruelty forced upon her. Many people knew she was a healer and not a witch. I've shame enough in my own family. In fact, as I'm sure you'll hear about soon enough, my mother was accused of witchcraft by Molly Percy. But we were luckier. The accusation didn't stick, and my mother won her slander case against her accuser. Still, things got worse with Hugh Percy, Molly's husband."

Her husband Thomas suddenly cleared his throat. "Please, Sarah, that's enough of that for now. Let's talk of other subjects with our new friends."

I must have looked stunned by these revelations for she paused and looked at me for a moment and then back at her husband.

"Do you need me to stop? Am I upsetting you?"

"Oh no, I'm fine," I assured her.

"You can hear about it later, if you want," interjected Simon, "But for now, I agree with Thomas. I don't think either of us care a lick about Hugh Percy nor do we want to ever think about him again."

"So, I guess your new husband won't be telling you of all the weird and devilish things that happened with these two men here in regards to Hugh. Praise the Lord, Hugh and his wife are no longer here in Springfield. Sometimes there really are witches you know," she explained.

"Enough of that, dear wife. You don't want to scare your new friend. I've an idea. Suppose we come together again this evening after all our chores and obligations are done with for the day. We'll celebrate properly."

He turned to his wife, Sarah. "And you, no more of this kind of talk. We won't be worrying about a thing tonight. But for now, just one more mug, eh?"

He filled four mugs to the rim with ale. As he did, I exchanged glances of bewilderment with my husband. I'd been avoiding it, but I suppose one day the topic of witchcraft would finally force its way to the surface again.

For now, I was relieved to change the subject and realized that Sarah could have talked all day in her friendly and blunt manner. It was obvious to me that Sarah, having lost her mother only six months earlier, must have been lonely for another woman near her age who she could share her experiences with. I loved how she was direct about her own misfortunes, not trying to hide them. It truly put me at ease, and I knew that coming from such a place of candor, we would be fast friends going forward.

When we finally left, Simon walked me around our neighborhood on the lane going down to the wharf.

In those days, Springfield was at the height of its beaver trade. It bustled during the peak months of pelt trading from late fall to early spring when furs were brought in by Natives from all over the western territories. I was taken aback at first by the overwhelming stench of pelts piling up for days in a warehouse next to the upper wharf waiting to be shipped downstream.

"The larger house with small stockade across the street belongs to the Morgans." Simon pointed to the lot directly across from the Millers.

"You'll run there in case of danger from intruders if I'm not around. They're a kind and practical couple from Wales, in their thirties. Miles is a sawyer who cuts boards for Pynchon. He's also a butcher and his wife, Prudence, is always helpful despite being busy with her brood," he said.

"Do you like most of your neighbors?" I asked.

"Aye. Most of them come from good stock and are easy to get along with. Well, just about everyone. The lot over there, right across from us is the Stebbins family. John Stebbins can be a little cross sometimes, but pay him no mind, he just gets rattled easily when things get strange. He has heard some bizarre things like Hugh's wife, Goody Percy, saying that she and other witches had once frolicked in his fields. I suppose he's a decent man though and his wife, Anne, is certainly neighborly. John's father, Roland, lives in town too."

I looked a little anxious.

"Don't worry my angel. Everyone will love you. In due time, you'll get to know them all. Now, if you look across the other way toward the next road to the North, you'll see the Cooper's place, the one closer towards the river and the one higher on the hill behind our lot belongs to Francis Pepper, a bachelor who is happy to stay that way," he laughed. "Silly man doesn't know what he's missing." He put his arm around me as happy as a lark.

"Are you ready to meet my employer, Master John Pynchon?" Simon asked.

I shrugged my shoulders and smiled shyly not knowing what to expect.

"He lives at the brick manor over there. You might remember it from your childhood. Your Uncle John would take you there on his visits and sometimes I would tag along. But it was usually the senior Pynchon who you saw. I don't remember if you ever interacted with his son John. We'll go see him and then you can rest and get your bearings until we meet with the Millers again tonight. How's that sound, my love?"

"Anything for you," I said and took his hand to meet the big boss.

It was pleasant meeting Mr. John Pynchon. He was cordial and congratulated us warmly. He was busy and didn't spend a lot of time with us, but he allowed Simon to take another day off to help me get settled in.

Later that night, we drank our fill with plenty of toasts and stories. I came to learn how Thomas and Simon became close friends at the beginning of their employment with William Pynchon. I learned of some of their exploits with Native tribes in the area while helping Mr. Pynchon to secure the land in and surrounding Springfield and the challenges of early settlement. It was clear that Springfield was a company town from the start. The enterprise of a fur trading hub, the only one on the western frontier, was the idea of Mr. Pynchon, now an outcast from the place he spent so much sweat and toil creating.

I hadn't been in Springfield long, but it certainly seemed different than I first remembered it in my brief stay right after my mother died. Everything was smaller and simpler because I was no longer in the body of a small child.

I woke up in the middle of the night after our merriment dripping in a cold chilling sweat. Perhaps my malaise was caused by the abundance of ale that night; or maybe the talk of witches, accusers, and victims that Sarah put brusquely in my thoughts earlier in the day were to blame. Whatever the reason, I was forced to confront the sober revelation that my nightmares had not ended by moving to Springfield. They had only just begun.

Chapter 10

Springfield, Massachusetts, 1647 & 1654: Nightmares

Before awakening, I must have thrashed about the featherbed so much that I'd woken Simon before myself.

"What is it, wife?" He shook me awake the whole way. Confused as to where I was, I cried profusely and collapsed deep into the blankets. It took several minutes before I finally responded to the gentle rubbing on my back and was able to escape my night terrors.

"There now, Alissa. What's the matter, my love?"

I sat up into wakefulness, welcomed by his strong and comforting embrace.

"I'm sorry Simon. I was not myself. I saw some terrible things. Some of the same ones I always see in my bad dreams. But there were some new hellish images too. I wish they'd leave me alone. Even being in a new place won't make them go!" I sobbed into his shoulder.

Our little cottage was still dark, and embers gently fizzled in the fire. We could barely see anything except for what was revealed by the few rays of moonshine that entered the tiny, frosted windows on the front of the house. Shadows had long stopped dancing on the simple wooden walls of the hall near the hearth. Once I had quieted, Simon arose to feed the fire. Again, the flickering shadows resumed their dances, and I was comforted by the kind caring image of Simon's face.

"Do you want to tell me about them, Alissa?" he asked, stroking my hair.

I thought for a moment. What harm could it do? They chase after me like fantastical beasts anyway no matter how much I try to ignore them or forget them. Perhaps they'd fade if they knew that my protective husband had been made privy to them also.

"I always see dark moving water, Simon. And my mother is near it or in it, but I can't see her. I only hear her screaming for me in a panicked, terrifying way. I hear her clearly, but I can never see even a shadow of her. I try desperately to find her, to help her, but her voice quickly fades away, and I am left feeling empty and alone. It's always unsettling."

He pulled my hair out of my face and kissed my cheeks. "You're never alone with me, Alissa."

"I feel you with me now, but in the nightmares, I'm afraid I will always feel alone, desperately trying to find my mother and never reaching her in time to save her from an angry mob. It also leaves me with a deep feeling of sorrow and even regret. The feeling that I should have done something differently haunts me."

I paused and stared into the darkness before continuing.

"Simon, I remember so little of the horrible day that they took my mother and even less about the events that led up to it. Yet, it still troubles me. I'm afraid. For the first time tonight, I saw the crowd. There were scythes and muskets. Then everything went black until I saw the dark, murky, moving water again and Mother yelled my name. What am I to do?" I asked helplessly.

Simon's strong arms remained firm around me as he spoke in a gentle voice.

"Alissa, you will get past these nightmares once you have your own children and they become your focus. Until then, busy yourself with helping others and being as useful as you can. Try to avoid thinking of the past. We'll pray together that God grants you grace to not be tormented like this every night. May He give you protection from your torments once and for all. But no matter the case, I'll be here with you, helping you through."

I sobbed quietly as he sat with me in silence. Once my breathing had calmed and the sobbing stopped, he lifted my chin.

"Do you feel a little better now my love?" he asked.

I shook my head and laid down again, nuzzling him.

"I suppose we should try to sleep again. My first Sabbath day in Springfield is tomorrow. I don't want to look dreadful my first time in the meeting house in front of the whole congregation," I said.

"Alissa, close your eyes and sleep like a baby," he said, kissing my forehead softly.

It was a crisp cold day but easy to navigate through the town. The first snows had not started. Simon and I walked briskly to keep warm. Turning the corner onto the main street, the wealthy founders' imposing residences dominated the road. There weren't many though and soon we were able to make out the two bell towers of the little meeting house. One tower was the lookout to watch for approaching Indians and the other contained the bell. It was ringing and leading residents to its door.

The meeting house was tinier than I remembered it, not nearly as intimidating as when I was a small child forced to sit with Elder Hoskins' wife in the front women's pew. She had watched me sternly and without pause, willing me to absorb every word of scripture to avoid my mother's sins. I understood early in life that I could not prevent my mother's tarnished reputation from sullying my own. Mrs. Hoskins made that very clear no matter the good works I did. She said I would have to humble myself before the Lord and bow to His will. I was happy to be here with Simon instead. I'd get no such talk from him. I nodded at my new husband as we went to our separate seats in the simple communal room.

As expected, people regarded me with interest, happy to relieve their curiosity as to whom Simon decided to wed. Their reaction to me was mixed: a meeting house of polite indifference, genuine neighborliness, and awkward stares. But as soon as Sarah Miller joined me on the women's side of the meeting house in her adjacent seat on the same bench, the atmosphere became warmer. After she'd greeted me with a welcoming embrace, I could sense the rest of the townsfolk easing a bit in their initial assessment of me.

"I'm so happy to have another companion to sit next to me. You're in my mother's old place. Thank you, Alissa. It gives me comfort. And hopefully, you won't mind helping rein in the little ones with me. It's a bit of a challenge without Mum here."

"Of course, I will," I whispered, squeezing her hand. "I'm happy to be a comfort to you. I'm glad you're here too. You are also a salve for me. You've no idea how much."

As the minister and deacons walked in, I tried to make myself comfortable on the hard bench that would be my home for the long hours of sermons that followed that day.

Springfield had yet to find a permanent minister after Mr. Moxom left. On this day, we had another traveling guest minister. His repertoire was the same that I'd heard in the meeting house in Windsor — Bible verses, atonement for our sins, being on guard against the Devil who wanted to trick us and not letting him do so. Aye, I'd heard it before and would hundreds of times again before my death. But that was why we were supposed to be on this Earth: to be vessels of God's knowledge and lessons, and to bestow them on our children to purify the land we'd come to be a part of.

I remember sitting on a little stool at my mother's skirts listening along with her at the meeting house in Windsor. All those hours in the meeting house didn't seem to do her a bit of good. Did the ministers really think that all the lessons they had preached about were repelled by every fiber of her being? I'd never understand it. At least those were the thoughts shared with me by Deacon Hoskins who put me in his care after mother was taken away from me. I was glad that he and his unpleasant wife weren't in Springfield long. My fate was lightened when he'd decided he'd had enough of New England and went back to his home in England.

Uncle John had been at the ready to take me back to Aunt Rhody to live as soon as he heard the Hoskins were leaving. Simon came with him to pick me and my spare belongings up from the Hoskins before they left. They brought me to Mr. Pynchon's to make sure I was ready.

"Child, I know we've talked about you going back to live with your Aunt Rhody. She loves you and she'll do well by you. I wanted to make sure you're agreeable to go back to Backer Row. I know a lot happened there and if it is too much for you, we can figure out something else," he said.

"No! I want to be with Aunt Rhody! She's been kind to me, as much as Aunt Mary. Please take me back to live with my family!" I pleaded.

"But who am I going to tease now that you're leaving Springfield?" Simon asked with a big grin.

"Well, you'll just have to find someone else. I need to be with my aunt!" I shouted.

"Say, it isn't so! The sunshine is leaving Springfield. You'll be back one day to brighten our town again though. Won't ye?" he teased a little more in his boyish voice.

"Maybe I will but maybe I won't. Don't know, silly," I said with childish innocence.

"Ah well. I'll have to live with that then. But you promise me that you won't forget me, and you'll try to keep your head up and think of happy things."

"Alright. I will," I promised and grinned with a big gap in my front teeth. New ones were coming in.

"Alissa, can you go find Mrs. Pynchon in the back at the big hearth? We've a little more to discuss here and I think she's made you a treat. A little to eat now and a little to share with Aunt Rhody later," he said.

"Aye, I will do it, Uncle John." I exited the room as Uncle John closed a chestnut door. Always good at spying, I lingered to see if they would talk about me.

"It's a blessing the child remembers so little. Indeed, it's the only way she is able to go back," he said.

"Such a sweet little one," said Simon. "I hope it will be good for her to be with your sister."

"Rhody will be a blessing to her. I'm sure of that! And I'll make sure that Rhody has the means to take care of her. It's the least I can do. You're right. She is a sweet child. How I wished I could have done something to save her mother."

Then, there was only silence in the room. I remembered what he asked me to do and quickly sought out Mrs. Pynchon with her servants in the kitchen area with the gigantic hearth. The inviting aroma of apple tarts wafted through the air. As a child, I could only hope that it was a prelude to my time with Aunt Rhody.

On our way to Windsor again, I wondered, What was I forgetting? And if I remembered it, would it be my curse instead of a blessing as Uncle John described?

Chapter 11

Springfield, Massachusetts, 1655: Close Friends

Sarah and I had become attached since I moved to Springfield, and every day we became a little closer. I had never imagined upon leaving Windsor that I'd find a twin in my dear neighbor and new friend. She was five years older than me, so we hadn't been friends in Windsor. I barely remembered her from childhood although I knew I had seen her in the meeting house. I'd heard the name Marshfield and faintly remembered that it had been attached to controversy.

As the cold weather intensified, Sarah asked me to help her with her enterprise of making coats. She made them for townsfolk, traders and Indians too. Sarah was behind on several orders that needed to be completed. She fretted that with the care of her two young children in addition to her regular chores, she wouldn't be able to manage to keep up with all her orders. I was happy to oblige. It was a little extra money afforded to me as I built my household with Simon, and it reminded me of the sewing circles that my cousins held on Backer Row during the colder months.

Since it was winter and the peak of the beaver trade in Springfield, there was ample opportunity to sell coats to passing traders not normally in the town. There were thousands of pelts that arrived and were loaded into the cargo holds of ships waiting at the upper wharf. We witnessed a good deal of the trading, living near the dock, Mr. Pynchon's estate and the town center.

In those days, there were many groups of tribal contingents who came through town, all wanting to benefit from the pelt trade. Some knocked on our doors for our husbands to arrange trade with Mr. Pynchon.

Overall, I liked Springfield, despite the overpowering stench of the beaver pelts for part of the year. There were gossips in town, of course, but Simon was respected, and I tried to fit in the best I could.

However, the nightmares that had always been with me did not pause. They became even stronger after Sarah and I became engrossed in conversation about what had happened to her by the hand of Hugh Percy and her own mother's witch accusations.

It came up one day while we were sewing together, working on the coat orders and talking about our lives to pass the time. Sarah was generous in sharing the details of her life and encouraged me to feel no shame in telling my own story.

"Ah. Look at that stitching. Those little fingers are nimble. I don't think I could have done a better job myself," Sarah told me approvingly as she peered to look at the hem of a coat I'd just completed, the very first one that I'd finished for her.

"You do fine work. Your mother must have taught you well," she stated.

"I've had plenty of practice," I said. I explained how I'd spent many hours in the sewing, weaving and spinning circle with my cousins each winter. Stitching to me was easy and relaxing. I was happy to be useful to my new friend and proud to receive her praise for my work.

Sarah was the kind of person who was open to the world. She had no inhibitions, never hiding, always friendly unless given reason not to be. She complimented my quieter disposition and made me feel comfortable. It was easy and natural to become friends. We were connected in so many ways and each year those connections grew stronger.

"Do you remember much about your mother?" she asked. "You talked of your sewing circle but not once did you mention what your mummy taught you," she observed.

"Oh, I suppose that's true," I said putting down the needle and thread and smoothing the finished coat. "I remember very little of my mother. Just a few memories of us in the garden or cooking at the hearth. I feel guilty not remembering her more but I'm afraid," I admitted.

"Are you afraid of seeing her as a witch?" she asked me honestly.

"No. Not that. I know without any doubt that Mother was anything but a witch. She was kind and caring. She was a bit shy in much the way I am. Always so gentle. Even though the Hoskins, who briefly took me into their care, pressed me to believe that she was a witch, I never did. I knew with my whole body that they were lying! My mother was never capable of such a thing and believing so would have been a betrayal. How could I ever do that? Even as a young child, my heart was loyal and assured me that she was innocent."

I paused and fumbled with some thread. It felt good to talk to Sarah, but I was also so afraid that my hands started to shake. It was the first time ever that I had told anyone how I felt about my mother. But Sarah was so sympathetic toward me, I could open up like a rose in early summer.

"What I fear the most, Sarah, is feeling her pain, and knowing that I cannot do a thing to help her or bring her back to life. I also fear that with each memory, the loss of my beautiful mother will also become more debilitating than it has already been. It'll become even more of a terrible loss and I'm not so keen on carrying that burden on my chest. It would suffocate me to death."

Sarah looked at me with pity in her eyes and complete understanding. She could relate more than I understood.

"I know the pain you feel, Alissa. The horrible things said about my own mum make me so sad sometimes if I let myself think of those days."

Her baby had started stirring in the cradle and she pulled her up to her breast with ease before continuing her story.

"By God's saints, my mummy should have joined them with all the suffering she went through: abandoned by my father, left with all his debts and all the shame that came with it. What a scoundrel he was, leaving his family in the lurch like he did."

I shook my head in agreement.

"Aye. That's another thing we have in common, Sarah. I know what it is to feel abandonment by my father — a father who didn't stick up for my mother, didn't help her, just left and let her take on all the shame for everyone. John

Young didn't help my mother and he's never really helped me either. He's barely spoken a word to me since they took her away. I despise men like that. It's just not fair."

"Thank God in His grace, the same won't happen to us, Alissa. We've been provided for by men who will do us honor and not leave us like that. I know Thomas Miller and Simon Beamon are good men. At least we have that. But even they can't replace the bonds a mother has with her child, and we'll probably always feel sorrow for the pain they went through," she said as she glanced at the daughter at her breast.

I quietly sat on the stool and contemplated what she said. We both felt melancholy infusing into the room. It was good to talk honestly about our mothers, but it was tiring emotionally.

"Alissa, I would have hoped that was the last of the suffering my mum would have had to go through, but it wasn't so. As I told you the first night I met you, she'd brought us to Springfield hoping for a fresh start but that's not what she received from the Percys. I know what it's like to have your mother be accused of witchcraft. My poor mum, Mercy Marshfield, went from a shameful situation to another one where Molly Percy, Hugh's wife, made sure to make my mum's difficulties even worse by calling her a witch. You know too well that's a mighty dangerous thing to place on a person. Molly Percy didn't even know her, but she talked like a raving lunatic all the same! Of course, I don't doubt the influence of us coming from Windsor when we did. Your own mum had just been hanged," she explained.

I was visibly startled. "I'm sorry, Alissa. I'm just going to say it. Your mum was murdered by an ungrateful community she'd spent hours trying to nurse back to health. People heard about it for miles around, the witch part that is. Being a healing woman somehow got lost in travels. It was wrong. Her story got passed around far and wide and by the time we got to Springfield, Molly Percy had made up her mind that my mother had to be a witch since we came from Windsor."

"Yes, they did murder her," I admitted. In an instant, I was overflowing like a dam that had broken after holding up water for years. Sarah put her babe down, already satiated with milk and pulled me in tight in a heartfelt embrace.

"There. There. Just let it all go. You needn't hold back. Let the tears come as they may. It's allowed to grieve your mum here. You're always safe with me," she whispered.

I don't know how long I cried that day in Sarah's arms, but I do know it seemed like an eternity. Finally composing myself, I took a cloth from Sarah to dry my tears and wipe my nose. She even brewed me a little chamomile tea to soothe my nerves.

Once I was feeling a little better, I wondered what happened to her own mother.

"Thank you so much, my friend. What about your mother, Sarah? I don't recall hearing of her trial. I hope that is not how she died? I seem to remember you telling me at another time, she was vindicated." I asked for confirmation.

"Aye. It was a happier ending. And thank the Lord for that. Mr. Pynchon ruled upon hearing the case that Molly Percy had slandered my mother. The townspeople had already been dealing with the Percy couple and knew that Molly was not quite right in the head, but that Hugh was pure evil in his interactions. He made us all shudder. If anyone was a witch, it was him. Such evil deeds to the town folk for no good reason whatsoever."

Sarah's older child, only a little older than the baby, awoke from his nap and started screaming from his trundle bed. She picked him up quickly with her strong arms and started rocking him.

"There now, little one. 'Tis but a bad memory."

Then she looked at me.

"Hugh even tried to hex my children in the womb, Alissa. My wee ones know. They could feel the fits I went into at the end of my pregnancies along with the headaches and swollen feet. It was terrible. I even had fits on the meeting house floor at the site of the couple," she finished and turned to her child.

"There, there. Here's one." She pulled out her bosom once again and gave it to the child to drink.

"Even ask your husband. You must have heard how Simon had to testify against Hugh."

I nodded but had been afraid to ask for the details.

"I don't think I can hear anymore today about witches, Sarah. I'm just so tired. I'm sorry."

"No! I should be the one who is sorry! You just cried enough to fill a lake and I still talk about witches. What's wrong with me? Dear friend, it is I who need to apologize to you. Why don't you go home now and rest. No more coat making for today. If you want me to tell you the story another time I will. You just have to ask if you want me to. Until then, we'll talk of other things, and you'll go home now and have your peace," she said with wisdom.

"I think I want to hear a lot of your stories, Sarah. And, another day, I hope to do just that!"

She nodded and kissed me on the cheek. We smiled at each other knowing we shared a special connection that would make us inseparable friends from that day forward. The bond between us had been sealed by a shared outpouring of the heart. Sarah wasn't just a good friend. She had become a sister. In her embrace and her acceptance, I felt that perhaps one day, I could gain the strength to heal.

Chapter 12

Windsor, Connecticut, 1645-46: Girls of Backer Row

I suppose it's not surprising that I did not remember all that much from my childhood. Just snippets here and there. But after moving to Springfield and grieving with Sarah, those memories started to come back with a vengeance. My new memories helped to explain things that hadn't made sense in previous years.

Backer Row, the little street where we lived, was filled with children. I had no shortage of friends who I could play with and do chores with. Most of them were my cousins. We were close and would spend our days in each other's homes or in our families' gardens, always working together as if we were really just one unit. The exception was the two daughters of the deceased minister Reverend Huit, Lydia and Mercy. Lydia confided that her uncle, Deacon Clark, warned them that they were to avoid the influences of our family. I always thought that was strange. I didn't understand, but they didn't either or they wouldn't have played with us at all.

Many times, I'd reflected that I'd rather be unsure of what happened, distanced from pain, and steady in my current world, eventually one of motherhood and children than to be aware of what had occurred. Why shouldn't my thoughts remain far from the past? I reasoned, no good could possibly come from dwelling there. But I had no control over these random bursts of new awareness. With each new piece I saw from my childhood, even joyful pieces, I felt disoriented, like the Earth was moving beneath my feet.

When I came to join Aunt Rhody on Backer Row only a year after I'd left, it was empty of most of the family that lived there previously, and a sadness lingered. My friends were gone. I knew they'd left us during the dark time of disease, but I was unable to piece together how or why it happened. The details escaped me as did some of our times together too. Their absence left me feeling lonely and melancholy much of the time.

But finally, after many years, I started to remember the experiences that I had with my cousins, my friends and playmates on Backer Row. Any small image, texture, aroma, or taste could be a window into my past.

It started in my garden, planting onions and one such remembrance came to me innocently slipping out into the new world I inhabited. Sweet Sarah Sension, my neighbor and cousin, was laughing with me as we helped our mothers in the garden. Sarah was my Aunt Mary's girl. She was always bright and had the face of a little angel.

I also remembered the fearlessness of my young companion. It was no more apparent than on our little adventures together with the other girls of Backer Row. Those first memories led to others.

As young girls, the elders in Windsor village tried to teach us that the woods were a very foreboding place — a place of nightmares and torments. On the pulpits each Sunday, the preachers tried to fill us with images of demons stabbing us with their pitchforks of sin and luring us with temptations to do their bidding should we ever let down our guard and go to where they lived — the dark, deep and unsettled woods. There, we were also told, they had grand meetings and festivities of untamed merriment with Indians who were plotting to kill us.

My mother seemed to ignore their entreaties and dismiss their horrific images. She had a way of making it sound ridiculous based on the real experiences we had actually had in our lives. One day I was with my pack of girlfriends, I dared them to come with me and follow the stream that met the river. I'd found a wild patch of strawberries with my mother and wanted to show my friends. Just as we spied the river, we saw some canoes filled with Natives coming to town to sell their wares.

Priscilla, the oldest daughter of the Thorntons, looked on with alarm. "We shouldn't have come. Oh, how evil may lurk here! Why did you lead us to such a place?" she asked me warily. Priscilla, part of the older contingent of girls, was always pious and fearful. She could be kind, but of course tattled on our exploits a little too much.

Sarah Sension defended our natural curiosity and our Native neighbors. "Why cousin, stop this nonsense. You know quite well they mean no harm. They only want to sell us the goods from their labors so that their own children may prosper. Sarah too was part of the older group at eleven. "They will pass, and we will continue on our way. No need to show ourselves. Stay calm, cousin," she said trying to reassure Priscilla.

Hannah, Aunt Rhody's daughter, started to mimic Priscilla, dramatically bringing her hand to her mouth and acting shocked. "Oh, shall we be kidnapped by the Natives today? I'm Priscilla and the Devil told me it is so!" The horde of us laughed.

A miffed Priscilla attempted to defend herself. "You do not take me seriously? It will be at your own peril. We must listen to our parents and elders. They know the true ways of the world," she said.

"Come now, Priscilla. We listen to our parents, but we must not put words in their mouths that have not been spoken. Please, let us pick the berries I told you about. We can bring them back to Mother. She will not mind and can help us make something delicious with them."

"Aye, Priscilla," Sarah turned to the visibly disturbed girl and spoke with sympathy. "It will work out, cousin. We are still a mere few minutes from our own home lots. You worry too much just like your mother. It will be fine as long as we are together in a group."

"Come on!" I said before rustling the branches hanging over the path. Why did Priscilla always have to carry on so? Before too long we reached the place of plentiful berries.

"There they are!" I pointed with excitement after seeing even more berries than there were a few days before. After we'd picked a good amount of them and covered our baskets to protect them, we retraced our steps in the woods and across the meadow.

"How I should like to see what life would be like with the Indians! Doesn't anybody ever wonder about that?" asked Hannah. "What do the Indian girls like us do all day? Are they not picking berries in their own meadows?"

"I wish we could meet them," said Sarah. It's a shame that most of the Indian children do not come into town with their parents.

Anne, Priscilla's younger sister closer to my age, was mostly quiet but this stoked a keen interest.

"Father says we must pray for the Indian children. They are not as fortunate as we are."

"And why would that be?" I asked.

Priscilla came forward, always the expert, always the one who knew better than everyone else.

"Well of course because they have no benefit of knowing God, Alissa."

"How do you know? Maybe they see God too," I said.

Hannah placed her hands on her hips in defiance, always ready to contest the so-called wisdom of her cousin Priscilla.

"Aye, how would YOU know Priscilla?"

"Do you not listen to our ministers? Do you not hear what they warn us of in the meeting house? We must be on our guard against pagans such as the Indians. Have you all forgotten your lessons?" she screamed at us impatiently.

We were well out of the woods now and the clearing opened up so that Backer Row stood partially in view.

"Well, I think you just don't know," said Hannah. "How would you know anyway? You can't even speak their language to ask!"

"I just do," said Priscilla defiantly.

We skipped up Backer Row past Aunt Rhody's house until we came to mine.

"Mother will have an idea of what we can do with the strawberries," I said.

We filed into the cottage, proud to show her what we gathered.

"Mother, look! We gathered up the strawberries we found on the edge of the woods near the river. Please help us do something with them," I begged as the others joined in.

"What suits your fancy young ladies? A sweet drink? Or maybe some griddle cakes with strawberries on the inside? Strawberry muffins?

Strawberry gruel? What do you think?" she asked us.

"Strawberry drinks!" we shouted with glee. "Strawberry cakes too!"

"I see. So how about this idea? We take a few strawberries and mix them in boiled water, sweeten them with some honey and add just a few dried sumac berries for color," The throng of girls listened carefully.

"Then, we can put the rest of the strawberries into cornmeal griddle cakes," she explained.

"Aye, do both!" everyone agreed.

"Gather round the table girls, let's get busy," she smiled, pulling out cornmeal, flour and honey. We settled in around the table and enjoyed ourselves and the fun respite we had on this day from the litany of tasks we needed to do. Our families had to rely on themselves and each other. Our lives were only made easier because our families reused the farm fields that Natives had once cultivated.

"Priscilla thinks the Natives are dangerous," I blurted out. The rest of the girls carried on excitedly, talking all at once to explain our conversation in the woods. Mother understood and interjected.

"Priscilla you are not the only one to think this way, but may I ask all of you, are there not Natives that come to us from upriver to sell us their baskets and food and medicines on a regular basis who cause no trouble?" she asked. "Do you not remember the Indian man who works with your Uncle John? Let me tell you a story."

Mother was calm as she recalled her first encounters with the Natives, first in Massachusetts Bay and then in Connecticut. She explained how an old Native woman had been kind to her and taught her much of what she knew of New England's medicinal plants. There was something wild in her that would always be drawn to the forest and the people who inhabited it — something that no amount of godly discussion at the meeting house would tame. She couldn't be like the ministers. She tried to see the good in everybody.

And being my mother's sole 'blessing', she doted on me and wasn't much of a disciplinarian as some of the ministers advised parents to be. She'd often whisper to me, "I know you are good my Alice, my little Alissa." I was named after her and her mother before her, but she called me Alissa saying how flowing and beautiful it sounded. Unlike her, other women on Backer Row had no shortage of children. They were fruitful and did multiply as instructed in the Bible. I know mother wanted other children. I sensed a sadness in her despite her attempts to be outwardly cheerful.

In any case, Mother made us all happy that day and I'd like to think we offered her a little joy as well. The memory of sitting around my mother's table with my cousins as she told her unique stories was as sweet as the strawberries themselves in the drinks and the griddle cakes we made even if it did leave me with a longing to see them all again.

Chapter 13

Springfield, Massachusetts, Summer 1655: A Man's World

Sarah and I continued to come together almost every day to work on the coats or help each other with our household obligations. Life in Springfield took on a new rhythm, a steady cadence of the chores needed to be done for our survival intermingled with new social interactions with neighbors and a bond with Sarah which only continued to strengthen with time.

I received occasional letters from Aunt Rhody imploring me to visit, telling me how much she missed me, and sending the greetings of the rest of the family. Ultimately, she was very happy she'd joined her beloved sister Mary and the rest of the Sension family in Norwalk, Connecticut.

I didn't travel there my first year in Springfield as a married woman even though I desperately missed my family, and nothing would have given me more pleasure than to see them again. Simon would have loved it too, but it wasn't possible. Mr. Pynchon had already granted Simon free time to court and then marry me in Windsor. Our lives were busy and focused on settling in together in Springfield. Unfortunately, travel to the southern reaches of Connecticut would have to wait. I hoped that with Simon's occasional travels, an opportunity would arise to visit Norwalk later.

Life went along smoothly until I heard the news of Thomas Gilbert coming to town to marry his wife's sister-in-law, the widow Catherine Chapin Bliss, wife of Lydia's deceased brother Nathaniel. The news jolted me into distress. It had been only six months since Thomas had lost Lydia, maligned as a witch, by a brutal hanging in Hartford.

At first, I did not understand why I was upset by his remarriage. It was common for widows and widowers to marry quickly in most cases. After all, our lives in the colonies were not easy and a household required the toil of both partners. I didn't know the Gilberts well enough to warrant such emotion. The Bliss family condoned the marriage and supported their decision so that their son's family would not be left without someone to care for them. They were already familiar with Thomas. As far as they knew, he'd been a good husband to Lydia while she was alive, and he already knew the Bliss children as their uncle by marriage.

It was May and the yard and gardens were steeped in blooming flowers representing every hue in a rainbow. Still working on our sewing projects, we loved to be in the fresh air outside with the bright light of the sun shining on our work and making it easier for us to see and follow the tiny lines of stitching on the garments we sewed. Sarah's children loved the outdoors too where they could take in the warmth and play in their pens that we placed in the gardens.

"Did you see him?" Sarah asked me as I picked out a needle to thread a new color of thread.

"Who?" I responded.

"Thomas Gilbert, of course. I know you knew who I was talking about. What's the matter? Bad memories?"

"It's not fair Sarah," I said. His wife is dead, and he can go on as if nothing happened. It bothers me so. I know it's not his fault, but if it were the other way around and he had been accused of witchcraft, you know that they never would have let her go. She as the wife would have been called a witch too and died hanging right next to him."

"No. 'Tis never just when it comes to the lives of women," she nodded. "Never has been and I suppose it never will be. With Eve enjoying an apple at the suggestion of the Devil in the form of a serpent, we'll never be forgiven.

The ministers and other powerful men will use it over our heads at will to hold us down forever. I don't understand why it's so bad that Eve ate an apple. Why would God put a whole garden there for sustenance and not allow a woman to use it to sustain herself and her man? It's a woman's instinct! Aren't we all trying to get our apple orchards to prosper? I really think something went askew in the translation of that story," she said looking around and putting a finger to her lips. "I trust you'll not repeat anything I say that could be construed as blasphemy!"

"You're always safe with me, my sister," I laughed. Then I paused and became serious thinking of my mother's demise. "I suppose it best not to say those things in the company of others. It's our secret," I confirmed.

"My mother's situation was even worse than Lydia's. John Young never stood up for her, never comforted me, and was the first to get as far away as he could, following the Thorntons down to Stratford. Do you know that he never even visited her at her prison cell, not in Windsor, nor in Hartford? Just abandoned her and me. I hate him, Sarah. I shouldn't, but I do. I doubt he'll find another wife who will be as kind and patient as my mother was with him, always dressing his wounds caused by strange skin eruptions. She'd wrap his chest too in liniments because he was always coughing and having congestion, a type of pleurisy. He was a lot older than her and treated her more like a servant than a wife. At least that's how I saw it," I explained. "She never complained as if she had agreed that she owed him something."

I was irritated and kept rocking back and forth on my feet. I'd even pull at my nail beds until they bled. It was a terrible habit, one of nervousness, but I couldn't stop it.

"Let me make you some chamomile tea again Alissa, to calm your nerves," Sarah coaxed me to sit at the table.

Suddenly my agitated thoughts shifted to other worries. "Tell me the details, Sarah. I should know," I said in a rare moment of bravery.

"What details, my dear?"

"The details of being bewitched during your time with child? Could that really have been the case?" I asked. Something deep inside was nagging at me.

What was the connection to being with child and witchcraft? I couldn't quite understand where it was coming from.

"Are you sure you really want to know?" she questioned. "Why worry about things that have already passed?"

"I don't know. I need to understand everything. I need to clear up the constant confusion in my head to see if I can make any more sense of things," I said.

"If you truly want to know, I should go to the beginning again."

I shook my head. "Aye, please tell me."

"Alright. The town folk in Springfield knew Molly Percy was peculiar so people didn't always believe her. She spouted off all kinds of fantastical things and even said her husband was in league with the Devil and that she was afraid of him. That last part we believed because he'd done so much evil, had harassed so many people, and everybody else seemed to fear him too. His cold stare was enough to make the hair on one's arms stand straight up. I was filled with dread every time I saw him," she explained and took a sip of her own portion of the steeped chamomile.

"Mum was not going to be abused any further by Molly's accusation of witchcraft against her. In a local court session with Mr. Pynchon himself, he determined that Molly Percy had slandered my mother and the Percys were told they had to compensate Mercy, my mum, for unfairly hurting her reputation. Well, that Hugh! You should have been there to see his reaction! He almost exploded like a ball blasting out of a cannon when he heard he was going to have to pay my mum for her suffering by giving her twenty-four bushels of corn. He was furious at his wife, but not her alone. He also showed up at my mother's doorstep. He pressured my mum to drop her quest for justice. He expected her to just let it go."

I thought for a moment before speaking. "He sounds like an awful neighbor by all accounts. I never asked Simon what happened precisely between the two of them. I confess that I'm curious, although I'd hoped to avoid all talk of it with him. Besides, Simon's careful not to speak about any of it with me.

But you can tell me about it now, Sarah. I feel strong enough and don't want the thought of it lurking in the shadows anymore. In fact, I need you to bring it out into the light of day so there are no surprises."

"Look at you, acting all brave now. Ok. I'll tell ye, but I don't want Simon to be mad at me for sharing a story he hasn't told himself. If it ever comes up, promise me that you'll assure him I didn't force the telling of it,"

"I promise. You're my sister now. I'll defend you should it ever come up," I assured her.

"Alright then, Alissa, but you must help me get the meal ready by peeling some onions and chopping some parsnips. That's the price I require for the full story," she said laughing. "Let me get the wee ones settled first and get the water boiling." She got up and threw more kindling into the fire and put a large cast iron pot to hang over it as we got busy with our work.

"You and Simon will be eating with us tonight," said Sarah. In truth, Sarah and I ended up cooking together often just as we sewed together. Once we were settled in again and Sarah's children attended to by their Aunt Alissa, Sarah tried to recount the incidents that my husband had had with Hugh Percy.

Pushing a stray hair back into her cap, she began, "I don't recall Simon ever having issues with Hugh Percy's wife. I suppose he avoided her after any weirdness with Hugh but his experiences with Hugh were quite disturbing."

"Tell me how," I asked, finally ready to understand my husband's past.

"The first time I remember something strange happening was during the harvest season. Simon told us that Hugh had demanded that Simon place a sack of flour on Nutmeg, Simon's mare. Hugh wanted some help and wasn't in the mood to carry his flour. By that time, most people in town, not just Simon, avoided interactions with Hugh at all costs because they were destined to turn out poorly. Simon refused Hugh's request. He said although he'd wanted to avoid Hugh in the first place, it was the rude way in which Hugh expected Simon to help him that he found most repugnant. Simon was also concerned for his mare who was just recovering from an injury. He was careful that the horse shouldn't carry too much weight and thought his own sack of flour was weight enough," Sarah bubbled with excitement as she told the tale.

"Hugh was angered by Simon's refusal and felt rebuffed. Not more than a few feet from the mill, Simon fell off his horse with his own heavy sack of flour as Hugh looked on with evil in his eyes. Poor Simon fell off Nutmeg not once but thrice with nothing to spook her. He said he could only suspect his own clumsiness once but not every time he fell as the normally gentle mare had been tranquil as they first started out up the main street. Eventually, Simon got home but he was rattled by that encounter. The strangeness of it shook him to his core. He was sure Hugh had bewitched him."

"Aye, 'Tis peculiar. Simon handles horses quite well, even under the most challenging circumstances," I agreed and dutifully continued to chop onions as I listened for more.

"But that wasn't all. No! It didn't stop there. The following February, Simon knocked on our door, deeply troubled. Havoc with the company's cart and horses followed after refusing Hugh's wishes again. Simon was nearly killed," she said.

"No! You mean to tell me it was that serious! What happened?"

"Well, Simon was minding the company store but closed it early because he had to get some lumber. The horses were already harnessed and attached to the cart. That's when Hugh stormed in asking for a piece of whitleather he needed to fix his flail, his favorite weapon, kept by his bed at night in case of attack by marauders or intruders.

Simon wasn't about to leave the horses unattended any longer attached to the company cart and bade Hugh come back later. His request didn't seem that urgent. Well, Hugh was seething in anger after that. He cursed at Simon and threatened him. Told him that he'd remember him for treating him so poorly. That was Hugh. Always took everything so personally and threatened people when he couldn't get his way. Never tried to get along or understand another soul. It was always about him and if people couldn't do what he wanted exactly when he wanted it, he was going to view it as a personal insult."

Sarah stopped and took a sip of the remaining tea. She got quite excited telling the story.

I was already done chopping the onions and stopped to listen more intently before moving on to the celery and parsnips.

"Sarah, tell me all of it. What happened with the cart and horses?" I asked stunned, thinking about how Simon had avoided sharing this story with me.

"So, finally Hugh left since he had no choice and scoffed at Simon as he led the horses and cart into the forest. Later in the day, Simon was coming home with the lumber he'd promised Pynchon for the company store. It was secured under the cart, and they were moving along just fine when suddenly, the horses startled, and Simon couldn't get control again, as much as he tried. He got jolted out of the cart as the horses raced forward, kicking one on the way down so it would veer off to the side. He was lucky not to be run over. As it was, one of the wheels tore the hem of his jacket and the cart only came a couple feet from his head before it crashed into the stump of a nearby tree. He said it took a while to calm himself before he could steady the animals. After that incident, he was sure that Hugh had vexed him," she finished.

I was silent as I thought of how afraid Simon must have been and then I thought of my mother. She'd never conversed with the people around her in the way Hugh had. Yet, in Windsor, people were so quick to blame and condemn her to be a witch. I never understood why.

"That same February our relationship with Hugh Percy disintegrated further when my dear husband became severely injured in an accident. By that time, Thomas wasn't trustful of Hugh at all. He'd seen me have my fits and was convinced Hugh had been the cause. A bunch of the men, including my Thomas and Goodman Cooper, and Hugh Percy went to the wood lot to fell and cut the bigger trees. It's very dangerous work as you know, and they had to rely on each other. They seemed to be getting on fine and it even surprised Thomas that they were merry together. But then, Hugh decided to break away from the group when they stopped to eat their food at midday. He sat high on a branch and peered over everybody else. They asked him why he went there. My Thomas, not trusting him again, said it was to find out what other wives had packed for their husband's meals. He knew Hugh to be the one of the most jealous sorts of men he's ever met. Hugh said nothing and stayed where he was high on the branch overlooking the rest of them. Nobody said a thing after that, careful to hold their tongues so Hugh might not be provoked.

After they ate, the men got busy with their tasks again. It was quiet, eerily quiet, except for the sounds of their work when all of a sudden, a saw slipped out of Thomas' hands and gouged his leg. He couldn't walk and they had to tie his leg with a cloth to stop the bleeding and carry him from the wood lot back to town. Thomas was fortunate that his leg healed. It could have been much worse if the saw had cut any deeper or if an infection had set in. I tended to him night and day to make sure he stayed well, Alissa. But he was flustered and thought surely it was caused by Hugh's acts of witchcraft again. He's got an ugly scar to remind him of it," she explained.

"That's awful, Sarah. I'm glad Thomas survived, and he didn't lose his leg. But now, what I want to know the most is how your pregnancies were affected, Sarah? You still haven't answered that question. You said you'd already had fits before Thomas went into the forest wood lot with the other men on that day. Wasn't that the case?" I asked.

Sarah let out a deep sigh. "The pregnancies were most difficult at the end. And the sight of Hugh and his wife and all his talk of cursing and threatening my mum made them worse. I just didn't feel well to begin with, and my legs were swollen more than they'd ever been. You wouldn't have even recognized me. My head ached so badly sometimes, it felt like I was being pierced by the sharp blade of a sword. Then the fits started. One time in the meeting house, others saw me, like the minister Moxon's daughters, and they fell into fits as well." She paused and looked at me gauging to see whether she had said too much.

"Alissa, I'm fine now that Hugh and his wife are gone. I delivered my little ones soon after the worst of the fits. My babies were the ultimate protection because the fits stopped once they were born. We don't need to worry about those things anymore. You understand me? I realize in talking about all this that I never want to think about those awful things again."

I nodded, "Aye. I've heard everything I need to hear."

"Ah, that's good now. You needn't worry, Alissa. There's no need to ever speak of Hugh Percy further." I smiled. She was right. We need not talk about Hugh Percy or his wife Molly ever again. I was glad I'd never met them. But still I felt sick that my mother had been reviled too. She was nothing like them. I was sure of that.

I threw the rest of the vegetables I'd chopped into the pot with the few scraps of fat and meat Sarah had already boiled. As the stew simmered, we turned to Sarah's children as they played.

Seeing the children, I turned to her and said, "Aye, you're right as always. From now on, we'll look to the future."

"So be it," she said, winking.

Chapter 14

Springfield, Massachusetts, 1655 & Windsor, Connecticut, 1645: Expecting

Simon and I were busy our first year of marriage together. He was keen to prosper quickly with a new wife to support. Even though we were newlyweds, that first year Simon took seven voyages down the falls to Windsor to trade for Pynchon and others in Springfield.   Occasionally, he let me go with him. It was exciting and scary at the same time to navigate the falls. Halfway through the first year, I started not wanting to go anymore.

I didn't know why at the time, but I could feel myself becoming clammy and sick to my stomach. It was hard to stay on task with my chores. Sarah and I were doing our washing at the babbling brook behind our homes.

"Why Alissa, what's the matter with you?" Sarah asked as she grabbed my side seeing me start to tumble and try to brace myself against a small boulder on the edge.

"Come, lay in the sun for a bit," she coaxed me and took a palmful of water and dripped it on my neck. "Lay there until you feel better," she said.

"I'll do that, Sarah. Let's take a break from the washing for a little while. I don't understand my queasiness. I've been feeling a bit nauseous every morning now for the past few days. Do you think…" I paused.

She scrutinized my face. "You're a bit different, Alissa. Aye, your face is even a little fuller. And you haven't been quite yourself. A bit more tired than usual, eh?" Suddenly, it struck her. "Why, Alissa! You're with child! You have to be. When did you last bleed? Has it been a while?" I nodded yes.

Seeing my beaming smile was all she needed to know.

"You're glowing. You're going to be a mother!"

She jumped up and hugged me.

"Simon will be so happy to hear that we've got a baby coming into our lives! I didn't understand what was happening and was afraid something might be wrong with me."

"Nay, you're splendid, my girl. Nothing's wrong! It's just as it should be. I can't wait to meet your little one!" said Sarah

"I do worry though, Sarah. Aunt Rhody told me that my mother lost at least one child. I hope I do not suffer in the same way."

"I only want you to think about holding your own little baby. Your mum's fate doesn't need to be your own. It will be fine. I will take good care of you and so will all the other women on the lane," she assured me.

"Alright. I promise to think of only good things. With you here with me, I can be strong."

"That's lovely Alissa! What a great mum you'll be and how nice for my two to have playmates. Or rather, my three! Alissa, I'm to have another baby also. Our babies will be the same age!" She clasped both my hands obviously pleased to share another experience together.

"Really? How can this be? You haven't seemed sick or overly tired," I exclaimed in awe.

"I wasn't very nauseous with this babe so I didn't realize until yesterday. And as far as feeling tired, the other two keep me running. Even if I were tired, I'd never have the chance to slow down. Thomas pointed to my belly last night. He noticed it was a little fuller. I hadn't even thought about the last time I bled but when I realized it had been a while, that had to be the reason," she explained with great excitement.

"Thomas said I've been a bit frisky under the covers. I was like that the last time too. All the more ready to please the husband when I'm with child. Or I should say I'm eager for him to please me," she winked.

I laughed. Sarah could be quite blunt when it came to expressing her amorous desires. Her lack of inhibition helped me to feel more comfortable in my own skin.

"We really are sisters now," I smiled.

Feeling much better, I got up from the ground with her help and hugged her tightly.

Simon was excited to hear the news. As the weeks passed, my belly was starting to visibly show and Simon doted on me even more than he normally did.

"Careful of the child," he said quietly if I became upset in the night or if I started to lift something a bit heavy. When I was tired, he would direct me to rest for a few minutes.

I dutifully sat down and viewed my belly pushing through my skirt. Sometimes he would stop what he was doing and sit with me, rubbing my belly and assessing how fast it was growing.

Was it another Alice? I wondered. Would she have to endure what I had endured? And would I have to go through some of the same female concerns that my mother had?

****

"Do you know how furious you were when you landed in this world?" Mother said as I laughed with glee in the big wood basin that she washed me in. "Are you really the same child?"

She tickled me with the cloth and tried to wash under my arms making me giggle even more.

"I guess you realized it wouldn't be so bad after all. I changed and so did you once we got to Windsor," she said. "We finally knew we were where we belonged."

"Were you furious too, Mother?"

"Oh no. I was melancholy my dear. I was sad that I couldn't make you happy and I suppose sad for feeling alone much of the time too. But it was better once we got here to Windsor. We could laugh with our cousins and be with family. You grew out of your colic. And your father could go and be alone in his farm fields across the river without any bother from us. It worked well for everybody."

While mother didn't say it directly, I knew I was her only consolation after her marriage to a mostly silent husband who preferred to keep to himself. At least until he needed her to help him.

Mother grabbed a blanket that was warmed by the fire and folded me in it for warmth after I bathed.

"I missed the Tinker family so much!" she said. "I had to be with them. I told your father there was no other way. He had to do it. He had to take us to Connecticut. I insisted," she pulled me into her lap and hugged me.

"How old was I when we walked the great path to come here? Was it scary traveling here?"

Windsor was the only place I had ever known. I spent most of my time on Backer Row, in my own home or at my cousins' and a good amount of time with everyone else at the meeting house a couple days of the week. Sometimes young children would also go into the farm fields for harvest time.

"You were still just a baby. It was around the time of your first birthday. You didn't think the journey was scary at all. In fact, I think you were very happy. You stopped fussing and looked in wonder at the world around you. You loved being on the trail to see other travelers and stop and rest at Native villages. They were all enthralled with you and one Indian man even gave you a little rattle made of natural shells. I wrapped you to me with a broad cloth so you could still see I was with you. I think you loved the motion of walking in a steady rhythm to go somewhere new. And you moved your little head around to try and find the sounds of songbirds calling to each other or woodpeckers tapping their way to insects deep in rotting old trees.

The act of bringing a new baby into the world gives one pause. During my final months of pregnancy, I thought a lot about my childhood, at least what I could remember of it. I know my mother tried to give me the best. She couldn't help what happened to her. I knew that truth deep in my bones. What kind of life was I bringing my own children into? Of course, as every mum does, I hoped they'd be happy and prosper and that I'd always be a good mother to them.

My childhood in Windsor was pleasant, always surrounded by love. But the love that came to me was dominantly from my mother whose side I never wanted to leave in the beginning. All my cousins and aunts, many of the women on Backer Row, were my circle of love and strength.

My Uncle John, their brother, was the man who pulled me up the most, kept me laughing, and made sure that my cousins and I came out of our gloom after hours of damnation and religious teachings from the pulpits. The family would always come together on those days and share a meal.

However, it wasn't a perfect life with the man who was called my father. I knew I'd done better than my mother on that score. And as a father, he was never affectionate toward me and paid no attention to me. I had his name, but that's about all we had in common. He was either lying in bed complaining about feeling unwell, out in the fields or talking with other men about the events in Windsor.

I hadn't thought about John Young for many years. I'd tried specifically to blot him out of my mind. It wasn't until I became older that it became easier to forget him altogether. But now my thoughts were rattled with new memories oozing out of me like popped pustules needing to heal. When I was a child, in the time I knew him, he spoke very little to me except to tell me which chores to do next and brief comments about the status of our household. So, it was natural to me to refer to him as simply John and not father. He didn't seem to care but mother, once she saw me do it, took me aside and gave me a slight verbal thrashing.

"Alissa, this will not do. You must not call John by his Christian name for he IS a father to you. He provides for you and protects both of us. Do not be an ungrateful girl. You must call him father for now. Do you understand me?"

She became angry and distraught, which was not the way of her character in general. As she looked at me intently, I submitted to her wishes and called him father sensing it was important to our survival, but it did not change my heart. I would never be close to him nor ever wish more of him than the basic rudimentary societal standards that fatherhood demanded.

More often than not, mother slept with me due to the routine gasps of air and grunts from his repeated illness. There were no amorous tossings and turnings inside their curtained bedstead. Nothing like the reports of the older girls on Backer Row who said the frequent movements and moaning behind the curtains of the bedsteads of their parents were what made their mothers so fertile.

My parents' relationship was more one of duty and reliance. It was clear in the memories that started coming to me.

"Tell John Young to fix it," Mother told me. The tool I was using to help Mother in her garden had broken where the handle met the spade.

My father was an older man of very few words. As I entered his woodworking shop and approached him, he looked at me in a scolding manner. "What's this?" he asked from behind his worktable.

"Please fix it, Father, so I can help Mother again."

He snorted at me and shrugged his shoulders. I looked down at the earthen floor covered in wood shavings, preparing myself for reprimands.

"Girl, how come I must repair things so often when you're around? I don't have time for this foolishness. Give it to me now and leave me in peace. Find something else you can do to help your mother until it is fixed. From shallow and pale eye sockets, he peered at me and waved a hand for me to leave his workshop. He was skinny and his clothes sagged awkwardly from his body.

"Why is he grumpy all the time?" I asked Mother who was kneeling and planting carrot seedlings when I returned to the garden. In essence though, I was numb to his scolding and his complaints. Most of the time, I stayed rather distant from him and felt relieved when he went to work with the other men in the fields or did his woodworking for community projects.

"Well, Alissa, you know by now not to pay him much attention. Pray for the poor man. He never feels well and is probably getting another one of his bouts of illness. You too would be cross if you felt so poorly much of the time," she reminded me. She helped me to see that we must always try to find empathy for the suffering of others.

Nobody knew what was wrong with John Young. Sometimes he seemed well and carried on without a problem, but at other times his condition could get so bad that he was bedridden, and all his joints ached. He relied on Mother to help him soothe those joints with her ointments and salves or calm his aching head which he complained was like having a wild horse stamping down on him with a strong hoof. When his bouts were particularly bad, his heart would ache, and his breathing seemed more labored. Mother tried her best to feed him well, but he could never fully gain weight.

Sometimes I think the villagers looked at Mother with suspicion, that perhaps she was not a good wife and was unable to nurture him enough to meet his needs. But the truth was, John Young had dealt with his illness long before he met my mother. He was only too happy to have her medical care to ease his suffering.

Our neighbor, Priscilla's father, Thomas Thornton seemed to know John Young well. I think they might have even been related in some way but I'm not so sure. It seemed strange to me to live with a man such as this, call him father and yet know so little of him. In the end, his absence later in my life meant nothing at all to me. I was indifferent— much better than being devastated as I was with the loss of Mother after her brutal death.

"Alissa! My lovely wife! Ye grow bigger with child each time I come back!"

My thoughts were disrupted by the sight of my husband dripping with wetness. He'd just come back from one of his trips and it was pouring with rain. I was so tired that I was getting ready to go to bed early. I couldn't help but smile looking at him shaking off the water that dripped from his hat. It was silly. Why was I even thinking of my past? Simon would be a wonderful father to our children.

He took off his overcoat and hat and walked towards me, finally hugging me carefully. "How long now, my love? You've changed a lot this time. I thought I'd better get the last of the trips to Windsor in quickly. Seeing you being bigger with child, I know I need to stay close by," he assured me.

"Sarah says there's still time to wait but not too many weeks before we'll have a wee one waking us all of the night. Are ye ready?" I asked.

"I suppose I am," he said. "The little ones next door and their parents have taught us well. We'll both be ready," he winked.

Chapter 15

Springfield, Massachusetts, 1655, &
Windsor, Connecticut, 1645: The Support of Women

It brought me great comfort to be pregnant and have my baby at the same time as Sarah Miller. The two of us relied on each other more than ever before. We were orphans in essence, distant shamed fathers and our mothers both dead. Sarah was afraid for the first time.

"My mum was there for the first two babies coming into the world, I'm a bit fearful without her here. I know I shouldn't be and I'm not normally prone to worry, but it's strange without her for the birth of this one," she said, holding her belly.

"I know my mother would have been a comfort too. I can't even imagine what I need to do without her here. I'm glad you're here though," I said.

"Oh Alissa, I'm a fool, only thinking about myself. At least I remember what my mum told me to do. Remembering it will give me strength. But you never had the chance to experience that even once. I'm a bit of a lout for only thinking of myself. Listen, I'll help you through it. I'll share my mum's advice and your body will also know what to do. Prudence Fields, the midwife, and the other women here experienced in childbirth will assist us too. You'll have plenty of help. You need not worry," she hugged me.

I was finally allowed into the birthing room with my mother and my aunts. Aunt Anne had just given birth to her fifth child, a boy. Thomas Thornton, Anne's husband, had also just come into the room to see his son for the first time.

Anne looked adoringly in her son's eyes and then at Thomas, hoping to get his approval for a task well done. He squeezed her hand in acknowledgement, but that was all. Taking the baby from her, he made his pronouncement.

"My dear second son, disciple of God, ye shall be called Samuel after the great prophet who implored people to repent for their sins with unparalleled zeal. A wise judge and counselor was he to turn the people toward the Lord. May your work to this end be blessed, young Samuel," he added.

Little Samuel started to squirm and cry in his large rough hands and so he passed his youngest son back to his wife to feed.

"God is pleased on this day! The glory is His!" He made this one last declaration on his way out the door before kissing his wife on the forehead.

"She's labored for hours to bring that one into the world," I overhead Mary commenting to Rhody. Mary knew how difficult it had been for her sister Anne, having guided all her sisters' children into the world as the local and family midwife.

"That was his generous praise," Rhody whispered in response raising her eyebrows and looking back at Mary knowingly.

"Such an open-hearted and gushing brother-in-law," Mary scoffed. Just then she caught sight of me and realized she should keep her thoughts to herself lest they be repeated in ways that she would regret later.

"Alissa, you've come to be with your mother and see the new babe in the family?"

"Aye, Aunt Mary," I said quietly. By that time Anne's oldest children surrounded her and Priscilla looked on more proudly than anyone. She was eager to hold her little brother for the first time.

It was then that my Aunt Mary noticed my mother moving slowly about in silence, cleaning the room and placing everything that Anne needed next to her. She seemed sullen and sad as if she was holding back tears. It stood out among the room of other joyous hearts.

"Alice, there you are. Please come sit with us," she motioned to my mother to rest and get off her feet for a while.

"But there is still much that Anne and the baby need," she murmured.

"Please, Alice, leave it for now," Mary insisted. My mother often helped Mary as her assistant at births and this time was no different, but I'd noticed she no longer seemed as excited and happy as she once was when she talked about the births she'd watched. She'd somehow lost the thrilling feeling that accompanies seeing new life come into the world. Aunt Mary must have certainly noticed too.

"You need fresh air. Please come with me," Aunt Mary guided my mother by the waist outside. Curious as my nature had always been, I followed them silently and remained within earshot.

They were in the side yard, hidden from the stoop by some bushes. The children inside were trying hard not to be boisterous and Aunt Rhody did her best to hold them to their best behavior so little baby Samuel and his mother would not be disturbed. No one was paying attention to Aunt Mary and Mother in the side yard except for me.

"Alice, you have changed of late. How can I help you? I sense there is deep sadness within your soul," Mary addressed my mother gently.

The thought of someone noticing her, willing to be a witness to her pain, was all my mother needed to bear her heart to her trusted cousin.

"Oh Mary, I am a horrible person, I am. I should feel nothing but joy when I see a new child being born I am happy for Anne and I am happy for everyone, especially my beloved family members when they bring a healthy child into this world. It's just that…" she paused and teared up. "It's just that it touches on something lacking in my own life. I want so desperately to have another child, Mary. It will never come to pass."

I peered through an opening in the bushes to see Mary stroking her hair in a motherly manner at that moment. "I know Alice. John Young is too old and sickly. It must be him, not you," she tried to comfort her.

"Mary, I only wish to have children with the man I love. Yet, people talk. They condemn and judge all the while knowing nothing of what I go through. Mary, I know they talk of me behind my back. I'm the only one in town that I can think of to have just one child after a marriage of several years," she explained. "They think I am not doing my duty. They think I am willfully making John Young sick. They do not understand my heart and my deep desire to have more children. I thought marrying John Young would help my situation, but I see it now for what it is, a curse."

She held on to Mary and she wept for several minutes as Mary tried her best to comfort her.

"Alice, you must handle the situation with grace and humbleness. You must not let on to how you feel to others. They will regard you as jealous and ungrateful if you do. I've seen the pain of women yearning for their unborn children. It's as if they know their souls are there waiting to be born but are trapped in the other world. Perhaps the conditions in this world are not ready for them and hamper their ability to enter their families' lives and their dwellings on Earth. I understand you, Alice," she said kindly.

Mother softly cried on Mary's shoulder as she listened.

"Hear what I have to say, dear cousin. Situations change and lives change all the time. Do not give up hope. You cannot know what lies ahead. The Lord may have other plans in this way for you still. Do you understand?" she asked.

My mother nodded and gave a faint smile.

"I feel so deeply that another child IS waiting for me, Mary. I cannot ignore him," she stated.

Mary looked at her strangely. "Alice, don't do anything that you would regret later or do anything to get yourself or anyone else in trouble."

They stared at each other knowingly for a while until Mary finally broke the tension in the air.

"Come, dear cousin, let's get back to Anne and the babe before others wonder if there's a problem. Are you ready to go back?" My mother nodded again and with that gesture, Mary took my mother's hand and led her back into Anne's home right after I disappeared inside to join my other cousins.

"Alissa, you did it!" Prudence wiped the little wrinkled baby clean and cut the cord that had connected us. Sarah brought him up to me and laid him against my chest as she covered us both with warm blankets.

"I'm so proud of you!" she grinned. "Your mother would be proud of you too, Alissa," she added.

I was exhausted but couldn't keep my eyes off the other-worldly babe that couldn't take his eyes off me. He seemed to know who I was.

"Who is this?" Simon asked excitedly after having just entered the room. He kissed me and accepted the swaddled child into his arms.

"He's Simon, your eldest son. The first of many," I said optimistically.

"Well now, Simon, you're a handsome yet strange looking little one. Did you properly thank your mother for doing such a fine job of bringing you into the world? What do ye say?" My husband listened as little Simon cooed. "No? Not yet? Well, we can't have that! That's the first lesson son, honor thy mother and thy father! Did you notice the order of that?" he asked teasing me.

Then he looked at me seriously. "You've done a fine and wonderful thing, Alissa. I know it 'twas hard for you without your mum here. I hope you had what you needed," he squeezed my hand and kissed me.

I looked around at all the caring women in attendance, assuring him that even without my mother, I'd be fine.

"Indeed, I did," I told him. "I have the best friend in the world caring for me and the best neighbors and midwife. The Lord has given me and our family a precious gift in the good care from these women."

I was a mother now and it had started to heal me.

Chapter 16

Springfield & Northampton, Massachusetts, 1656: To Save A Witch

Mary Bliss Parsons, the wife of Joseph Parsons, once of Hartford, then later of Springfield and finally of Northampton, was in trouble. The third location of her existence afforded her no comfort. Instead, its' citizens bestowed numerous accusations of bewitchment by her hand. The reasons for it were many. It started with rumors of her very peculiar behavior in Springfield. Mary Bliss Parsons was not a normal woman. For what normal woman would have to be locked up at night by her husband? He said it was necessary so that she wouldn't go roaming around the lands abutting the river when she should have been in bed. Some say the loss of a child had made her crazy in such a way that mourning her son never stopped in its most dramatic stages. And she could find anything lost to the amazement of all. This also made her a cunning woman, I was told.

Mary Bliss married Joseph Parsons in Hartford a year before my mother's tragedy. Her widowed mother and siblings followed her to Springfield after she wed. But they couldn't be a comfort to her when her second baby boy died at only five months of age. From that point, until she finally gave birth to another boy, she was seen roaming the marshy land in the middle of the night, the moonlight allowing witnesses to it. Those who saw her said that at times she was with another woman whom no one could identify. And at other times she was alone wailing from afar.

About this time, Hugh Percy's wife, Molly, had witches on her mind all the time. So, when our friend Mary who danced in the swamps next to the river at night became the topic of town conversation, Molly Percy thought for sure that she must be a witch..

Not long after Molly Person's unfounded accusations, Joseph moved with Mary upriver to Northampton where Mary had a falling out with her neighbor Sarah Bridgman. Sarah Lyman Bridgman and Mary Bliss Parsons were no strangers to each other. They had both come of age in Hartford, met their husbands there and moved to Springfield after their marriages. Goody Bridgman's neediness combined with Mary Parsons' strong personality and lack of care about what others thought of her meant they would never be friends even though Sarah Bridgman had tried while in Springfield.

Utterly rejected by Mary Parsons, Sarah Bridgeman began her lonely quest for revenge. Mary, the younger woman, had never been respectful of Sarah Lyman Bridgman. Mary was like her sister Lydia, hanged as a witch from Windsor, who also never cared what anyone else thought of her. These Bliss women were always strong and opinionated, raised that way by a mother who thought her daughters should be treated like queens for their rare and intimidating beauty and their keen intellect.

It made sense that since their relationship started poorly even in childhood, it had little chance of getting better as adults. Goody Bridgman always coveted what Mary Parsons had. Of course, she denied this, but it was obvious to all who knew her. When both women moved on from Springfield with their families to Northampton, their relationship took a turn for the very worst. Sarah announced in no uncertain terms that Mary was her rival by the way she behaved as a gossip and found fault and malfeasance in everything that Mary did, eventually calling her a witch.

Goody Bridgman took every opportunity to make sure that her new community knew of Mary's strange behavior prior to coming to Northampton. Of course, she failed to mention that the stress of losing her baby and her father in the same year at the height of Hugh Percy's strange behaviors and Molly's malicious rumors naming Mary as a witch might have been contributing factors. No, Goody Bridgman carefully weaved many doubts into the heads of Mary's fellow neighbors in whatever ways she could and implored others in town to do the same for any misfortune that came to their doorsteps.

I was content to hear about the story from afar, not wishing to be involved in anything pertaining to accusations of witchcraft. I was satisfied that my husband was no longer involved in testifying during any kind of trial concerning witches. So, when I heard that Joseph Parsons had recruited Mr. Pynchon and Simon to testify on Mary Parsons' behalf, I was nervous.

"What are you telling me?" I asked my husband, confused as to how the situation in Northampton had reached a breaking point.

"Alissa, you don't understand. It's getting dangerous for Mary. Goody Bridgman's spite has gotten worse. She's accused Mary Parsons of killing her baby she lost a few months ago and now she says that Mary's responsible for a severe injury of her eleven-year-old son who hurt his knee while trying to retrieve his cow out of the swamp," he explained.

"So, what does it have to do with you, Simon?"

Joseph Parsons has complained that the situation has gone too far and he is suing Goody Bridgman for slander on account of his wife."

"So, you're saying you'll give a good word for Mary?"

"Aye, woman! I've no need to see another innocent hang! We have to put a stop to Goody Bridgman's menacing words before they cause too much mischief for Mary — deadly mischief. Of course, I'll help her," he exclaimed.

I sighed, relieved that he was on the side of innocence, but I still had concerns.

"Tis the right thing to do Simon, but I fear you may draw attention to the story of the woman in your own household," I admitted. "Me."

"Alissa, do not fear. People are focused on Mary Parsons and making up tales about her. They won't give a thought to you or what happened to your mother. No one will even think of you. They know me and they know I'm fair.

They remembered that I testified against Hugh and his wife years ago. 'Tis important because they know I'll be truthful about what I think. This is a case of slander. Nobody's on trial for being a witch, Alissa. Joseph is right to do this and you'd best be assured, I'd do the same for you if it ever came to that." He grabbed my chin gently so that I would look into his eyes.

"You've no need to fear. I'd stand up for you, my love, with all that's in me. But nobody has ever said anything to anybody about you. Nor should they. You haven't had disputes with anyone."

I nodded and then looked at the floor for a few moments, ashamed that I had only thought of myself.

"Aye, Simon, go help your friend Joseph protect his wife." I vowed to be silent about any further misgivings I had about the trial and to keep any fears to myself.

Each night, after the town folk told their stories in court, Simon recounted to me what had transpired. The testimonies for the slander trial, Parsons vs. Bridgman started in August of 1656 and went through September. John Pynchon or Mr. Holyoke wrote them down. Of course, people gossiped and so we heard more details about the deplorable things that Goody Bridgman had accused Mary Parsons of doing through the accounts of our neighbors, friends and even acquaintances passing through town.

By this time in Mary and Joseph's life, Joseph was doing quite well and had already amassed more wealth than most of the others in town. It was his time in fur trading that gave him the wealth he needed to buy even more property and own a retail store. He'd even purchased a warehouse in Boston and a wharf to help keep goods that supplied his store. Mary, for her part, kept having sons. She was no longer visibly distraught for the child that died and had become a shrewd helpmate in her husband's businesses.

Goody Bridgman had not grown up as modestly as Mary's family had. She was used to living well, but when she married her husband James, her material fortunes fell while witnessing the rise of Mary Parsons'. It was obvious that Goody Bridgman was jealous. She'd even gone so far as to say that Mary's good fortune was a gift from the Devil for doing his bidding.

In her testimony to Mr. Holyoke, she repeated the claims that she'd shared with her friends and others in the communities of both Northampton and Springfield with the specific details of her accusations. She accused Mary of causing her baby to die, saying that there was a great blow to the door just a few days after she delivered him into this world. She noted her impression that the babe was immediately changed by the shocking noise. Her servant looked outside but saw nothing there. However, when she looked through the keyhole, she saw two women with white cloths on their heads and was certain there was wickedness about and that her child would soon be sickly and die.

She went on to say that she thought Mary was the one to cause a severe injury to her eleven-year-old son after he went to retrieve one of their cows in the swamp. As he entered the swamp something hard hit him on the head. Soon after, he stumbled over logs and his knee went severely out of joint. Laying in his bed after the incident, he said he saw the specter of Mary Parsons sitting on a shelf taunting him. He also thought he saw her run away followed by a familiar, a black mouse. Her husband corroborated her story and said even though they could not see Goody Parsons on the shelf, her son cried out that she would pull off his knee.

I was deeply disturbed by the Bridgman's accusations for they were based on stories, stories anyone could make up about someone else they didn't like or were jealous of. Of course, my thoughts always came back to the unfairness of what happened to my own mother.

I suppose Mary Parsons was lucky in one way. Her mother was her staunch defender. As soon as Margaret Bliss had heard what Sarah Bridgman was saying about her daughter, in true courageous family form, she went to confront Goody Bridgman. But Goody Bridgman refused to back down and to Mary's own mother's face, she confirmed that she had heard that her daughter was suspected to be a witch!

The Bridgman's weren't the only ones suspicious of Mary Parsons. The Hannum couple complained of her outspoken nature and unlikeable personality. Goody Hannum testified that Mary Parsons always found fault with the quality of her yarn that she hired her to make. Mary complained that it was full of flaws and lacked the proper quantity of threads. When Goody Hannum checked her own work, she saw that it was lacking threads, but swore it was not so after she completed the work. Mary had also expressed interest that one of Goody Hannum's daughters should live and work for her. The daughter was excited and wanted to, but Goody Hannum denied her the opportunity, afraid that Mary Parsons really was a witch. Soon after, the daughter became sickly and would not help her mother at home. Goody Hannum blamed Mary and her supposed witchcraft for having that effect on her daughter.

Goodman Hannum reiterated what his wife said but went even further with his accusations. He slandered Joseph Parsons by saying he treated his wife and children abusively. He also noted that a lusty cow of his took ill the day after Mary came to their home to find fault with his wife's spinning. In addition, he lost a pig that had been healthy and assumed once more it was Mary's fault because it got sick the day after she chastised him for mistreating her brother. Finally, he said that on the way to Windsor, one of his oxen was bitten by a rattlesnake. He said it wasn't far from his thoughts that Mary would be the cause of such things.

There were others too that blamed Mary for causing misfortune and connected it to her strange behavior after she lost her baby.

With each story, I fell deeper into sadness. Anyone who suffered loss and acted strangely could later be accused of being a witch.

"Please, tell me no more!" I implored Simon. I'd vowed to keep my feelings to myself, but I was upset and couldn't hide it anymore. I could no longer patiently listen as he told me things that suffocated my very being and instilled dread in my soul. I could no longer witness the cruelty of others.

"As you wish, wife. But there are others who are coming to her defense. Not all are suspicious and cruel. Do you wish to come with me when I testify before Pynchon? I think it would do you good to hear the testimony of someone defending Mary."

"Maybe, you're right, Simon. You may tell me about those who have come to her defense if you choose to. In any case, I should get to know the hearts of the men and women in Springfield and Northampton to get a sense of those who are prone to talk nonsense about others," I said, wiping my brow from the August heat. I was tending the fire to cook us supper.

As my husband informed me of each new person who came to Mary Parsons' defense, I was a little more relieved but also wondered who had come to my mother's defense if anyone. Mary was fortunate to have not only Hanna Broughton but also Ann Bartlett testify that Goody Bridgman's baby was sickly from the time it was born. They'd helped to care for her and Goody Bridgman too after her birth.

John Broughton, who had skinned William Hannum's cow after it died saw it took on too much water and even heard Hannum say to his wife not to fear because the cow's death was natural. John Webb verified the fact. And as to the rattlesnake incident when Hannum's ox was bitten, George Alexander, Samuel Allen and Goody Webb were all there and testified uniformly that they saw nothing unusual about the incident that would pertain to witchcraft. It too was a result of the natural consequence of stepping near a threatened rattlesnake.

Unfortunately, those who were formerly from Springfield remembered Mary's fits and peculiar behavior when she lost her second child and tried to use it against her as proof she was a witch. It made me shudder for I knew my friend Sarah Miller had also had her fits.

William Branch and our former neighbor, John Stebbins, churned up old memories recalling how Mary walked on water out to the swampland, yet did not get wet. All the old rumors and outright lies came back to haunt her. They repeated stories of her suspected supernatural powers at always being able to find the key which her husband used to lock the door at night to prevent her from going into the swamp.

Simon went to testify on Mary Parsons' behalf in front of John Pynchon on the nineteenth day of September, 1656. We walked arm in arm on the way to the Pynchon mansion. Simon held my hand and observed my belly and face growing plump and healthy. I was with child a second time, just starting to show.

I sat down as Simon sat in front of John Pynchon's large desk. He took out his quill and ink and began to write as Simon gave his testimony. I couldn't have been prouder of him for defending Mary. I knew he would have done the same for my mother had he known her. My earliest fears that he could turn on me and suspect me to be a witch because of his testimonies against Hugh Percy and his wife Molly were unfounded. I knew that without a hint of doubt when I heard what he had to say.

"About the time the witches were apprehended to be sent to Boston Mr. Moxon's children were taken ill in their fits (which we took to be bewitched) and at the same time was Mary Parsons, the wife of Joseph Parsons and others taking with the like fits,…" said Simon.

My thoughts went to Sarah and her fits while she was pregnant at the same time.

"…so that they were all carried out of the meeting it being Sabbath Day as Mr. Moxon's children acted so did Mary Parsons, the wife of Joseph Parsons, just all one. And I have diverse times been with them all, and I could discern no difference in their fits. And once I carried Mary Parsons home to the Long Meadow when she was in her fits, and when she was at home and came to herself, she wondered how she came there, and by the way as I carried her behind me, I was fain to hold her up upon the horse. And, I discerned that she did not understand herself nor where she was. And she would often cry out of the witches and call to Hannah Smith that they might creep under Goodwife Warriner's bed (from whence I took her to carry her home) or else the witches would kill them she said, And I have at other times been helping to hold her when she hath been in her fits and have found it as much as two men could do to hold her in her fits," he finished.

It wasn't long after Simon's and Mr. Pynchon's testimonies that the Magistrates Court in Cambridge made their decision. October seventh of that same year to be precise.

The word was that throughout testimonies, Mary boldly protested the accusations against her and maintained her innocence as did her mother and her brothers.

In the end, Joseph Parsons won the slander case on behalf of his wife against Goody Bridgman. She had to pay a fine of ten pounds to the Parsons and seven pounds to the court. Sarah Bridgman was directed to make a public apology in both Springfield and Northampton. Mary Parsons was vindicated.

The court, in looking through the testimonies, had its doubts about Sarah Bridgman's allegations for she would not let her son, the one who had said Mary Parsons wanted to pull off his knee, even testify. Did she lie and put words in his mouth? She'd admitted being jealous and also to maligning Mary's name to neighbors. What more could she and her husband, who had also done his share of trying to tarnish reputations, expect?

Sadly, the feuds, bitterness and jealousies against Mary Parsons by the Bridgmans would never be finished. They viewed her even more suspiciously thereafter and continued their gossip of Mary in newly hushed tones. Mary's reputation was irredeemable to the wider community. It was a curse. Once the doubt was cast, it was set for life. The second time the Bridgman's would officially accuse Mary of witchery years later, they'd make sure she suffered.

Chapter 17

*Springfield, Massachusetts, 1658 &
Windsor, Connecticut, 1646: Loss*

Feeling a snap followed by severe pain, I let the wood pile fall from my arms.
I was alone except for my little boys. Everything went black as I reached for
the fireside chair, holding on to it for dear life. I heard ringing in my ears and
felt clammy. All of a sudden, a rush of wet fluid ran down my leg. Finally, my
head cleared and I felt alert again, I looked over my pregnant belly to see
blood soaking my skirt. I lifted my shift out of it to find the flaxen cream color
transformed to bright red. I knew the smell of it meant death. I sat and
breathed slowly until I had enough strength to start calling out for Sarah.

Little Simon hobbled out of the house and was crying while his brother
John slept in his cradle. That's what first alerted Sarah to a problem. As she
approached him and was closer to our home, she could begin to hear my faint
screams. By the time she found me, I was white as a ghost and the labor pains
had started.

"Oh, dear friend, what happened? Dear God, help her!"

She quickly rounded up the other neighbors who were home. Francis
Pepper ran to fetch Simon who was at the company store.

Prudence Morgan took the boys and Goody Miller ran for the midwife
while Sarah had older children in the neighborhood watch her young ones
while she stayed with me.

As she started to walk with me to the featherbed, everything became black again and she had to guide me down to the floorboards instead. I became awake on the floor once more from a strong contraction and slight pressure of a miniature-sized babe slipping from my womb. Sarah was wiping my brow and praying over me when she heard me moan in pain.

"Something has come out, Sarah. Not the baby?" I cried. The contractions made it clear what was happening. I'd done this before.

She carefully looked under my skirt and pulled out the foreign thing that had slipped out between my legs.

"The baby's come too early. I'm sorry Alissa," she said. Sarah pulled her up into her arms so I could see.

Slightly bigger than my hand, her eyes were closed and she did not breathe. Sarah wiped clean the little lifeless one and wrapped her in a little blanket, handing her to me. "Look at her and say a prayer for her that she might be with God," she said, shaking her head.

The poor, pitiful little creature had no eyebrows and her body was full of little peach fuzz. Her skin was thin and she looked strange. I'd only felt her moving inside me for a few weeks. I regarded her in shock as the midwife ran into the room with Goody Miller, soon followed by Simon.

"Let's get her off the floor!" Simon directed everyone in the room.

"Best let her deliver the afterbirth first," said the midwife. "Get her a pillow and another blanket for now." She knew there was a lot more blood coming. "We'll carry her to her bed when she is finished," she said.

Simon held my hand and stared at the lifeless little thing in the blanket.

"What was it?" he asked in sorrow.

"A wee little girl, Simon, not fully formed."

"I'm sorry my love," he said, kissing me on the cheek.

The midwife was able to coax the afterbirth out and a strong fist on my belly stopped the rapid bleeding. The next day, Simon buried the body of our lifeless child who came too soon. I found my way to the featherbed eventually, but when I did, it was there where I wanted to stay for days.

Despite having my two boys, I had worried incessantly about this pregnancy. My world collapsed for a time, and I was forlorn and inconsolable. It didn't matter how Simon tried to help me or how kind his words of comfort were. They could not touch the pain in my soul.

And even my dear friend, Sarah, could do nothing as I sat distraught for days. Sarah tried to comfort me, but I dwelled on the many stories of other women whose pregnancies had ended abruptly, or even worse, the stories of the mothers who were devastated to find out that the baby they had labored to bring into the world was already dead. I knew it was even worse for those mothers whose children had started out as healthy. Those mothers had already bonded to their babies, but they weakened and died eventually anyway. What heartache!

I should be grateful for the children I already had, I thought. I knew that many pregnancies never came to full completion, but it did nothing to appease my great anxiety about the situation. I'd seen many women become distraught to the point of barely getting out of bed. With each lost child a part of them was gone. I had become one of them.

I am convinced that only a woman can understand the full angst of losing a child. It was even worse for those women who tried so hard to have children and barely could. People looked at them with pity and suspicion, like they were doing something wrong or that their mothering intentions were twisted with malfeasance.

I thought of Mary Parsons and her similar loss of a child and the strangeness in her behavior that followed. She was never the same. Her personality became unsteady and strange at times. I hoped I would keep my head more than she did and refrain from wandering in the bog at night. But with my deep sadness, I wasn't inclined to go to the swamplands near the river or anywhere else. I didn't fully understand why I should react with such a suffocating force around me.

I tried to go about daily life, but there was something about my emotions that made them feel much deeper and pertain to more than just this single pregnancy loss. Simon helped as much as he could to do extra care for the children, as did Sarah. Even the other neighbor women came to help, although I know some of them looked at me with pity.

One evening, Simon approached me worried and upset.

"Alissa, I don't know what to do for you to help get you better. Plenty of women lose a child. Why do you think you've taken it especially hard?" he asked genuinely concerned.

"I don't know Simon. I feel overwhelming guilt and anger. I know we are lucky to have the sons that we do. But this child was a girl. Are the women in my family cursed? Should I be punished for being my mother's daughter? Is God trying to prevent any females from coming into this world from my womb knowing who my mother was? Does He not understand that she wasn't who they said she was? I feel terrible for thinking that way, but I can't help but carry the guilt and also great anger with me."

"I should accept it and be humble, but I want a daughter, Simon. What is the reason God would deny me one?" I demanded.

"Alissa, there will be time. You're still very young. I refuse to believe this is a punishment. You and I have done nothing wrong, but rather we are faithful servants," he tried to reassure me.

"But what if you shouldn't have testified for Mary Parsons? What if God is angry that you did?" I said, not thinking clearly anymore. I should have been glad that Simon came to Mary's defense, and I was. I didn't even understand why I would say such a thing at the time.

"Alissa, you're not seeing things as they are!" he cried out in alarm. "I pray for you, that this cloud of darkness passes before we lose more than a child," he said frustrated, thinking of what could follow if our lives did not return to normal.

When he left me alone in the dark room, I started to sob myself to sleep. I knew I had to make things better again, but I didn't know how. I felt as if I'd alienated the person whom I was closest to. I prayed in earnest too that I could come to terms with what had happened with the loss of our child and why it touched me so.

As I slept, I do believe my mother or an angel came to me as if a miracle. She let me know what I was carrying was not a burden that was all mine. It was through my dreams that many more memories started to come back.

Mother and I were in the deep woods. We sat on the riverbank of the Rivulet and she stared out not hearing a word I said, almost as if she was ignoring me. But even as a child, I knew her head was in another place. Was it riding along the gentle ripples created by jumping fish, I wondered. Finally, losing my patience, I pulled on her arm until she came to be with me again.

"What is it, Alissa?" Can't you let me be in my daydreams for even a few minutes?" she demanded impatiently.

It was not like the mother I knew, one so distant and oblivious to my own desires and needs.

She looked at me pitifully and then burst into tears.

"I'm so sorry, my love!" she said and hugged me tightly for an eternity. "Of course, you don't understand. Please forgive me."

"Please Mother, tell me what happened," I said. "I didn't want to burden you, Alissa, but the day before last when you spent the night with the Thornton children, I lost another child. I wanted so desperately for you to know what it's like to have a brother or a sister," she said. "I'm sorry I failed you and everybody else."

"You didn't fail me!" I grabbed her arm. "You're the best mother anyone could have! I like being an only child. And I have plenty of cousins and friends to keep me company. Don't worry about me, Mother. If I have a brother or a sister one day, it will be nice, but I don't need one," I smiled.

"I'm sure nobody else feels like you failed them either," I added, thinking of my father John Young who didn't care for children, even me.

"Always such a sweet girl," she said kissing me on the head. "I will get better for you. You are the main reason I can get through this again," she squeezed my hand.

"Come, let us go back and bake something delicious," she said, rising from her perch over the river. "We'll cover it in edible flowers to make it pretty too. That might be the perfect thing to cheer me up and it's a well-deserved treat for you too."

That night, an incident occurred while my parents thought I slept. I was having a hard time falling asleep, but not wishing to worry my mother, I closed my eyes and laid still when she came to check on me.

By this time, I had gotten used to my parents being less harmonious and cooperative with each other. The year before my mother died had been difficult. They seemed to squabble over many things, some of them inconsequential. I never understood. My mother always tried to approach me with cheer, but I knew that she wasn't happy. Admitting the losses of her pregnancies was one thing, but I sensed there was more.

"She's sleeping now," I heard my mother say. "I need another baby. It's a longing John and it's better for us both if there is another one," she said.

"Why do you approach me, woman? I have no control over the situation. I agree. It's best another child be brought into the world, but the concern is mainly yours," he said.

"Aye, but you can help. Go to your little hut across the river and stay a day longer hunting or fishing when you go on your trips into the forest. Give me the time I need," she explained.

"Gladly, I will if it gets me away from the constant complaints and requests that I cannot honor for my own sake. Go do what you need to do but only in the confines of what you promised. And you'd better be careful, Alice. From what I see, you've already drawn more attention than you should. I have my needs too. That is all I will say for now."

"You say so little, I'm surprised you said anything at all," she snapped.

He glared back at her and huffed outside for a few minutes. When he came back in, he went straight to bed saying nothing. He looked beyond her as if she didn't exist. Mother tip-toed in quietly after him. As I opened my eyes and spied on them in the dark, she turned away from him, creating as much space as possible between them in the little bed.

In my child's eyes, the conversation they'd had was impossible to understand. It was strange to hear after my conversation with her on the banks of the river. But I observed over the next few months, before her demise, her behavior becoming stranger, she disappeared for hours at a time. She said she had to leave to take care of people with her herbal cures, but I wasn't so sure that she disappeared solely for that. And when I asked how she was, she seemed scared, lost and desperate to have that baby she so wanted.

She started saying, "When your baby brother comes, we shall be a happy family. "When your baby brother comes…"

"What if he doesn't come, Mother?" I asked her one day.

"Oh, one day, he will come. The baby who left will return. And this time, we will go to a place that he likes better than this. And we will all be living as one happy family. Trust, my love, that these things will come to pass," she assured me.

Remembering my own mother's grief at losing more than one child helped me to understand that my own loss of a child was weaved into her story and her own fears. I was unsettled because I knew what had happened only a year after she shared those losses with me.

I couldn't let that happen to me. I understood what my husband had hinted at earlier. It was important to go back to normal. I willed myself to do it for my own survival and that of my family's. In the end, it felt good to come back and I thanked my mother or her angels for showing me the way. Falling back into my routines with Simon, my children, and Sarah was the safest place for me to be.

Chapter 18

Springfield, Massachusetts, 1659 &
Windsor, Connecticut, 1647: Suspicion

The loss of my child many months after the Joseph Parsons' slander trial against Goody Bridgman did not portend the future. I was fortunate. I remembered Rhody's advice to wear my children around me like a cloak of protection. The next year, I gave birth to another child, another healthy boy, and with her words always in my ear, I gladly had many more after that.

With each healthy child, I breathed a sigh of relief and became more embedded in my community and more immersed in the routines of daily life. With each child there was a little more to do. Sarah also continued to build her young family. Together, we worked to clean, cook, spin, weave, brew, garden and raise our children. Being so busy during the day and the early part of the night helped to occupy my thoughts and dispel fears and obsessions about the past. With Sarah next door often guiding me, and me helping her too, we could do what both our mothers could not from their graves.

But at night, my thoughts of the past continued to come to the surface after drowning in my head and bogging me down for years. They flooded through me in torrents at times, another life that was begging for my attention.

As more memories came to light, they drew me in with a pull of nostalgia at first, starting out more lightly like the gentle ebbs and flow of a river glistening with the tiny jewels of reflected sunlight before eventually leading to more shocking turbulence over darker waters.

Priscilla, Annie's older sister, had always been overbearing. And when Annie and I played, she was bossy over me too. She always demanded attention as I played or spent time with Annie, who was closer to my own age. Poor Annie was under her thumb, but Priscilla was part of the family and so we had no choice but to accept her as bossy as she was and give deference to her when she inserted herself into whatever we did.

Priscilla was Thomas Thornton's favorite child. Perhaps, it was because he could see his own piety in her. Like her father, she thought she knew what was best for everyone, always giving advice that was never asked for. To please her father and show her virtue, Priscilla had the habit of reporting back to him and chiding us for behavior she thought was ungodly.

Having grown up with Priscilla, I was used to her and didn't think much about the way she was. There were certainly many other girls like her, trying desperately to please their fathers by showing their high moral character and behavior. It wasn't until after her little brother Samuel was born, that it became harder to be around her. It was also harder after I understood how sad my mother was about not having more children. Priscilla boasting about her newest siblings and the marvelous things they did, made her even more insufferable.

The three of us were spinning and carding wool with our oldest cousins, Sarah and Hannah, one day as they watched some younger ones. Priscilla was full of pride for little Samuel who was growing bigger by the day.

"It pleases my mother and my father that I am often with little Samuel to help watch him, change him and feed him. Mother says it will help me to understand how to be a mother."

"You must be feeding him a lot, Priscilla. He is a nice fat baby," I giggled. The other girls laughed with me.

"'Tis a pity you don't have a little one in your house to teach you those things, Alissa." she said. "There is so much to learn before becoming a mother. That will be our main duty one day. Don't worry. You can come and learn with me, and I will teach you," she added with authority.

Sarah came to my defense immediately. "Priscilla, Alissa is fine. She is around all her cousins. We are all learning together. Just because you have spent more time with a babe of late does not mean you know everything!"

I was burning with anger. How dare she belittle me so? Samuel was a sweet baby. I probably would have bragged about him too had he been my little brother but to hear Priscilla do it incessantly was irritating. I would have been glad to learn with Samuel, but I loathed her criticism and her bragging.

Instead of controlling herself, Priscilla kept her focus on me. "Why doesn't your mother have another baby?" she asked.

Everyone stared at me. They must have known something was wrong by their expressions of concern. I could feel my lower lip curling in and was on the verge of crying. Why was my family so different from everyone else's?

"Stop pestering the girl!" screeched Hannah. "Children do not know the answers for why their parents do as they do! Nor should they ask!"

"Well, I know," Priscilla said with confidence. "My parents do everything they do to be pleasing to God and that is what everyone should do. Our ministers teach us so."

"My mother wants another child," I murmured. "It is not her fault if her son was taken away from her. She wanted him with all her heart," I emphasized, quickly wiping aside a tear that I didn't want anyone to see.

We were taught not to be emotional, to always be controlled and humble. For a child, it was impossible. Even for some adults like my mother who was dealing with so much pain, it could be difficult to remain calm and nearly emotionless in the public square or the meeting house. Even amongst f riends and some family members, becoming too passionate or sensitive was frowned upon.

"Perhaps God is displeased with your mother," Priscilla said.

I wanted to punch her.

"Don't say that about my mother!" I snipped.

Hannah spoke up again, "Stop it, Priscilla. Can't you see Alissa is upset. Why can't you leave the girl alone? Stop being cruel!"

"Well. It's not my fault that Aunt Alice goes to trade with the Natives as she does. Maybe that is why God is displeased. She should stay away from them."

"Mother needs to trade with them to get medicine! I hate you, Priscilla! I never want to speak to you again. Come Annie. Let's go!" I grabbed Priscilla's little sister's hand and stomped out the door with her in tow.

"Oh, you mustn't say such things back to Priscilla. She will be awful to us from now on. I have to live with Priscilla not you! I know she shouldn't have said those things about your mother, but you must make-up with her or else I'm going to get in trouble when I go home," Annie pleaded.

"She's always awful to me," I said, still seething.

Just then, Priscilla came out with the other girls, her head lowered. Hannah and Sarah must have shamed her to come out and apologize. They were both behind her, nudging her to go to me.

"I hope you still don't hate me. You shouldn't because we are cousins."

Hannah gave her a nasty stare and nodded toward me again.

Priscilla continued, "I'm sorry, Alissa. I deserved your anger, but I hope you don't really mean that you never want to talk to me again. I shouldn't have said the things I did. It was wrong of me even though adults can and do say the same kind of things."

I stood defiant and formed my hands into fists. "What kind of adults say those things about my mother?" I demanded.

As Priscilla started to open her mouth, Hannah jumped in.

"Priscilla hasn't heard anything about your mother specifically, Alissa. You know how sometimes adults do talk after they've been to the meeting house. The ministers are always encouraging the adults to watch over each other and all of us lest anyone is tempted to stray," she explained.

"Aye, Satan lurks about, and he'll try to tempt anyone to upset the will of God." Priscilla said.

"I don't want to talk to you!"

I screamed at Priscilla again. Couldn't she just say she was sorry and then go on with things?

"Why are you talking about these things? Just go away," I said.

Sarah came up to me.

"Alissa, it will be fine. It's gotten out of hand," she said, squeezing my arm gently. "Everyone, listen, let's just stop talking and get back to our work. We are all cousins. We must get along and agree that there will be no hard feelings or nasty talk toward each other from this time forth."

I looked around silently and then stared at Priscilla and she at me.

Finally, she smiled. "Alright, I agree. My head hurts and I want peace too."

I nodded in agreement also.

The older girls, Hannah and Sarah, made some silly gestures pretending to be me and Priscilla putting our swords down to rest as Annie looked on laughing. Finally, Priscilla and I caught on and were giggling too, running across the yard and pretending to fight with swords.

At the height of our revelry, I noticed Hannah stopped suddenly. She quickly smoothed her skirts and pulled some loose hair into her cap. The rest of us were puzzled until she offered some clues. Her face flushed a brilliant shade of red that I'd never seen on her face before. Once she pulled herself together, she stood properly at the gate and looked toward the dirt road of our lane. We all understood what was happening once Johnny came into closer view with his cows in tow.

She pretended to look away for a few moments like she hadn't noticed him at all and seemed surprised when he called out to her.

"Good day, Hannah! What are ye doing there?" he paused with a guiding stick in hand. Looking at him, her face became even more crimson.

"Good day, Johnny," she smiled shyly and then froze without saying anything further. Sarah had come up and nudged her. The rest of us couldn't help but giggle at Hannah's awkwardness. Hannah looked like she was going to faint.

Sarah interrupted the silence. "Hannah, you were just about to tell Johnny what we were doing," she smiled at her cousin and raised her eyebrows.

"Aye," she quickly responded. "We were just taking a break from our spinning and sewing while our mothers were helping with the harvest. We're watching the young ones today too. And what might you be doing?" she asked.

"Taking the two cows to pasture. Well, don't let the little ones wear you out. I'd better go. The cows are getting restless." He tipped his hat and continued on his way, prodding the cows to go further down the lane.

We were silent as he passed us, but our broad grins let Hannah know we were quite aware of her attraction to him and we would not let her forget about it.

"I saw how he looked at you!" teased Priscilla.

"That Johnny sure is handsome," said Sarah.

"I know nothing of what you're talking about," said Hannah, blushing again.

"Do you think we're blind?" asked Sarah. Even the younger girls can understand attraction when they see it!"

She looked at Annie and me while Mary nodded with us even though she really was too young to understand.

"I saw you looking at his broad shoulders with your gushing glances. I'm sure you also noticed the new whiskers on his chin," Priscilla continued to goad her. "Aye. I'm sure Hannah also noticed his new deep manly voice!" she laughed.

"Was it that obvious?" asked Hannah. She had finally relaxed and started laughing as well. "I hope he likes me too! I want to know."

"It looked like he did, but I don't know much about boys," I giggled.

With that, we gathered the smaller ones in our care and returned to our chores that taught us about motherhood. With the older girls, becoming more aware of the boys in our neighborhood and in the meeting house, it would not be the last conversation about budding relationships, and the mysteries of what our parents did behind closed bed curtains.

Chapter 19

Springfield, Massachusetts 1657-1661 &
Windsor, Connecticut, 1646: Divination

My children became my buffer from the world. With every child born, especially my sons, the world continued to feel a little safer than it had before. Simon also brought me a comfort that I had never fully known before I married him. My footing in the world was less precarious and my existence forgiven further with each pregnancy and child that I bore.

I was fortunate because most of my babies lived. They didn't succumb to disease like many others. I took my mothering seriously and knew what to do to keep them well. I knew my knowledge of remedies and child rearing had come from my mother even though I didn't remember her specific advice. I'd watched her take care of the sick so often that I must have learned something.

I took my duties as wife seriously and always tried to please my husband. It wasn't hard to do for I truly loved Simon and our bond was strong. It was different from the relationship I observed between John Young and my mother. I had been lucky to have so many cousins to help me learn how to act in a loving relationship. I remembered our times together fondly as we explored the idea of motherhood and marriage, but I also looked back at some moments of shame.

"I shall not wait another minute to find out if Johnny likes me!" Hannah stated with impatience. One day he smiles and stops to greet me, but when he is with his friends, he acts like I am not there," she said in frustration. Our group of girls was gathered again. Our mothers were attending to a woman in labor and we kept each other company by continuing with our spinning and sewing.

"There are ways to find out," said Sarah. "I would like to know who my husband will be," she admitted truthfully.

"As would I," agreed Priscilla. We all knew she became quiet like a mouse when Elias Smith passed her on the green during meeting house or military days.

"And we don't care!" I laughed with Annie.

Priscilla ignored us. "But isn't looking into the future a sin?"

"Not if our intention is to ask God and not the Devil. If we pretend the string is the Bible then God will know," explained Hannah, searching for any good explanation and determined to find out the truth of Johnny's heart.

"What if you just asked Thomas?" Sarah referred to Priscilla and Annie's oldest brother who was close in age to Johnny.

"I've tried, but he tells me to stop pestering him," stated Priscilla. He is of no help at all and knows nothing of love! My big brother will be a bachelor a long time!"

"There is only one way," announced Hannah. "If we have a key and a string, we can find out the answers to all our questions about love and marriage."

"It's supposed to be a Bible and key," corrected Priscilla.

"But we don't know anyone who has a Bible. Only the ministers have one and they would frown if it were taken from the meeting house," said Sarah.

"Sukey Gibbs told me that it will work just as well to use a string and key. She's done it before," said Hannah who sometimes looked to the oldest girls of Backer Row for advice. After all, they were approaching the age of marriage.

"And did it really work?" asked Sarah, frowning and still a bit skeptical. Her infatuation with boys hadn't fully blossomed.

"Yes, Sukey Gibbs said that George Wilton has been coming to court her on a regular basis. She would not have known to act more interested unless she had asked the question with the key and thread," Hannah continued to argue her case for using the tool to see into her romantic future.

We were at Aunt Rhody's place. Her boys were with their uncles taking care of their livestock.

"Does your mother own a key?" asked Priscilla.

"Aye, we could even do it now while no one else is here, but we all have to promise that what happens here today will be kept a secret forever and ever. Turning to look at Annie and me she asked, "Even if you don't care about boys or marriage, you must keep our secrets. Do you understand?"

Annie and I looked at each other first and then grinned impishly. We were grateful they were not kicking us out of the room. We wanted to know how everything worked and we were enthralled by the older girls' silliness when they thought about their married futures or their crushes. For Annie and me, being mothers and wives seemed like something very far away. I wasn't so sure I wanted to be married after seeing my mother so unhappy with John Young.

Hannah opened her mother's intricately carved dowry chest. Mrs. Tinker purchased it for her from John Moore when she married John Taylor. Its oak and pine wood panels were beautiful, with intricately carved foliage and flower motifs. Aunt Rhody had a tinier wooden box in it where she kept her most important papers. Underneath the papers, Hannah carefully pulled the key from its hiding place.

"Here, we can use this," she whispered. "Let's try it before my mother comes home. Remember, it's our secret!" We nodded in reverence of the rite of passage we were about to commence.

"Come to the floor and sit," commanded Hannah. The rest of us dutifully listened and gathered around the key to which Hannah had attached the thread.

Priscilla in her piousness made a pronouncement. "We ask that the Holy Spirit know that we humbly attach the string to the key and ask that it be used as a Bible would be used, to give us information we need to find the mates that the Lord hath chosen for us."

Annie and I stared in awe as Hannah explained what the proceeding would be.

"With this key and string substituted for a Bible, we humbly ask the Creator to verify who our helpmates and marriage partners will be through 'Aye' and 'Nay' answers. We ask that you show us how Thee will answer a question with the answer 'Aye.'"

I almost held my breath as the skeleton key began to swing back and forth on the string.

"We humbly thank you and further ask for Thee to show us the direction of the key for the answer "Nay" to our question." As she held the key straight above her, it began to move in a circular path.

"Are ye sure that the key is not moving from the quivering of your hand?" asked Sarah, still not fully convinced.

"Do you dare to question the Holy Spirit?" chided Priscilla, quickly silencing Sarah and making her keep her doubts to herself.

"It has now been established the ways in which the Holy Spirit will communicate with us, and we may proceed. Who is ready?" she asked.

"You go first," Priscilla whispered to Hannah.

"Holy Spirit, please bestow on me the knowledge of who my mate will be. Have Thee chosen Johnny for me?" In an instant, the key and string acting as a pendulum, began to swing forward and backward.

"I knew it!" Hannah beamed. "I humbly thank Thee, Holy Spirit. Your turn, Priscilla."

Priscilla took the key and thread from her in a careful and solemn manner. She stood.

"Holy Spirit, I humbly beg of Thee, please let me know if Elias Smith is the boy I am to grow up to marry. Please direct me."

She tried to hold her hand as steady as possible. The key changed direction and circled above the floor and below her hand. It was a "no" answer.

"If that is what God wills, I accept he is not to be my husband." She bowed her head in disappointment.

"Who's next?" asked Hannah.

"I don't want to know," I said.

"Me neither," said Annie sheepishly.

Sarah crossed her hands. "I don't blame them," she said. "I don't want to do it either. I changed my thoughts on it. It feels strange to think about."

"Fine. No one said you had to," said Hannah.

"Now that you know, what do you intend to do about it anyway? And how can you be sure that it's not the Devil really telling you what you want to hear?"

"It's the Holy Spirit and not the Devil!" Hannah defended herself. And now that I know, I will prepare to be a wife. I will keep learning and practicing." She paused. "I wonder what it's like to kiss a betrothed or a husband? Sukey Gibbs said it takes practice to know," she wondered aloud.

"Ha ha ha!" Annie and I roared with laughter and Sarah let out a big grin.

"It's like this," Annie and I puckered up giving quick kisses to each other on the mouth giggling.

"Silly girls! You look like two hens pecking at each other," chided Hannah.

"I doubt you two shall ever have husbands!" added Priscilla. "It's like this I imagine, smooth and long kisses holding lips together for a long time." She put her hand up to her face and began kissing her hand at length.

"But you have to get your head in the right position too," said Hannah.

"Go ahead, show us," dared Sarah.

"Fine. Priscilla, pretend you are the husband. She put her hands around Priscilla's waist and they started to kiss, pressed against each other, at first knocking heads and bumping noses. Hannah tilted Priscilla's head to the side as they continued to kiss each other.

Being so engrossed in our lesson, we didn't see Aunt Rhody silently slip into the house.

No one was more shocked than our Aunt Rhody when she walked in on our little innocent trial and observed her daughter and her niece embracing.

"Girls, what are you doing? Be grateful that someone else was not the one who walked in to see you doing this! Why?"

"Mama don't be cross. We were just talking about boys and wanted to know what it was like to be a wife," said Hannah. "We don't know what it feels like to be kissed by a husband. We just wanted to know how it felt."

"You'll find out when you're married," she said.

"I'm sorry, Aunt Rhody," said Priscilla, hanging her head in shame. "We really meant no harm."

"Mama, we don't want to be bad at kissing. What if the time comes and our husbands are not pleased with us? Or what if we feel stupid because we don't know what to do? We were just practicing. Are we truly the only girls who have ever thought of this?" Hannah asked.

"No. I suppose not," Rhody said thoughtfully, making me wonder if she had done the same with her sisters as a child. She became serious again with us.

"What is this? she asked, spying the key on the ground. "Why did you take it out of my chest and what are you doing with it?"

"Nothing, Mama. Just a game," said Hannah.

Aunt Rhody must have recognized what we had been doing.

"Girls, you will keep these things to yourselves and never tell anyone. It would not be looked at with the lens of innocence by our ministers or some others in town. Do you understand me?" she asked sternly, not taking her eyes off us until satisfied.

Everyone shook their heads.

"We shall say no more of it," she declared. "It's time that you get back to your chores."

We were relieved she hadn't delved more into our conversations regarding the purpose of the key or heard our conversations about desire, love and mating.

How many other young girls thinking about their futures as wives and mothers had the same concerns or curiosity? We couldn't have been the only ones.

What we didn't realize at that naïve stage of our youth was that some of us would be blessed in love and others not. I hoped that none of us experienced the unhappiness that I'd seen revealed in my own home because of a marriage where two people were estranged and unhappy.

Chapter 20

Springfield, Massachusetts, 1661 &
Windsor, Connecticut, 1646: Change

The robins flitted about looking for twigs to finish building their nests. Leaves had started to grow and fill in the empty spaces between the branches of the local trees, once again casting some shadow on forest floors. The sky was blue and clear. The warmth of mid spring was always welcome and full of hope as we readied the fields for another planting season. As we came in from our endeavors that day, Mr. Pynchon arrived at our home on horseback.

"I have a letter for you, Alissa. From your kin in the south of Connecticut with the instructions to deliver with great care and expediency," he said.

With unbridled excitement, I took the letter from him and gave thanks. I excused myself and sat in the back on an open bench I often used while doing outside work. Opening it with great care, I wanted to take in every delicious moment of contact with my kin. I knew I'd read the letter many times. I did think it was a bit peculiar that Mr. Pynchon would personally deliver a routine letter of communication from my family, but I didn't dwell on it. It always raised my spirits to hear news from my aunts, Mary and Rhody, in Norwalk, in the very southern reaches of Connecticut along the sound.

Dear Alissa-

We regret to inform you about the news of the passing of John Young in Stratford. He died on April 7th and was buried the very next day on April 8th. God rest his soul.

Stratford was a town not far from Norwalk. In fact, they were closer to it than Windsor was to Springfield. So, they'd heard the news from both passersby and my uncle, John Tinker, whose boss, the Governor John Winthrop the Younger, often sent remedies to address John Young's many ailments and generalized weakness of body.

John Young had been plagued by illness for many months. His bouts of sickness and consumption came more frequently, and he had to be cared for by the goodness of his neighbors as it became harder for him to get out of bed each day. Alas, he died an invalid. Despite his many months of illness, he left no will, claiming no heirs. His estate will remain with the town for the next seven years according to custom and unless kin come to claim it.

I was stunned as I read the contents of the letter. At the same time, the news of the death of John Young stirred nothing it my soul. It remained numb. I had been given his surname at the time of my birth, but the more I thought about it, he had been a father to me in name only. How typical of him to leave no will and claim no heirs. If he had cared for me or thought of me as his daughter, he would have done so.

Certainly, he had heard that I now had several sons so the fact that I was a woman could not have been the issue. In one of my moments of trying to forgive as preached by our minister, I'd written to him two times. I never received a response. There was no excuse since he could read and write. His books were a testament to this. Aye, there was no doubt that he knew I had sons. As always, he chose not to acknowledge me in his will or by responding to my letters. So, this most recent news was unsurprising but still sad to me. We had lived under the same roof and broke bread together for many of my early years. He'd refused to ever try to make a connection with me, his spirit barely touching mine in common humanity. Abandoned by him long ago, his latest rejection still stung and surprised me since I was normally numb to it now.

"What is it, Alissa?" my husband Simon asked.

"Wait. Let me finish and I'll tell ye." I put a finger to my lips and continued reading.

If you and Simon would like to make a claim on John Young's estate for your sons' futures, please let us assist you. You and Simon will always have a place to stay in the region with kin who will not hesitate to fill your bellies with good food and put a roof over your heads as you work out the legalities of this situation. Our brother, your uncle John Tinker, is happy to represent you and your sons should you decide to make a claim for them as his heirs.

As for you, dear Alissa. We hold you as always in our hearts and prayers. There is not a month or season that goes by without tender thoughts of you and your family. Regards to your wonderful family as it grows in love, prosperity, and numbers. And highest regards to our dear cousin Simon Beamon, your husband. We are so happy he continues to love and watch over you.

We will send you another letter later of any personal news. But for now, rest in God's love and keep yourselves well.

Aunt Mary and Aunt Rhody

"John Young, my father, is dead," I said, my voice cracking. I was confused about how I felt. I preferred to feel nothing. But now I was hurt again from rejection, angry that he hadn't even thought of my sons.

"Simon, I need you to know the contents of the letter for the sake of our sons," I informed him. At that young stage of our marriage of six and a half years, my oldest son, Simon, was nearly six years old, John was four, Daniel was two, and Thomas was still a baby. They were too young to understand. But their father could go claim John Young's estate for them.

"I'll read it for ye," I said.

Simon shook his head in disbelief when I was done. "Wife, I'll do whatever you need me to do, but you must decide what's most important to you. After all, John Young has scarcely been a father to you. Once he sold his lot to Walter, he went to Stratford and never looked back. Never sent for you. Never so much as a letter stating his regards for you or the family or his congratulations after our marriage."

"'Tis true Simon, but the ministers did force me to go out of his home after mother's death. They were concerned that I had not received the proper upbringing in it. However, my father was relieved, not discouraged when I left. I could see it in his eyes. He never petitioned for our situation to be different and was happy to move on with his life without me."

"But I wouldn't give it too much thought as he didn't think about how this might affect you or your children."

I thought for a moment. My husband was right. The vengeful part of me wanted to claim John Young's land for my sons even if it would be the only thing that I'd ever gotten from him.

"Do you think he had much of an estate?" Simon asked.

"I don't know, and it mustn't be a deciding factor. I must not let my anger make any decision for me. I shall think about it for a few days. In fact, I will pray that my heart will be ready to forgive him again. Let us talk no more of this today. It will become clearer to me," I said.

"As ye wish my love," he kissed my cheek and went to the barn to sharpen some tools.

I continued with my routines, busy with the boys and all the chores a mother is required to do until one night another dream jostled into the inner reaches of my head, showing me something that had made no sense as a child.

I didn't remember falling asleep early. Someone had carried my tiny body to my trundle bed and tucked me in. I don't know how late into the night it was, but my detached father was shouting at my mother. She was crying. All the cousins that had come to be with us earlier in the evening were gone too.

"You promised me, Alice. You'd best keep the promise. Neither one of us can afford any changes to the original agreement. I will not budge. And, keeping things as they are is in your best interest. We depend on each other. Without the two walls connected, the construction falls. Is that what you want? Please tell me, do you really want that?"

Mother continued sobbing.

"Answer me!" He made her look at him by grabbing both her shoulders. "Do not do something that will ruin the both of us!" he warned her. "Why didn't you think of this earlier? How could you not understand how this situation would play out?"

Mother straightened and stood defiant. "John, how would I have known? I heard nothing for many months. I was afraid. What if he never came back? How was I to care for Alissa? You also had no idea how it would all end up. You know you didn't either! You and I agreed to help each other blindly. But circumstances change! And, you have no right to place all your regret upon my shoulders! I know I'm not perfect but you, you take advantage of this situation as best as anyone could. Do you think I enjoy incessantly massaging your limbs and making you specific liniments when you don't follow my advice anyway? Why do I do it?" she screamed back at him.

"Quiet, woman! You damn well know why! Watch your tone before all the neighbors hear us!"

"Then just leave. Go to your little hut in the fields across the river! I know how much you love going there so you have time to stop pretending that you're a father. Just go! It's not like you do a very good job of it anyway. Nothing will be resolved tonight." Her last words trailed off into a whimper and she collapsed into a puddle of emotion on a chair near the hearth.

My angry father looked at her with disgust as he grabbed a few biscuits and cut himself a piece of hard cheese. He grunted loudly as he put them into a small sack with some dried meat. When he couldn't get her attention, he grabbed an extra blanket along with his prepared sack and walked straight to exit. Taking his hat from one of the hooks, he placed it on his head and darted out the door, not looking back once.

Instead of upsetting my mother, his disappearance seemed to give her more relief. From the little perch of my trundle bed in the next room near the open door, it was clear they were both better separated from each other. My mother's remark about pretending to be a father baffled me. I didn't understand her. She'd become angry with me before if I didn't call him "Father" in public but now in private she said he was "pretending to be my father" and accused him of doing a horrible job of it. I suppose at that young age, I truly could not make sense of it. Perhaps though, I didn't want to. I pushed the thought of it away and got up to try to be a comfort to my mother.

When my mother saw me up and approaching her, she quickly wiped away any obvious tears left behind and put an instant smile on her face.

"I should've known you'd get up again tonight. I shouldn't have let you fall asleep so early. I guess you were tired from all the little games you played with your cousins. Come to me and sit on my lap. We'll tell stories to each other until we're both sleepy," she winked.

"That would be fine, Mother. But where did Father go?" I asked.

"Such a dedicated farmer that one is," she said trying to divert herself from what had just transpired between them. "He wanted to sleep in his fields, watch over the new plantings and be ready at sunup to get to work. Between you and me, I think he wants to hear the pair of owls he heard the other day right after dusk. The pair live over there in a clump of river trees along the banks. It's eerie the way they call out to each other. Almost like lovers in distress," she explained.

"Are you alright, Mother?" I asked. She looked at me quizzingly to assess if I'd heard any of the argument with my father. Even if she thought I had, it was a topic that she was anxious not to discuss.

"Of course, Alissa! Now, let's get to telling stories. I'm not as good at it as your Uncle John but I'll try, my sweet," she said kissing me on the forehead. She started to tell me about her own mother and how she lived with the Tinkers and was born in their cottage where her mother used to stay.

I let myself become engrossed in her story. I never asked why she and John Young had a fight that night. It was obvious that she wouldn't want to talk about it with me.

The next day, Simon was sitting in the yard, whittling a part for a wheel on our wagon that needed to be fixed.

"Simon, I've made a decision. I'll write a letter to Mary and Rhody today," I announced.

"I see. If you want me to go and stake a claim, I can go for you, but it will have to wait until the fall, it being spring now and the planting season just beginning. Best to go after the harvest but return well before winter starts."

"It doesn't matter Simon. We don't need to go for that. I'd still be happy for a visit to my aunts and cousins."

He paused and held his chin in thought. "I respect whatever decision you make. I suppose another option could be that you have your family closer to Stratford claim it for you. As your aunts have said, your Uncle John could even represent you."

"I'm not sure that I wish to make a claim," I reiterated.

He stopped what he was doing and put a loving hand on my shoulder, "I'm still dumbfounded that even though he was sickly for months, he didn't take the time to get his affairs in order."

"That's true, Simon. John Young left no will. He had no concern to do that. He did not care. Aunt Priscilla told me a while ago that Thomas Thornton is no longer in Stratford, so he cannot easily be a witness. He left for Ireland years ago to minister to the Irish Catholics and convert them."

"That won't be a problem my love. Your other family will vouch for you like we discussed earlier. The real issue is how you want to finally end your relationship with John Young. Are you ready to let go of the bad memories?"

The more I thought about my memory the previous night, I knew it was better to reject anything to do with my estranged father and do what was right. I had no relationship with John Young and hadn't for years now. It probably wasn't worth the time or the effort. I didn't care. I knew my sons would have plenty of land in Springfield and beyond if they wanted it. Simon would make sure of that. Was John Young's estate rightly mine anyway? I had my doubts more than ever before.

"Will God forgive me for saying I really don't care about John Young? Aye. Let the property sit there for seven years. What small connection I ever had to the man has been shattered anyway. Why drag it on?" I asked logically.

"I cannot say I blame you for feeling as you do," Simon assured me, squeezing both my shoulders and looking on intently with concern.

The thought that John Young had chosen to do nothing to save my mother or show any particular kindness to me after her death would always haunt me. A few acts of kindness might have given me at least a stronger foothold in this world. It all fell on Aunt Rhody to do that and others like Simon and my Uncle John. I made my final decision.

"John Young was much older than my mother. She had always devoted herself to helping him feel better with his ailments. And, under her care, he did better. Without her, he became sick again for months. He could have written his will to at least respect the care my mother gave him by giving his remaining earthly goods to my sons, but he chose not to. No! I'll not request anything from his estate. It would be betraying my mother once again. His estate can sit there and rot for eternity," I stated, hands defiantly on my hips with my head up high and proud.

"As you wish, my love," Simon hugged me with all his might.

And so, it ended — my family's connection to John Young, forevermore. He was never spoken of again in my home. Nor did I make the trip to Stratford to see his grave. I was free of him and his betrayal of me and my mother. My only regret was not seeing my aunts. That day I decided that I'd only keep a place in my heart for those who I could count on, who truly loved, cared for, and protected me.

Chapter 21

Springfield, Massachusetts, Fall 1662:
Darkness Seeping In

The fall of 1662 was a strange one for me. Dark childhood memories came tumbling before me as similar events unfolded in my waking world.

In September, I received a message from Hartford that my Uncle John Tinker was taking care of his business and handling some of the Governor John Winthrop the Younger's affairs while the governor was away in London beseeching the King for a charter for Connecticut Colony. The messenger stated he would come for a visit and would stay with Mr. Pynchon. He was well acquainted with the Pynchons because Amy, Mr. Pynchon's wife, had gone to stay with his boss, Winthrop the Younger, for several months as she got through her illness in New London. They were close friends and John Tinker was always welcome there. Simon and Uncle John got along well too. I was excited for the visit and busied myself preparing and planning for our special rare visit with the man who had helped me so much in my childhood.

I anxiously awaited more news about my uncle. The leaves were swirling down to the ground and the skies hung gray and overcast when I caught a glimpse of a young man I didn't recognize. He was making his way slowly toward our home. He hopped off his black mare and tied her to a post near the threshold. I ran outside to see what he wanted. Bringing his hat from his head to his chest, he bowed to me in a solemn manner.

"Ma'am, I come on behalf of John Tinker. I am Silas Jones, his assistant. We came to Hartford several weeks ago to take care of some business."

"Aye, I know. He sent me a letter announcing he'd visit when his affairs in Hartford were in order."

A feeling of dread enveloped my chest.

"Where's my Uncle John?" I demanded.

Silas took no pleasure in telling me the shocking news.

"I'm so sorry, ma'am. Your uncle has passed on suddenly. I know he treasured the thought of seeing you again," he hung his head.

Simon had come to the door after me, listening to the conversation. He could see how pale I had become. Quickly grabbing my waist as if I were a thin sheet about to drift off, he carefully guided me to sit and asked Silas to come and rest as well at the bench and table outside. He brought us both drinks: weak beer to revive me and a stout to quench Silas' thirst after the long, sad journey from Hartford. He also returned with water for Silas' mare.

In my shock, I remained mute and thought of my uncle's family. Uncle John had five small children who stayed with his young wife in New London. She was named Alice just like my mother. How devastating it would be for them.

Silas told us about the bustling inn in Hartford where they stayed. It was busier than usual for the court session. It was there that he died the morning they were to leave.

"They think someone poisoned him, missus. We know not who it could have been, but he had a few enemies in Hartford. It is fair to say," said Silas.

"But why?" I asked. Uncle John was likable, personable and the right-hand man of the governor.

"Let's just say he was enemies of Governor Winthrop's enemies by extension," Silas lowered his eyes before mumbling, "'Twas the accused witches he tried to help that made him more enemies. He forced their hands to let the Dutch witch go."

I hated that word WITCH. In fact, I never wanted to hear it again. It had ruined me from ever carrying on as a normal person. I was still unsure of myself, scared of everything and anything that might be around a bend. I'd been plagued by nightmares for years and still I didn't remember most of the details of my own mother's demise.

"Witch you say!" I glared at him. "Silas, how can they still be searching for witches?"

"You hadn't heard about everything happening in the town of Hartford, ma'am?" he asked.

"I hadn't listened. I hadn't wanted to. But now I must if you say my uncle was involved. What started all this?" I demanded.

"Please bear with me ma'am. I'm from New London and I can only tell you what I know from being in Hartford of late. The story about witches in Hartford started in the spring when a woman named Goody Ayres came to bring soup for her little neighbor girl, Betty Kelly. The woman, Judith Aryes, was quite fond of Betty I understand since she'd lost a daughter and only had sons. She'd brought the soup she'd made herself when young Betty was sick and fed it to her." He paused, unsure about going on. I knew he saw the fierceness and impatience in my eyes. Simon nodded that it would be alright.

"Please, Silas. Finish your story." I'd heard the beginning of it before. Sarah had tried to keep me informed of the insanity that was occurring in Hartford. But I'd bade her to stop. I had no patience to hear about witch trials anymore. But now that Uncle John was dead, I had to know how he'd involved himself with defending alleged witches once again, something that might have been the cause of his death.

"What happened to Betty, the sickly child?" I asked yearning for the answers to how her death could possibly relate to Uncle John.

"She died," he stated, "but not before she'd pointed the finger at Judith Ayres, the neighbor who'd loved her and wanted her to be well. According to her father, Goodman Kelly, she'd screamed in the middle of the night that Judith Ayres had pinched her and was in league with the Devil to harm her. Betty wanted her father to grab the broad axe that very night and go kill Judith Ayres. If you asked me, it sounds like the child was possessed."

I shuddered. It was eerily familiar. Simon listened intently and respected my need to ask questions.

"But what does any of this have to do with my Uncle John?" I asked, needing to stand again. I repeated, "Please tell me. What does this have to do with my uncle?" I was losing patience.

"When Governor Winthrop left the colony last year to obtain the charter, he warned Mr. Tinker to be on guard for incidents such as this. He implored him to do his best to smother witch accusations and panics in his absence. He'd worked so hard to tamp them down once and for all. He had genuine concerns that his assistant governor, John Mason, was all too happy to let witch fears and accusations set in again."

"And, he was right," said Silas.

"But what did my uncle do and what could he do in Mr. Winthrop's absence?" I asked.

"Well, he wrote to Mason and beseeched him to steady the ship and keep calm, but Mason called in an old friend, Bray Rossiter who he knew from Windsor, a doctor."

The tiny hairs stood on my arms. I knew that name. I knew there was some connection to my own story.

"Missus, you look pale. Do you need to sit down again?"

He noticed my shock at hearing these familiar names. Simon grabbed my arm gently and led me back to the bench.

"I will be fine Silas. I need to know what happened to my uncle," I steadied myself.

Simon encouraged him as well. "Go on with your account of what happened, Silas. Let's get to the end of it."

"After Bray Rossiter examined Betty's dead body and said her death was caused by witchcraft, there wasn't much your uncle could do. The fire was already raging and spreading further into the community. However, he could be helpful on one front. He'd been asked to help with freeing one of the accused witches from New Netherland. Her family had been living in Hartford. She had powerful kin who requested her release, but Mason needed convincing. That's where your uncle came into the story in the most important way. Alas, your Uncle John successfully negotiated the release of the accused young woman, Judith Varlet, a beguiling Dutch beauty, to the lieutenants of Director General Stuyvesant. Your uncle was cheerful that at least he was able to do that. However, I found him dead, frothing at the mouth, writhing in confusion and slowly dying on the day he intended to come see you. I'm so sorry missus. I truly am."

I sank deeper into my chair. Sadness encased me. Simon grabbed the pewter pitcher and refreshed my drink. I couldn't cry while Silas was there. I knew when the dam burst, it would drown me for several days.

"I bet he knew something — something so foul that he was killed for it with a lethal poison. Or maybe he was getting in the way. I guess it doesn't matter now," Silas finished softly.

"No. I can't believe he's really gone," I said quietly.

"Neither can I. He was a great man," Simon squeezed my hand and held tight.

"Aye, that he was!" Silas responded and then turned to me again.

"Missus, he wanted to visit you. He said it was important. I don't know what it was about, but I do know he was eager to be with you and Simon again. He wanted to meet your newest children. And lastly, he wanted to give you this."

He handed me a small leather pouch filled with coins.

"Your uncle had done very well of late in his business dealings as a merchant and wanted to share the bounty with you and Simon. You were very dear to him, he said. As much as his children in New London."

I teared up remembering his generosity as a child living with Aunt Rhody. He always left something to help her take care of me, usually wampum or coins. And he frequently brought me and Rhody little gifts: pretty textiles or small trinkets from the continent of Europe.

"I humbly thank you for bringing this to me as he would have if he had lived to see another day. But I must insist that you bring it back to his wife."

"No." He pushed the little bag away. "Your uncle insisted that you should have it. There is estate enough to care for the needs of his wife and children. This is but a small token of his desire to help you in your life. Please take it. I do not want his spirit to be cross with me."

"Thank you," I murmured, staring at the small pouch.

I pulled myself together and made Silas a basket filled with some bread, cheese, and dried beef for his ride back to Hartford. Simon engaged him in conversation and let him know how grateful we were for his visit.

"Fare thee well, Silas. I thank ye for coming out of your way to tell me the news. I'll never forget my Uncle John. Please send my best wishes and my condolences to his wife. It won't be easy for her now with five young children to raise on her own. Please make sure they are cared for. I will write to his sisters and let them know what happened."

"It's already done, ma'am."

He bowed before me and Simon and thanked us for the food. He waved one last time after he mounted his saddle and headed back to Hartford.

As I shut the heavy wood door to my home, my heart felt heavier. I made my way to the bedstead where I collapsed. According to Simon and my children, I was in bed for days, inconsolable and not even in the present. They said I'd go in and out of wakefulness, crying, moaning, waking up from dark dreams.

By then, everyone had heard about my uncle's death. Silas had also stopped at Mr. Pynchon's to let him know that John Tinker would not be coming, that he would never come again. According to Mr. Pynchon, John Tinker was given a ceremony and burial by the state and his widow would not need for anything after his death. The estate of Governor John Winthrop, his employer and dear friend, would see to that.

I imagined that by the time I came to my wits again, Aunt Rhody and the other siblings would have heard about John Tinker's death, but I wrote them letters all the same wanting to be close to them in some way once again. I talked very little and finally remembered some of those moments that were so difficult for me. John Tinker, my uncle, the storyteller, made me feel joy when I needed it the most. I remember laughing so much with my cousins as he told us all kinds of wild tales about the wilderness and worlds I could only imagine. Such a kind smile, an endearing grin, and allowing always an atmosphere of ease and comfort in his presence. Those were the nice memories, but some were much more difficult. No wonder I lost my wits for a few days immersing myself in memories of him and my mother again. The hardest of all was walking with him and Aunt Mary as they held on to me when the constable led my mother away forever.

I was morose for days after seeing the vision of her, the very last time I saw my beautiful mother in chains, hair disheveled and clothing dirty and torn in places. Uncle John was there for me and mother. He always was during the darkest of times.

John Young was nowhere to be found that day. He didn't see my mother off. He didn't seek me out or try to bring me comfort. It was as if John Tinker was my real father and John Young, a convenient imposter. It was his name only that I carried.

As if the heavens opened with that thought, I cried heartily. Could it be? I knew in my heart. I had the same hair, brown and curly. Some said I took great resemblance to the Tinker cousins of shared great grandparents far back in the old country of England. Who was it that protected me and encouraged my marriage to Simon so soon after they convicted Lydia Gilbert? It was Uncle John, of course. He always seemed to appear when I needed him the most.

He was certain I'd be safe with Simon Beamon, the amiable servant of John Pynchon who he knew well because of his connection to Governor John Winthrop of Connecticut. 'Twas if my mother herself were talking to me after John Tinker died, telling me all the things she would have liked me to know when she was alive if the time had ever been right. Ah yes! Of course, it made sense that John Tinker was my real father, even if I couldn't be sure.

And it was he who'd go with Aunt Mary to Hartford to visit my mother before she died, and I'd heard he was the one with Mary who brought Mother bedding and food so she shouldn't have to suffer so much during her last days on Earth. I loved my Uncle John, my possible father, even more when I thought of all this.

But why hadn't my mother ended up with him? Why did she marry the old and grumpy, John Young? That part, I'd never fully know. At least, I knew I did love John Tinker like a father for he'd been a father to me every time a need arose. That's what mattered.

I made up my mind then that I'd go to Hartford in the future. I'd find his grave and thank him profusely for the love and care he showed me while he walked among us. My dear husband, kind soul that he was, wanted to pay his respects to John Tinker too and agreed to go to Hartford to attend to his grave.

We couldn't go until the following spring, but I found where his body was laid to rest in the burying ground and left a handful of bluets there to show my gratitude and respect. I prayed that he would find the soul of my mother and guide her to peace if that was possible. I hoped that he could be at peace himself and that whoever caused his death would suffer for it.

As I sat next to his final resting place, a flood of another kind of memory came to me along with the tears. I finally remembered how he took me to a secret place in the woods. He whispered that he placed my mother's body there. He made me swear an oath to never tell another soul about it. It was covered in the wildflowers she so loved. He transplanted many for her over the years. His tenderness in placing her there and giving her child, me, a safe place to grieve my mother, confirmed the suspicions in my heart. Only a father would give such a gift to his child for a mother that was condemned to death, a mother labeled as the consort of Satan.

Knowing John Tinker's love for me and the care he gave to both of us comforted my soul. In some ways, it fortified me for what was to come next because past demons show themselves when one becomes stronger.

Days after visiting the Burying Ground in Hartford, the sweetness of John Tinker's blessing on my life was forced into the background. Reality continued to impose itself on me in nightmares. The story of how the witch panic began in Hartford and the death of young Betty Kelly had stayed with me. Why did she fear her neighbor was hurting her? I thought of all these stories as I did the mundane chores of daily life: sweeping or sewing as the children napped or preparing for dinner. Feeding the hearth late into the night, the stories started to make more sense.

The doctor Bray Rossiter starting the witch panic in Hartford with his pronouncement of the child's bewitchment was all too familiar to me. He had been the doctor in Windsor at the time of my mother's accusation! Aye! The truth was revealing itself to me. He'd lost a child too during the great time of illness. I sensed strongly that he was partially to blame for my mother's demise. Had he acted in the same way in Windsor? Had he studied the bodies of the dead children and also declared they were bewitched? I intuited more details would come to me.

Aye, there was more. Once I allowed myself to see so deeply into the past, I was hurled into the world of my childhood where I realized the identity of who was most responsible for my mother's witch accusation. IT WAS PRISCILLA! Something had spooked her before her death.

Through staring at the fire as if in a nightmare, I glimpsed a sickly Priscilla Thornton. She thrashed in her bed, feverish, and bedeviled. My mother came to comfort her, but Priscilla screamed, deeply disturbed as if she'd seen the face of evil. Over and over, hellish images came to me. Priscilla, sweating in her shift, as she tossed and turned on her feather bed, crying out, asking God for forgiveness, and telling her father that she was much troubled by the Devil. Then, I saw my mother doling out some soup or one of her herbal teas, trying to give her comfort but Priscilla cried out and said my mother was the Devil's consort, a witch who disturbed her. The story was similar to what had happened to Betty Kelly who accused her neighbor of bewitching her in Hartford.

It also unleashed the memory of my mother coming home one evening very upset. The whole Thornton family had taken ill. Mother was known for her skills as a healer. Ah yes! I understood! Of course, it was much to the dislike of the town doctor Bray Rossiter! He was jealous of her.

While the memories were hard to witness, I was grateful that so many of the fragmented remembrances I'd had from the past were starting to come together so that I could finally understand what had happened. My mother had always met the disapproving eye of that doctor. He was suspicious of her from the start for she made good use of Indian medicines as she went about her calling of nursing and comforting the sick. Most would choose to see her in their illness because of her gentle and kind manner. She was not arrogant like the doctor who thought he was above everybody else. As Priscilla lay in bed, that doctor came at the insistence of her father and did nothing to truly help her. He was as powerless as anybody else to cure her.

So, when my mother tried in a last effort to help her, Priscilla was already at death's door. Who knew what she really saw before she met our Lord Jesus. But Mother said she was much troubled by darkness and Satan and begged for God to be with her. Priscilla had led her life trying to be pious and was more concerned about doing the right things than most children her age. She knew it was the one way to truly please her father. Ultimately, she failed. As she lay dying, did she fear in her dark fantasies that her imperfections and failures had led her to be tormented by someone who had a pact with Satan, a witch?

I learned later through the gossip in the town that Priscilla had accused my mother of sending her specter to torment her. She was convinced that my mother was hurting her while she slept and was causing her to suffer. No wonder my mother was so upset! She'd known Priscilla since she was a baby and had grown up with her own mother, Ann. But Thomas, Priscilla's father, demanding of perfection and piousness from his children and a devil-fearing man himself, must have listened when Priscilla called out my mother as an instrument of the Devil.

No wonder the story of little Betty haunted me so! Betty Kelly had done the same thing to Judith Ayres as Priscilla had done to my own mother. Deep in their sickness, they couldn't recognize the kindness of someone who loved them trying to help them feel better. Both of their protective and pious fathers grasped on to everything they said and once their children died, they were thoroughly convinced of supposed evil done! And the doctor was there both times to say their deaths were caused by bewitchments. In truth, two unfortunate women accused of witchcraft were only trying to help two sick little girls they loved feel better and get well again.

It had taken me years to put together what had happened. Too many long years! I don't think I could have done it as a child. It would have tortured me to great harm. But now, I could look at it and be grateful to understand. I also realized I'd hated Priscilla for sowing doubt and blaming my mother. I'd have to beg God for forgiveness for my hatred of her. But the more I tried, the more difficult it was.

There was something more to this sad story. I knew it. I felt uncomfortable as if I were Priscilla's accomplice. How could that be though? I wasn't there at her bedside. Mother forbade it. She was afraid that the sickness would take hold of my body too. She'd watched too many people die and she wasn't going to lose her only daughter, she said.

Whatever my ongoing discomfort was, I'd have to live with the feeling for much longer. It was a secret locked tight in the core of my being. It might never unlock itself and be visible to me.

Chapter 22

Springfield, Massachusetts, 1662-1675: Build-up to War

War was imminent. For years, we took it for granted that our Native relations would continue as they were, living in peace. The locals taught us much about farming and helped us survive by selling us corn when our own supplies were low. The townspeople of Springfield had gotten along with our Native friends, but most English were careful not to get too close. Resentments started to build and the underlying reasons for them became more apparent with time.

For well over a decade, John Pynchon bought Nipmuck lands and encouraged more colonists to come to the areas surrounding Springfield. Many inhabitants bought more land as well. Simon was one. He purchased parcels to develop from the Natives in Old Skipmuck near the Skenungonuck Falls. So did Sarah's husband, Thomas. Sarah's brother, Samuel Marshfield bought such a large amount of land from the Natives in Agawam that they didn't have enough left to plant on. The court forced him to set aside acreage for their use so that they wouldn't go hungry.

Over time, many Natives disappeared, some to sickness and others moved on to wilder places to the west, missing the life they once knew. Some started to protect and isolate themselves in forts and constructed a walled one on Long Hill in Agawam to the south of Springfield.

We English and others from across the Atlantic continued to spread across the land taking what was once part of Native territory. Our numbers were like those of locusts attacking a planted crop of wheat, leaving Natives to become isolated and more impoverished than ever before once the fur trade had almost stopped. They'd been forced to cede land that they'd put up for security to buy English goods in hopes of more beaver skins to trade. But the beavers were almost gone. And we, in our greed, had taken as much as they could bring us. In the end, the scales of plenty tipped toward the English, leaving the Natives with very little.

Our past Native friendships became less important, and we embedded ourselves eagerly into the landscape. We reshaped it and tamed it and destroyed what was once wilderness to remake it into something useful to us and "claim it for Christ" as our ministers told us. We'd learned the survival skills that the Natives offered us, but we soon discarded our teachers, always wanting more and taking more. If we couldn't have the animals they'd trapped for us, we'd use their former lands to our advantage. And anyone with a mind to try to understand how they felt might be branded in a negative way.

It stirred an uneasy feeling in me, even though our colonial leaders told us it was part of God's plan for us. Not only could I see that it was not fair but something about it reminded me of my mother. I knew she'd spent times intimately learning about plants used for healing with an older Native woman. Images of her talking to local Natives who still planted their corn in Windsor when I was a child started to come to mind. She knew some words of their language. She greeted them and asked about the herbs gathered in their baskets. My mother seemed more comfortable interacting with them than most English were.

I also remembered my Uncle John Tinker and Uncle John Taylor bought a large tract of Indian land in Windsor. I was too little to remember much about it. But it was vast and beautiful along the Little River. Uncle John was almost fluent in Native tongues and when we went to visit him on what became Tinker's Farm, many of the Windsor Natives still fished along its banks, farmed or gathered groundnuts and walnuts as they always had.

Remembering exchanges with Simon and the local Natives at Pynchon's trading post in Springfield as newlyweds allowed me to see the stark contrast of the environment before the war, one of imbalance, hard feelings and regret to an earlier one of hope and prosperity. I began to wonder if it was really to the advantage of the English to leave our former friends with nothing. We would soon find out.

It was no surprise that the Natives around Springfield and greater New England began to feel conquered and dismissed. It was inevitable that they would want to gain back some of what they lost, but it was too late. Metacomet, known to many as King Philip, took a last stand and influenced many other Natives to fight for their survival.

In that environment, the drum beat of war pounded even louder with each passing day until there was acceptance that violence would surely happen. Even surrounded by dark talk and the voices of vengeance and complaints about King Philip, the powerful Native sachem, and his Wampanoag Confederacy oozing into every crevice of our lives, I tried to remain distant from the reality of it. We began to fear local Natives who had been friends in previous times, and they feared us as well. It was strange since our town had been founded and grown because of its ties to Indian trade.

The treaties of early days were broken, and the Natives gathered acting to unite many tribes into purposeful revenge and take back what they thought was rightfully theirs. The fact that settlers kept going west, always hungering for more, inflamed the tensions further. Promises were never kept to contain our settlements to the east of what had been agreed to by the English in years past.

One night at one of our usual suppers together, Simon and Thomas explained to Sarah and me that the final act which sowed the most distrust and ruptured Natives ties was the English murder of Native John Sossamon, King Philip's brother. That winter before the war, Natives were convinced he was poisoned by one of our colony leaders. Even though his alleged killers were hanged the following summer, Prince Philip could bear no more of the English.

In our own lives, we'd talked of ways to prepare for war. Its imminence became more apparent than ever at the end of summer. We'd been harvesting crops all day down by the Big River. Working together to make sure we could bring in the crops as soon as possible, no one could be spared from doing the work. The Wampanoags had already attacked several towns in the East and the Nipmunks had joined in the fight as well, laying siege to towns further west. The militia of the colony was busy at work to stop attacks upon English villages, farms, and attacks on European travelers.

That evening of our great harvest day, Sarah, Thomas, Simon and I came together with our throng of children after working hard in the fields. Our older girls had prepared pasties of beef with turnips from the side garden. We drank thick beer heartily to nourish our bodies after a long day, finally taking in the benefits of having tended our crops steadily all summer.

As we sat on our benches at an outside table, I noticed the lines starting to become more deeply etched on Simon's face. Thomas's hair had turned completely white over the past year. Sarah and I noted often in our conversations that both of their jovial natures had been subdued from the anxiety and burden of keeping their large broods safe. The stories of violence reached us each day and our husbands had to carefully work out how to maintain peaceful relationships with the local Natives.

I listened with appreciation to what Simon had said. I couldn't imagine my life without his wisdom and care. Where would we be without him? I thought to myself.

"Another good day without being pulled into war," Simon clanked his pewter mug against his friend Thomas's, also filled to the brim.

"Aye, we've been lucky so far, but can we manage what's placed at our feet for the long term?" asked Thomas.

"Do you think it's inevitable, the war?" I asked sheepishly.

"Maybe so. With these two men here, their charm and their sense of fairness, the local Indians must know not to start anything. We've been friends with many since early settlement," added Sarah.

"If only we could shut out the rest of the world, we might be fine. But I fear that's wishful thinking. Best to be prepared and do what we can with the harvests," replied Simon.

"We've tried to live with the vast array of interests of the Agawams in the South, the Woronocos in the Westfield area, the Nipmunks near the Chicopee River and finally the Nonotucks further north. Any disruption could upset that delicate balance. The fury that the Native's leader, King Phillip, has unleashed has burned many fragile agreements to keep peace," Thomas sighed.

"Enough of this. We worry one day and another we worry more. What does it ever help? I don't want to talk about any of it tonight. You men have had your say. So, let's put it to bed just for tonight, eh?" asked Sarah.

I nodded in agreement. One could go crazy thinking about it all. And being someone prone to anxieties in life, her invitation was a welcome relief.

Our men accommodated our desires, but our merriment and break from the talk of war did not last for more than an hour.

Before too long, Francis Pepper and Thomas Cooper were on horseback to come see Thomas, Simon, and Miles Morgan across the lane. They tipped their hats as they approached but were serious and direct in their mission.

"There's a need for immediate resolve to get our affairs in order. We've just come from the outskirts of town. Very soon, a contingent from Hadley will be here. There's been an act of war with Natives that's bound to affect us all in Springfield. We've come to gather men to meet at Mr. Pynchon's to greet them and get the details about the latest news."

Thomas and Simon sprang into action. They made sure our older boys were armed before they left in case any mischief should arrive on our doorsteps while they were gone.

"I'll keep an eye out from Pynchon's," Simon assured me. It wouldn't be hard to do since it was only a couple of streets away high on a hill.

Our brief merriment ended, Sarah and I busied ourselves with cleaning up after our supper, getting the little ones to bed, and most importantly, preparing for a possible Indian attack. It wasn't long before our men came back with the news that colonial troops, tired from the ambushes to towns from east to west, demanded that the Nonotuck Natives in their fort near Hadley lay down their weapons. They told us the Indians refused and absconded themselves into the deep night giving chase all the way to Sugarloaf Mountain. Our troops attacked them without success. The Nonotucks held them off and eventually slipped away.

The men who gathered that night knew that the attack against the Nonotucks would enrage the Indians of the region who had started banding together and were emboldened to keep fighting. Even though the Agawams had helped us earlier by providing information that protected us, they were no longer trusted. The colonial leaders who came to speak with Pynchon urged him not to disarm the local Agawam but rather take them as hostages to Hartford to insure their loyalty to us.

It bewildered Simon that Pynchon should take that tactic. He had to have sensed that it wouldn't work. There were only so many hostages that they could take to Hartford. Holding our friends of forty years as prisoners for weeks to ensure their cooperation was nothing more than madness. They'd valued their lands and way of life, but even more so, they valued their freedom to move about as they pleased. It wasn't their culture to stay in one enclosed place as we English did. The plan was doomed to fail. Thomas noted that many words were said, and Pynchon faced grave tensions from within and without the town. Under severe pressure, he agreed to send Agawam hostages to be imprisoned in Hartford.

As Simon predicted, the remaining Agawam, feeling betrayed, easily succumbed to the hundreds of other Natives of other tribes calling for war and expulsion of the English from their lands. The next few weeks were blurry to me. The colonial authorities called John Pynchon and his soldiers to fight in Hadley. The remaining Agawam kept to themselves and stayed in their fort fearing for their kinsman imprisoned as hostages in Hartford.

While Pynchon was away and our strongest militia members gone, the Hadley sachem Wequogan had been secretly planning an attack on our settlement. A small group of warriors went to Hartford to free the Agawam hostages. On their way back to the Agawam fort, they passed through

Windsor and an Indian named Toto who served the Wolcott family heard about their plans. Whether coerced or voluntarily, Toto told his employers of the scheme to raid and destroy Springfield. The Indians never imagined that Toto would betray their strategic secrets to attack us.

The warning did not come fast enough. Hundreds sneaked into the Agawam fort as they prepared to lay waste to our town and its inhabitants. It was early October, and our lives would never be the same. At Long Hill, the location of the Agawam palisade, the Indians of many tribes gathered to plan our demise. They slipped in secretly and thought of revenge and survival. From atop their barricaded hilltop, they had visions of Springfield burning, erasing forty years of English settlement.

Chapter 23

Springfield, Massachusetts, October, 1675: Destruction

Even though tensions with the Natives had been building, a final warning from Windsor that Springfield's inhabitants were truly in grave danger was difficult to absorb. Aye, other frontier towns had been terrified by Indians taking their revenge on the white man for ruining their way of life, but we'd always had close ties to the Natives in our region. I was also used to peaceful relations having grown up in Windsor where the Poquonocks, Podunks, Tunxis, and others who had stayed in the area after their tribes were decimated by smallpox, had always been a common sight.

Toto, the Poquonock tribesman who alerted us, was the grandson of the Sachem Nassahegan, who had sold land in Windsor to many settlers. In this one Native family, one could try to understand the losses of Native communities. Once being rich in land, now many were forced to work for the English — no longer the rulers of their former domains. The Indian way of life was disappearing for many of them without land to traverse freely for hunting and farming.

Under cover of night, the messenger arrived from Windsor and woke up our townspeople to make us aware of the planned attack for the morning.

Captain Morgan sent one of his men to post the news at Hadley. Our men organized families into three fortified houses. Mind you, many of our older sons and some men folk were already away with Mr. Pynchon serving with the militias at Hadley. At first, we were worried since much of the harvest was now done and was the means for our very survival for the rest of the year.

I had been sleeping deeply before awaking with a jolt to the shocking sound of hard knocking on our door that morning shortly before the sun came up.

"Indian attack coming! Beware! Indian Attack! Be ready!"

Simon jumped out of bed, threw on his doublet, and grabbed his musket in the corner on the way out.

He looked at me hard.

"Have the children ready and grab the small metal box with the valuables. Be ready to leave in a few minutes. We might have even less time than that."

I nodded knowingly.

John and Daniel joined their father. Simon talked with the other men on our lane after the rider passed. Miles Morgan had made a blockhouse, a small fortification on his property and had added protections to his home as well. According to the plan we'd talked about since the beginning of the war, Sarah and I would go there with our youngest children and girls in case of Indian attack. We'd already rotated food stock there on a regular basis and seemed as prepared as possible. Our immediate neighbors from the lane would meet us there. The Millers, Beamons, Coopers and a few others were all huddled together with our many children. Others in town would meet and board themselves at John Pynchon's brick home that would be difficult to destroy. A few other fortified homes also provided refuge for our fellow townspeople.

As the sun rose and time passed that morning, nothing happened. Crammed into the small fortress of Morgan's making, we patiently waited for hours. Some of the men, including my Simon, believed that that the information brought by the Windsor messenger was simply wrong. They relaxed and Thomas Cooper, then a lieutenant, along with Sarah's husband Thomas Miller, decided to go to the Long Hill fort to have a parlay with the Indians.

Cooper was certain he could talk the Natives out of whatever nefarious plans they might have. He'd traded with them for years as had most of us and was certain that he could persuade them to work with us again by appealing to our years of cooperation and trade with each other. Mr. Glover was so doubtful that anything would happen, he brought his renowned book collection back from Pynchon's home. Others were doubtful too as they remained on the lookout to keep their families safe.

Even if the Natives were to carry out something, another messenger had already been sent to Hadley to warn John Pynchon of the threat to his town. Deacon Chapin and Reverend Glover met to offer prayers to an angry God all the same. It seemed like everything that could be done was being done.

However, I continued to worry. The face of my dear friend Sarah was concerned. She stared at me about to cry.

"Alissa, I have a terrible feeling of what's to come, I do. Please pray to God that my dear husband and our loyal neighbor, Thomas Cooper, will be safe. I can't explain it, Alissa. Please pray with me."

I squeezed her hand and nodded to assure her. "'Tis never a mistake to pray Sarah. I imagine God appreciates it in any situation."

"Children," I called to the many wee ones we watched over, "Get down on your knees. Let us pray for the safe return of Mr. Cooper and Mr. Miller and ask God to maintain the peace of this place for years to come. May He change the hearts of anyone who would think to hurt us and watch over all the men who guard us and protect us." As I said it, I thought of my older sons, John and Daniel, stationed outside with their muskets still at the ready as well as Simon Jr. who was with the troops in Hadley.

The prayers brought us peace for a time until shouting and musket fire seemed to come out of nowhere. The faint smell of burning grew stronger with each gust of wind.

Sarah Miller panicked. She gripped my arm, eyes wide with shock. "No! Where is my Thomas? Alissa, where is my Thomas? Why hasn't he come back?" She released my arm and ran to leave the blockhouse just as some of our older sons were filing in.

"Stay back Mother! We can't do a thing to find Father now. Stay still and be very quiet. The Indians are on their way."

Off in the distance, the sound of war yelps and shrieks wafted closer from a southern direction. We couldn't see what was happening from the blockhouse, but the screams could have curdled one's blood. The whoops of Indians and smoke that filtered through our little safehouse gave testament that all was not well.

Thankfully, Sarah had listened to her son and held her little ones as tight as she could. True to the warning given, the Natives were coming from the South from their fort on Long Hill. We wouldn't understand until the next day that the Agawams had been joined by King Philip's warriors or that several among us had already perished in the attack.

But with Sarah's sons' pronouncements, we knew that neither Thomas Miller nor Mr. Cooper had returned to our lane. I still prayed that they were safe, hiding in marshland along the river or elsewhere in the thick of a nearby forest. We could also hold hope that they were taking refuge and giving aid in another dwelling in town where a need might be greater.

Then, I worried for Simon and my older boys who were still defending us from their perches outside the Morgan's residence and the blockhouse. Some of the older boys held their muskets firm from their positions at the top of the blockhouse, firing through little holes when the enemy was in sight.

I trembled and continued to pray as I held my own young children. It was the only thing I could do. I felt helpless. The chaos and commotion lasted for a good hour. The morning was over and the sun normally shining through to reach the fields and into small windows was hampered by thick clouds of smoke. The sun was as trapped as we were inside our hiding places. But after an hour, the welcome sounds of running horses, those of Appleton's and Pynchon's forces arrived from Hadley, giving us great comfort and relief. With gratitude, we heard a throng of English forces again, shouting out orders to drive the enemy further away.

I made my way to Sarah who was mad with fear, and I hugged her with all my might.

"Sarah, it's almost over," I whispered. "Hold on a little while longer and we'll see what's happened. Thomas is probably defending another one of our fortifications. Just hang on. We shall soon see," I tried to soothe her.

Giving her hope was not only for her but also for me since I was still unsure of the fate of my own husband.

The constant din of chaos eventually began to subside. Sunlight began to traverse through any cracks and other openings in the blockhouse. It became eerily quiet and still. We continued to huddle together, dreading the curse of what might come next. Finally, the men in charge decided that the danger had passed. Daniel yelled through the door that the marauders had finally been chased away. When the men of our party signaled that it was safe to go outside, I squeezed Sarah's hand. We'd both hoped to find our husbands.

Sarah and I walked gingerly out of our little fortress together with the youngest children in tow. We were thankful to come into the light and hoped to find fresher air despite fires smoldering everywhere. Unfortunately, our worst fears materialized before us. Nothing could have prepared us for the shock of what we saw at that moment.

Outside the massive door of our blockhouse shelter was a landscape that was unrecognizable to us. Most of the town had burned and collapsed into smoldering embers. Across the lane was nothing but the blackened ruins of the town. Both our homes and barns behind it were completely gone. We were not alone.

Most neighbors lost everything, including the Coopers down the hill. It was only the Morgan's residence and blockhouse that were still standing in our immediate neighborhood. A couple of streets away to the South, we saw many others emerging from John Pynchon's brick house that still stood high above the ashes. Almost every other structure as far as the eye could see was gone. It would be a while before the air cleared of the putrid smell from the destruction of our lives.

Seeing the hellscape, my heart sank. There was nary a sign of Simon or Thomas. Just then, John found me again and motioned for me to go with him.

"Mother, come quickly! Father was injured during the siege. We carried him into the Morgan's root cellar in the heat of battle."

"Pray, tell me, where is he now? How did they hurt him? Take me there at once," I demanded, not imagining what kind of state I would find my beloved in. By then, they'd carried him up to the Morgan's home. I was told that Elizabeth Morgan, Mile's second wife, tended to him once he was there. Miles had cut out an arrow that was embedded deep within my dear one's leg.

I found him pale, lying on a featherbed, unable to stand due to the deep wound in his right thigh. He was moaning in pain with his eyes shut. Surrounding him were Simon Jr. and Daniel as well as some neighbors. I hugged them each with the force of a mother bear.

Then, I slowly came up to my husband and kissed his cheek, whispering, "I'm here, my love". He opened his eyes and gave me a faint smile.

"You're alive Simon! My dear Simon. Thank God that you've made it through. We'll get that leg to heal my love. I promise you, we will. I'll tend to you night and day until you're better," I smiled at him tears streaming down my face.

He nodded gratefully and squeezed my hand to let me know he'd do his best to heal and stay with us, his family. But I could tell he was in too much pain to talk.

I kissed him once again and whispered, "Simon Beamon you take your rest for now. You've had quite the day. We'll work to find you some rum so we can ease the pain a bit."

He nodded ever so slightly before closing his eyes. I knew it would be a difficult recovery for him. Miles Morgan told me that the arrow had pierced him down to the bone. Miles warned me that when I dressed his wounds, I'd see a gaping hole in that spot from where he'd had to excise the arrow.

"This is not the kind of butchering that pleases me. The bone looks a bit shattered too. I pray your man will walk again," he sputtered as he wiped across his whiskers with his hand. "They got him good, probably used poison on the tip too. It's a miracle he's still alive."

Looking at my distress, he started to restrain his speech.

"I'm sorry, forgive me. Don't mind the likes of an old man like me," he said in his thick Scottish accent.

I nodded in understanding and stayed with Simon for a while, holding his hand to give him strength. Once I was assured that he was asleep, I gathered my wits to address the many questions that my younger children would have.

On my way out, I wanted to thank Elizabeth and Miles for helping him, but instead I could only look pitifully across the room and see Elizabeth wailing as Miles and other men carried her lifeless stepson, Pelatiah, into the parlor. A tomahawk penetrated his skull. I left them alone to deal with their grief and motioned for my oldest sons to meet me outside.

"What do you know about what happened to Thomas Miller and Lieutenant Cooper? Have you heard anything?" I asked as I watched my dear friend Sarah stare blankly where her house once stood.

She cried and called out to him. "Thomas? Thomas, where are you? Your children and your wife want to know. Thomas? Where are you?"

The boys still hadn't heard anything. I ran to Sarah and hugged her as if I were her mother.

"There now, Sarah, we'll find out what's become of him." I tried to reassure her.

She collapsed into my arms. Both of us sobbed into each other's shoulders, our clothing smelling foul and desperate. We could only pray that both Thomas Miller and Lieutenant Cooper would show up again as the smoke started to clear towards the evening.

We were still piecing together the shock of what had happened. All two hundred troops that Pynchon had brought from Hadley were milling about the town to assess the damage and taking account of who survived and who did not.

I don't know how much time passed that Sarah and I were standing there, leaning on each other for comfort. Our children were gathered together, and the older ones were caring for the younger ones.

"Sarah, Mr. Pynchon may well know what's happened to your husband. Come with me. We need to seek him out."

She nodded meekly and followed me, clasping my hand tightly. We headed down what was left of Main Street enroute to Pynchon's brick house. Surely, someone would know there. However, before we arrived, we saw Mr. Pynchon on horseback coming toward us from the South. With a somber tip of his hat, he stopped his horse and slipped out of the saddle.

"Goody Miller, I bid you to come inside my home and sit with me and the reverend. I have news for you." He asked a servant in the infantry to seek out her older sons.

"Find Goody Cooper and her eldest sons on the upper wharf lane and bring them back to my home as well," Pynchon instructed.

Sarah winced, looking as pale as ever.

"Please, Alissa, I beg you to come with me."

I said nothing but took her hand and led her to Pynchon's brick mansion.

Seated in the parlor, Mr. Pynchon addressed Sarah and Goody Cooper.

"With great sorrow, I must tell you that your husbands are dead, taken by Our Lord and Father, earlier this day," he said, bowing his head in respect.

Both men's wives remained still, trying to digest the meaning of Mr. Pynchon's words. Their children held on to them and nodded in grief. They listened intently as Mr. Pynchon continued to explain what had happened to their heroic fathers.

"Your fathers were good men. Both worked for my father and me for many years and helped build this community. They truly believed that they could negotiate with our local tribesmen to stop the attack. However, the Natives were already too influenced by King Philip's successes this year and have become more desperate of late to have their lands back," he said. The Beamon and Miller families understood.

"Witnesses near the southern border of town recounted that as Lieutenant Cooper and Goodman Miller neared the Mill River, not far from the Indian's hilltop fort, they were attacked. Thomas Miller was instantly killed, his body found in the open field at the base of the hill. Lieutenant Cooper managed to survive the immediate onslaught even though he was severely wounded. He commanded his horse to return to town, but by the time the creature stopped his gallop in front of my own house, Cooper's soul had already left us, his body too weak to go on from the seriousness of his injuries. I am very sorry.

Your husbands and fathers were like family to me." He bowed his head once again.

With the finality of his story, Sarah and Goody Cooper wailed in despair and sorrow, surrounded by their children joining them with tears. For each woman — no more husband — no more father to her many children — and no home to go to. In the course of a day, there were more personal losses than anyone could have imagined.

Mr. Pynchon tried to assure them that we would all help to take care of them until the community got back on its feet. He recounted further developments so we would understand the extent of the damage he'd noted since surveying his town in the aftermath of the attack.

"Pentecost Mathews, the wife of John Mathews hath faired not better than your husbands, I'm afraid. She was found shot dead outside what was left of their home. It was also burnt down. In addition to your dear husband, our brother Simon Beamon," he stated looking my way, "our brothers, Edmund Pryngrydays and Nathaniel Brown, have also been severely injured. We pray that they will be able to survive."

It wasn't just the crying families who were struck with grief. Mr. Pynchon, having assessed the widespread damage of the town his father had founded and bequeathed to him to take care of, was also in grief as he gave us more horrific details of the destruction in a low, anguished tone.

"I wish I'd never had to be dispatched from Springfield to Hadley yesterday with some of our men," his voice cracked with guilt. "But alas, we were ordered by the Commissioners to give aid to Hadley. If only I would have had time to get back before most of the town was in ashes. It was a sad and woeful sight to enter it after it had been torched, some fires still burning. So much of it unrecognizable."

"Almost our whole settlement is gone. Everything, except a few structures and the barns across the river, is burnt to the ground. Both the sawmill and the grain mill, along with the house of correction, thirty houses and twenty-five barns since the last count, have been destroyed. Every home south of the Merrick's ceases to exist. Thanks to the Lord, about twenty structures on the outskirts of town were saved, but far fewer remain in the town. Only this building, Goodman Branche's, the Morgans' and a few others stand for another day."

"Captain Samuel Appleton also came here with his troops and chased out the last of the Indians upon our arrival. Major Treat, of Connecticut, has also come to our aid and left Westfield with more militia members once he heard the news. It is thanks to these men and their soldiers, that we have anything left and that we hope the Indians who did this damage have been driven off once and for all."

"So many are suffering. Mr. Glover lost all his corn, his home, and his books. Not even a Bible is left. So many had moved their grain, hoping to store it in safe places and many of those have burnt down too. We will all have to support one another to survive and share homes until others can be built."

He wiped his brow, looking more exhausted than I'd ever seen him. After a long pause to compose himself, he continued.

"Our saving grace is that the barns full of grain across the river were untouched and the marauders driven out before they could destroy those supplies. We must share in our pain and share comfort when we can. It will be a long winter for us all, with not much subsistence to spare. The livelihoods of most are destroyed, and over forty families are in peril. Lord only knows how we will carry on beyond this stressful situation, but I beg you all to pray to our Lord to show us His mercy and save us from utter despair and destitution."

He paused again and surveyed the faces in the room full of desperation. He tried to assure us.

"I will write to the Governor tonight and request assistance to help us rebuild and give us the dispensation we need to make it through the long Massachusetts winter. I must go now. There are many things to attend to. I implore all of you to find the strength within yourselves to persevere. Together, we will overcome this tragedy."

He put his floppy hat back atop his head and lowered it 'to Sarah and Goody Cooper in an act of respect.

Outside, a force of two hundred soldiers awaited orders for how they could best help and how they could find their own shelter and sustenance in the days ahead. Indeed, Mr. Pynchon had much to think about.

I went to my friend's side after Mr. Pynchon left.

"Sarah," I called to her and grabbed her hand. "We will get through this together. We've been friends for very long and we will help your family. I am sure your brother Samuel will aid you also. These are dark days, but light will come," I forced myself to say.

It was hard to keep the faith, but I supposed it couldn't have gotten any worse. We hugged tightly knowing that we were in fact sisters to each other, and we'd overcome the dark days together. I also had Simon who I was determined would heal.

Chapter 24

Springfield, Massachusetts, 1675-76: Aftermath

Sarah and I held hands for strength as we walked back to see the impact of the raid on both our properties once more. My boys had just carried my injured husband to Pynchon's home to recuperate from his injuries. My poor Simon was in excruciating pain, and I prayed he would have relief from it in a better bed with his family surrounding him and encouraging him.

With thirty of the thirty-four homes in Springfield burned to the ground, and winter fast approaching, we were all required to make sacrifices. This included our leader, Mr. John Pynchon. With room to spare in his mansion and with our own homes burned to the ground, Mr. Pynchon offered to house the Miller and Beamon families. He felt responsible to provide shelter to Simon and the recently deceased Thomas Miller's family. He made sure that Lieutenant Cooper's family was housed in comfort at the Morgans' home and aided in their keep. All three had always been faithful employees to both John Pynchon and his father.

As we neared our properties, I gripped Sarah's hand a little tighter. The landscape was barren save for a rare building here or there. The stench of burnt homes and belongings remained strong, some embers still burning. My poor girl, she was a different person altogether — somber, devastated to lose not only her beloved but also everything she'd helped to build with him for over twenty-five years.

"I loved him so much," she cried as we reached the stones that had surrounded her home. The thick entry was burned but some pieces of iron hardware littered the ground where the door would have been. When we reached the threshold, she collapsed into my arms asking the same questions repeatedly.

"Why did this happen? Thomas always got along with the Natives. I don't understand. Has God forsaken me, Alissa?"

I had no answer for her other than a simple response.

"No, you're not forsaken, my dear."

After that, all I could do was hold her up to the best of my ability. But the truth was I also feared the same outcome. What if Simon did not survive? I knew that being a widow was one thing I was not prepared to share with Sarah as I turned to look at the charred emptiness of my own home lot with Simon.

The only thing left standing were the hearths where we had kept vigil day and night to cook and bake the food we prepared for our families' sustenance. Even some of the iron pots were left hanging there. I sighed at the thought of gathering anything useful in that moment. We were both too exhausted to survey for anything of utility.

"Come along, Sarah. Let us go back to Mr. Pynchon's. There's no use in yearning to see what was here just a short time ago. I don't think either one of us can face this ugliness right now. It's better for us to walk along the path of the river and the vast marsh — a place where almost everything remains as it was. It's prettier than Main Street, yet familiar and will bring us some peace to go there."

I pulled her down the upper wharf lane in the direction of the river.

We walked slowly, arms around each other in silence. I prayed to hear the typical sounds of splashing water caused by jumping fish and the calls of birds in flight. Something to make us both forget, even for a moment, the horrors of destruction. Even the wind swishing our skirts and stirring the lingering leaves of two lone oak trees gave deep comfort. The way the wind whistled reminded me of a lute, an instrument I'd only heard once as a very small child when my Aunt Mary took it out of its hiding space and played it in a rare moment in which she became a girl in England again. As she played the other women in my family hummed with tones of hope and calm. Was it a sweet memory or was it a sign that life goes on? I started to hum the melody in my head, desiring that Sarah too would gain assurance and some hope by hearing it.

"Hm,. Hm, hm hm hm hm hm…"

"Down derry, derry down down."

"What a beautiful melody." she said.

"All I remember is that it was about loyalty to a slain knight. I wish I knew the words, but I think it was from when I was very little and can't remember."

"Never mind. 'Tis lovely all the same."

As we turned our backs to the Big River and began to approach the Pynchon mansion again, I knew I needed to leave Sarah and keep vigil with Simon. When I'd left him to comfort Sarah and catch a glimpse of our phantom homes, he had finally tired, giving him what I'd hoped was blessed relief from his pain and suffering. But something jolted me in that moment, and I knew I should take my leave of Sarah straight away.

"My dear sister, I must leave you for a time to check on Simon. I pray that he is still slumbering in a much-needed rest, I hugged her again and walked with her to greet her oldest sons in the yard where they could be with each other. I could barely leave her alone and was grateful that her sons were there.

Inhaling deeply, I gathered my strength for the next round of comforting. I started out slowly but then became frantic as I realized that my husband could be on the precipice of death, his soul not far from his friends on the other side of the veil of life. By the time I finished running up the stairs to find my man stirring in his sick bed I was out of breath and alarmed at his condition.

He was paler and moaned in his sleep. His dressings were oozing and turning to pus. His head felt feverish, and my heart sank with despair.

Mrs. Pynchon came into the room and brought her best herbs. Together, she helped me change the dressings to his wounds with fresh herbal salves and cooled his head and neck with water soaks.

"Thank you, Mrs. Pynchon. The wounds look much better now. But I've seen what happens with loads of pus like that after an injury before. Sometimes I'd go out with my mother who was a healer. I'm scared for Simon," I stuttered.

"Keep the soaks to his temples and his neck. Give him rum to drink when he stirs. We're lucky we have a little left. 'Tis almost out so pray it lasts as long as the pain. I'll pray for him all night. I promise you."

She laid a hand on my shoulder before leaving the room again.

It was three days since the attack and Mr. Pynchon told us that he had yet to hear from the Governor in Boston..

I was across the hall when he called his scribe into his parlor to dictate a letter to the leader of the colony, mourning the loss of almost everything that his father had built. I was taking a rest from tending to Simon while my oldest girls, the ten-year-old twins, Ruth and Mary, who wanted to be by their father's side, sat with him. When I heard Pynchon's pleas for help, it saddened me to think of the desperate situation we were all in.

Worshipful Governor Leverett: —

I desire to give you an account of the sore stroke upon poor distressed Springfield, which I hope will excuse my late doing of it. On the 4th of October our soldiers which were at Springfield I had called off, leaving none to secure the town because the Commissioners orders were so strict. That night a post was sent to us that 500 Indians were about Springfield intending to destroy it on the 5th of October. With about 200 of our soldiers, I marched down to Springfield where we found all in flames, about 30 dwelling houses burnt down and 24 or 25 barns, my corn mill, sawmill and other buildings. Generally, men's hay and corn are burnt, and many men whose houses stand had their goods burnt in other houses which they had carried them to. Lt. Cooper and two more slain and 4 persons wounded. That the town did not utterly perish is cause of great thankfulness. As soon as said forces appeared the Indians drew off, so that we saw none. Our endeavors here are to secure the houses and corn that are left. Our people are under great discouragement and talk of leaving the place. We need your orders and directions about it. How to have provisions, I mean bread, for want of a mill is difficult. The soldiers here already complained on that account, although we have flesh enough. Many of the inhabitants have no houses, which fills and throngs every room of those that have, together with the soldiers; indeed, it is very uncomfortable living here. But I resolve to attend what God calls me to and to stick to it as long as I can. I hope God will make up in himself what is wanting in the creature, to me, and to us all.

To speak my thoughts—all these towns ought to be garrisoned, as I have formerly hinted. To go out after the Indians in the swamps and thickets is to hazard all our men, unless we know where they keep, which is altogether unknown to us."

—John Pynchon

It seemed as if we waited an eternity before help came. Many townsfolk were ready to abandon Springfield forever. With both mills lost, we sent our young men into Westfield to mill our corn and wheat or pound it into flour ourselves with the long-neglected tools we used before the mills were built. There wasn't much to mill anyway with most of our precious harvests lost in the siege. We thanked God that Natives had not destroyed the barns on the west side of the river. Their contents were all that stood between us and famine.

And still, there was no peace. Later in the month, another Native attack killed three of our young men enroute to the mill in Westfield. Each trip after that was filled with foreboding and dread. The town of Hadley also endured the violence at the hands of local Natives who descended upon the town in the hundreds — killing, burning, and destroying in their wake. Those who were once friends had become foes. Fear, hunger, cold, and desperation: they were all present, but never welcomed in. We tolerated them only because we had no choice in the matter. What we feared even more was a vengeful and powerful God who could make it all happen over again should we stray from the righteous path. We continued our worship and toiled as much as we could to restore Springfield to a place that was inhabitable again.

Through that long winter, Simon's leg did not heal. He'd have periods where it seemed to become better, and the pus and the fevers would subside. But his wound was so deep. Even if it looked healed on the outside, the foul-smelling pus, heat and redness would open the wound again. He wasted away in bed, eaten up by continued pain. I prayed for an end to his suffering, hoping it would not mean it would also be the end of his life.

On a clear winter night, my love called out to me. He squeezed my hand with the little strength he had left.

"Alissa, I rescued the little dowry chest with your mother's things. The boys know where it is. He paused awhile before gaining his strength to say more.

"'Tis time. Please forgive me. I would stay if I could."

Outside, snow was gently blanketing nearby trees in beauty and extra grace as they glistened from the moonlight.

I knew what he meant.

"No, Simon. No. There's more to come. Please, rest Simon. You will be well again one day," I pleaded but deep in my soul I knew what was coming — a life without Simon.

He smiled softly and caressed my hand.

"You've been my whole world Alissa and I love you for sharing my life and bearing my children. But 'tis truly my time. We'll meet again, my love," he said clearly.

I finally smiled back and kissed him for what I knew was the very last time he would feel my touch. He looked at the children who had awoken and gathered around us together.

"I love you all," he said in a whisper. "God will keep you. Do not despair," his voice slowly trailed off.

Finally at peace, he closed his eyes and slept without pain and without purpose. Our children surrounded us in a soft embrace. We huddled together quietly sobbing before dawn showed its early light and Simon took his last breath.

PART III: SKIPMUCK

Chapter 25

Skipmuck (Chicopee), Massachusetts, 1676-77: A Move Near the Skenungonuck Falls

Sarah with her family and I with mine decided to abandon our barren lots in the heart of Springfield. There was nothing left. Even the simple items that might stir fond memories such as a family Bible with birthdates of children were gone. The first embroidered cloth made by the hands of a young daughter, the first trencher whittled with the skillful hands of a son, the first cradle made with the loving hands of a husband that rocked with each new life brought forth were all gone into ashes. Ashes to ashes and dust to dust. Sarah and I shared even more now. We two widows, with many mouths to feed, were both shocked and anguished by the loss of everything except for our children.

We decided that together with our families we would stay strong and rebuild. The fires that took everything away were not purifying. Rather, they left dark angst and despair upon our souls. To rebuild and look forward happily with faith and gratitude in our hearts, the old lots would not suffice. So together, we moved from the lane near the northern Springfield dock and went even further north to the outskirts of town where our husbands had bought parcels near the great waterfall from Mr. Pynchon a decade earlier. The Nipmucks called the cascading waters Skenungonuck Falls.

Simon had eventually wanted to move us here to farm a bigger piece of land, fertile from the river soils. It was above the falls on the south side of the river where I inherited rich farmland with my son Simon. John Pynchon even supported us by sending some of his other workers to help our sons build us new homes.

Before our arrival, two outposts to defend against the warring Natives were in place. One fort was situated at Nayasett below the falls and the other fort at Skipmuck was above the falls in a place that came to be known as Johnny Cake Hollow. We could run to the forts for protection in case of a siege.

Japhet Chapin, John Hitchcock and Nathaniel Foote started to talk of building a sawmill at Skenungonuck Falls, the place Natives called Green Fields and revered it for its fish and other bounty. With the beginnings of our little community on the outskirts of Springfield, new settlers came to join us.

I could hear the flow of the turbulent waters from my family's new home lot. If I listened for long enough, the cadence of the water helped me feel better on days that I felt my worst. It reminded me that I was carrying out Simon's plan for his family and I'd hoped his spirit was there among us as I helped my oldest to organize my other sons to fell trees, saw them and assemble them into our new home.

The land was full of birch and the Natives had used them to build their tree bark canoes for as far back as they could remember. There were also elms the size of small castles and stands of cedars lining the raging waters of the turbulent river with their deep, red bark. 'Twas beautiful and largely unsettled except for plots of a few brave men. The Chapin brothers who'd purchased and farmed the land from John Pynchon soon after he bought it were some of the first who decided to stay there no matter what was happening to our Indian relationships.

I was overjoyed that Sarah and her family joined us. We would still be neighbors by the grace of God. I was also appreciative of the move to the outskirts of our settlement to start fresh. However, I felt less confident in myself as the threat of Indian skirmishes were not over. A deep depression hung over me. Trying to have the energy to take care of my brood was difficult. I was paralyzed with fear on a continual basis for reasons both known and unknown. I needed my children wrapped around me as Aunt Rhody advised me to do. In addition to the children, I would always need my friend Sarah and she would need me too.

The violence of the war continued unabated, and I truly feared for my life and the lives of those who I loved. At the outpost in Nayasett where the falls gradually dropped to depths of seventy feet, two adults and a child succumbed to death after a Native raid at the same time. Goody Wright was taken captive and never seen or heard from again. On another occasion, five men were killed at the outpost in Skipmuck above the falls. We dared only traverse the trails in forested areas in fear of ambush.

Eventually the climate settled down. King Philip, the mighty Native leader and warrior of his time, died in 1676, a little over a year after Simon passed. A praying Indian named John Alderman, fighting on behalf of the English, killed him. In the aftermath of the war, towns and forests were emptied out of both European and Native alike. All told, there were hundreds of Europeans and thousands of Natives who had lost their lives in a sad clash of culture and desire.

Proud Indians were enslaved or converted. Many of us had confused feelings. It did not seem right that our former Native neighbors had been turned into refugees in their own lands, but at the same time, we also suffered, as Sarah and I could attest to. They took from me in their violence toward our husbands and the burning of our homes, as much or more as I felt I'd ever taken from them. I thought we'd paid them for their lands. What did I know from my perch of bearing children and then rearing them? All I knew was that it was a tragedy of horrific proportions. I'd never understand fully why former friends and trading partners had turned into enemies.

In the aftermath of war, peace would eventually come. But it was sporadic and occasionally we'd hear about physical fights or confrontations here or there for several years. Most Natives left, not content to live in the land of their birth subservient to the English. They'd chosen to leave to maintain their life and their sense of who they were. Two hundred Narragansetts were spotted crossing the Big River a mile down from the falls and at the wide mouth of the Chicopee River in rafts and canoes, finally disappearing forever beyond Westfield into unknown forests. Our former Nipmuck neighbors went north and our other neighbors, the Agawams, went to the South.

The war, with its constant fears and tragic loss, jostled in me even more unpleasant memories. I started to recall with a vengeance the darkest memories of my childhood. It was difficult how one tragedy often buried for years was revived by another more recent one.

The nightmares returned, but they were more intense than before. The pain of losing Simon and our home and friends in Springfield in addition to the constant terror and dread of another attack for several months prodded other horrors from my early life to finally reveal themselves. Horrid visions of pitchforks, fire, and an angry mob all flashed before me. The nightmares always ended with my mother calling to me in distress from the deep dark waters.

Until that time, I had remembered nothing of my mother's arrest. But the dreams were so dark that they scared my small girls who slept with me in my bed, a place vacated by Simon in his death.

Drenched in sweat, I screamed out. "No! Please! No!" I was whimpering when young Alice shook my shoulder.

"Mummy, Mummy! Mummy, what's wrong? You've scared little Abby. Mummy wake up!"

By the time I opened my eyes, I saw that Abigail, my youngest of two years, cried in worry for me. My sweet little Benjie, just two years older, was now awake as well and staring from his tiny trundle bed on the floor as if he'd seen a ghost. Simon could always handle my nightmares and knew how to soothe me, but for my children, I was a frightful sight. No wee one should ever have to see their mother suffering so, but what kind of suffering hadn't they seen already at their very young ages? It wasn't fair. I hoped to spare them such strife with the loving home Simon and I had created together. They suffered despite my dreams of a better life for them.

I was staring straight into the eyes of my daughter Alice, named after the woman I'd been having nightmares about. At first, I was scared to name my daughter Alice, fearing that the stain of having that name would carry on. But after my first three daughters were born, I started to feel remorse for not honoring my family's tradition of passing down the name of my mother and her mother before her.

But then, as I looked into little Alice's face, my own distraught with tears streaming down it, I hoped I hadn't carried on a curse to her. I wanted to stop crying for the sake of my children, but in those moments, I was a child myself. I could not stop sobbing after remembering my mother's arrest clearly for the first time.

In the midst of my weeping, I managed to say, "I'm sorry. Mummy is sad. I will be fine." I know I didn't convince them. Hugging each of the little ones tightly, I called for the twins.

"Ruth and Mary, please help give comfort to the little ones. I've had a nightmare. I must take my leave," I said.

I was acting in a way that the ministers found offensive. We were taught to keep our emotions to ourselves, and I failed at it time and time again. I certainly did not want to be so full of emotion with my children watching and worrying.

My twins stirred a bit and then rolled out of their feather beds.

"Oh Mummy, the dreams still terrify you."

Mary came to me and comforted me by stroking my hair in a reversal of our mother-daughter roles. Ruth looked on in empathy as she scooped up the littlest ones into her arms.

"We'll take good care of them," she said in her kind, yet serious manner.

"Thank you," I lowered my head, ashamed to be unable to care for my children, yet relieved that I could be alone with my thoughts.

I grabbed a shawl and went to sit on the bench outside in my shift, hoping that the sounds of the falling waters in the distance would give me peace.

I reflected on the nightmare that ruptured my reality. It pricked my memory like a pin digging into a deep old wound to clean out the pus that festered, finally allowing me to piece together the events of my mother's arrest for the first time in almost thirty years.

It was almost dusk on the horrible day the marshal of Windsor arrested my mother. Darkness descended ferociously upon us as the sound of a mob, a faint din at first, became a boisterous and chaotic clammer for riotous justice.

I huddled tightly into my mother and holding onto her leg with all my might, I tried to keep them from dragging her away from me. We hid by the side of the hearth in the darkest corner of the room in futility as we watched the door forced open with a deafening thud.

Where is my father? Where is John Young? I thought pointlessly. Why wasn't he standing in front of the door to fend them off? Some men in the hateful throng grabbed my mother, working hard to loosen my grip from her leg. Finally, they peeled me off of her with force as if I was nothing more than a leech.

I sobbed to see the true evil that took place that day. No wonder I was not strong enough as a child to remember these things. Looking into each corner of my memories, I still searched in vain to find John Young who was nowhere to be found. All I saw was a little girl, defenseless, unprotected, sobbing in a corner near the hearth, me.

Then the marshal put my mother in irons as I watched trembling. Realizing that she would be lost to me forever, I mustered the strength to scream for her and exit the door after the mob. She was placed into a cart and whisked away down our lane as the throng continued to yell insults. It was only as I stepped past the threshold that I caught a glimpse of comfort coming to me. Both Mary and Rhody had gathered outside the house and were panicked with concern.

My Aunt Mary swooped me up into her arms. Both of my mother's cousins had been desperate to reach me. They must have known that they could not save my mother from the mob who would have surely turned on them as well. Aunt Anne came outside, full with child, tearful, and sad. She seemed relieved that her older sister had me in her arms and nodded when her husband called for her to go back inside. She looked at us with melancholy but obeyed his command. They were unusually distant.

Finally in the comforting arms of someone who loved me, I let my feigned bravery slip away. I collapsed even further into Mary's shoulder as my world changed to a dark unknown.

"You'll come with Aunt Mary now, child," she said, trying to comfort me.

She held me near the hearth of her home as I sobbed for hours. Each time I asked her about my mother, she would repeat the same thing.

"Your Uncle John is going to find her, child. Try to sleep now."

John Young never showed up that night. I'd heard much later that he'd slept in his fields across the river. Our little house remained abandoned with its door off the hinges. Mary handed Rhody a sack and directed her to quickly gather anything of my mother's that might be of importance to me in later years.

"We will hide it and keep it well for Alissa," she told her sister, thinking that I had already fallen asleep. If there is anything that the magistrates or ministers would use to make their case against Alice, get rid of it."

That was all I could see from that night. The sack of things my Aunt Rhody gathered that night went back into the little dowry chest she gave me when I was older — the one I still hadn't had the urge or strength to go through. What good was it if it couldn't bring my mother back to me or take away any of the suffering she went through?

I thought of my own children then and how I needed to get back to the present and reassure them that their own mother's terrors had passed. They needed to know that I would remain there for them, continuing to take care of and love them. If only I could have known the same in my own childhood. As if he had read my mind, Josiah came outside.

"Mummy, the little ones are calling for you. They want to know how you are now. I'd like to know too. The girls said you woke with awful terrors."

I held out my hand to him. "I've got my wits about me again, Josiah. None of you need worry."

I arose quickly and managed to place a slight smile on my face. "The light has come. I'd best help the girls make breakfast so we can feed all of your growing bodies and start our day."

I was able to think of my mother in quiet moments during habitual chores during the day, and I was calmer when I did. I had to close my eyes with the little ones midday though. I don't think I'd ever felt that tired. It was as if I'd been a time traveler exhausted from a long and arduous journey. But I was no stranger to that kind of traveling in my own life and knew even though I was paddling through peaceful waters for a time again, the rapids would present themselves around another bend threatening to swallow me whole.

Chapter 26

Windsor, Connecticut, May, 1647: A Last Goodbye

I pricked my finger on the needle again. I was distracted and unable to concentrate. I let the needlepoint work drop on my lap and sucked the blood away from my finger.

"Careful," instructed Mrs. Hosford. "Remember, a godly woman creates a tidy needlework with organized stitches. Focus, girl. It will do ye good."

"Aye, ma'am." I spoke softly. I suppose she was just trying to help me but ignoring the fact that I was grieving for my friends and worried about my mother felt extremely cruel.

Mrs. Hosford put me through this routine every afternoon after the hard work of the early morning. The ministers had placed me in Deacon Hosford's home as a servant so that I would "learn the proper ways to behave" and fully understand what was expected of me by God. Every evening was the ritual of reading the deacon's new Bible. If I wasn't doing heavy work like hauling in wood, cleaning the house, or working in the fields or the garden, my body was forced to rest in the quiet posture of needlework or to listen to the Bible for hours with my head bowed.

Gone were the forays into the woods or trips to market with my mother or the sewing and spinning circles with my cousins, enriched with Uncle John's stories and contagious laughter. That had all ended with the death of so many of the children who resided on Backer Row and the arrest of my mother. The first death from my circle, that of Sarah Sension, my dear cousin, had been hard enough. But the last deaths of Annie, Priscilla, Thomas and Samuel were almost too much to bear. The fact that they seemed to be intertwined with my mother brought chaos to my soul. Five of my cousins were dead from the fever's ghastly outbreak.

I'd only seen little bits and pieces of what happened, although I continued to feel guilty as if I were responsible for the tragedies in some way.

"Repent for your many sins and humble yourself to the Lord," the Hosfords commanded. They thought they were saving my soul. But I thought it was supposed to feel good to be close to Jesus, not like the bleak reality the ministers had forced me to live in. And in the end, it only piled more guilt upon my soul.

Hannah, my lone friend and girl cousin near my age had tried to visit me, but the Hosfords had viewed her and Aunt Rhody with contempt. It was only Aunt Mary and Uncle John who were able to get through to me at the Hosford's under threat from some powerful people in respected places. I did not know who they were. John Young remained absent from me.

My mother refused to tell me what Priscilla said on her death bed. She was worried though. And after Priscilla died, her brothers and sister soon followed. A pregnant Aunt Anne was sick herself for much of their illnesses and the Tinker family feared she would lose her baby before the sickness was over. I did know that my mother was forced to use the last of her herbal medicines, the wild ones introduced to her by her Native friends. As she made the remedies into strong decoctions, I would pray with her sometimes, begging God for the survival of every sick child.

Over a week had passed since Mother was placed in chains. In my boredom and loneliness, I imagined saying good-bye to my cousins. I hadn't been allowed to go to the Thorntons while the fever was raging. The procession to the burying ground, ending with the sight of their little bodies wrapped up in shrouds being thrown into cold dark graves, gave me no peace.

The last time we had all gathered together brought no clues that it would be our final meeting with each other. We knew some people in the town of

Windsor were feeling poorly, but never ever thought some of us would succumb to illness. I managed to escape from it somehow. Perhaps, it was because of the infused herbal tea that Mother made me drink every day to fortify my body. I'll never know, but I was sure that my good health was part of the reason others looked at my mother with suspicion. My soul was not only steeped in guilt for living when many of my cousins had not, but also for thinking people's suspicions about my survival was a cause of Mother's death. Knots in my stomach were always there and I was afraid the mob would come for me next.

That afternoon in the hall, the Hoskins were discussing my mother, unaware that I was listening. I'd just come in the side door into the hearth room that I accidentally left ajar. Mr. Hoskins had been at the meeting house and came back to report to his wife about the goings on there.

"She mustn't find out that her mother will be sent to Hartford today," declared Mrs. Hoskins.

"I see her quiet and humbler now that we have settled her into a routine. We need her to stay clear of any demonic influence that her mother may further pose. I will not allow Satan to take hold in our home," she explained.

"You are correct to be concerned, wife. We cannot allow your pious encouragement to be undone. She should not go with the throng to see her mother being led to the river. The shallop should be arriving any time now," he said with relief.

I froze. I didn't have a second to spare. I wouldn't be able to see my mother possibly ever again if I didn't leave right then. In my haste to leave through the side door again, I knocked over a ceramic pot alerting my wardens to my escape. Elder Hoskins had a lame leg and had lost all past spryness, so Mrs. Hoskins ran to catch up to me for the both of them. I hoped I could lose myself in the crowd.

I sprang forward when I first caught sight of her. Once I was at a safe distance, I panted and gulped in air before running again as fast as my little legs would carry me. Mrs. Hoskins could barely keep up with me, the child in her charge. Finally, gasping, she let her middle-aged body stop, wiped the sweat off her face, and made pitiful attempts to call out to me. She realized that she wouldn't be able to catch up to me in time to prevent me from seeing my mother.

"Alissa, Alissa come. There is nothing for you to see. Come back."

Her words were meaningless as I ran to see my mother for the last time. My drive was fueled by the love of a daughter for her mother and nothing — not loads of gossip, not the ministers' warnings to stay away, not explanations of evil, or even Satan himself could ever have kept me away from her — the one who birthed me and the one who had loved me for my entire life. There was no contest. I would win out. I would get away if even for a moment before my mother was shoved unceremoniously into the boat bound for Hartford.

My hair flew in the wind after my coif had fallen to the ground. I continued up the road until I reached the town square. People were moving in a mass towards the dock on the river beyond the meeting house, past Captain Mason's homestead and past the Thornton's tannery, its stench following as well.

It was there that Mrs. Hoskins caught up to me. She tried to grab me by the wrist, but my Aunt Mary saw and scolded her and pushed her away, releasing her grip.

With Aunt Mary, I pushed my way through the crowd with a force I had never known and screamed at the top of my lungs.

"Mother! Mother!"

Mother, sensing me there in that moment turned to me. Locking eyes with her, I was immune to the chanting "Witch. Witch. Take the witch away!" I ignored my mother's face drenched in tears and dirt. I only saw her beautiful and loving eyes in that moment.

"Mother!" I screamed over the din of the crowd, my whole life in ruins with my only need in that moment — to receive the embrace of my mother. Uncle John was there protecting her from the angry, irrational mob, former friends and patients. He grasped my hand from Aunt Mary and pushed others away so that Mother and I, her only child, could be reunited one final time.

Mother's eyes barely held the fire of life in them. Her life was already almost extinguished from the betrayal of those people she had helped over many years. Going to trial in Hartford and the certain punishment for witchcraft at the gallows were only formalities. I knew at that moment, as I'm sure she did as well, that this would be the last time I'd ever see her.

Finally, Mason and others pulled her away from me, desecrating our sacred bond. The last image of her I remember is her being forced into the shallop, her shackled body broken and forced to sit, reaching her arms toward me and screaming my name, surrounded by dark churning water as the shallop set sail down river. The dark water — the gut-wrenching scream for me — the stuff of my nightmares.

Uncle John cradled me as I sobbed uncontrollably. Aunt Rhody soon appeared with Aunt Mary to console me as well, but Mrs. Hosford insisted that I go back with her. There were fierce words exchanged. From there, everything went into a fog except for my nightmares. Eventually forced back into the care of Elder Hosford's family, Uncle John promised he'd find a way to get me back to my own family. I know my life would have ended had he not kept his promise.

I remind myself daily to hold my tongue, to speak kindly with my words and my deeds, to continue to honor my mother daily, carefully recalling the fine details of her gentle hands and her comforting smile. And I see now, if for just an instant, her hand that reaches out to me to touch me one last time before she was walked to the shallop on the Rivulet.

Chapter 27

Skipmuck (Chicopee), Massachusetts, 1677: Remembering the Dowry Chest

A poppet is a simple little item, yet it can carry many meanings depending on the owner or the observer. One can be crudely made with twigs and swatches of linen. In the case of Native poppets, they may be made with scraps of leather and beading. Some are fancier than this, but most children are satisfied with the less elaborate version for their play. They need only their imaginations. Some families will not allow their children the joy of playing with these dolls. For them, these images made of knotted rags, pieces of wax, pieces of cloth or wood are instruments of evil, not simple playthings. But for others, some adults even, they are a symbol of hope, a prayer in action to assure that dreams have the possibility of fulfillment.

For me, seeing the poppet again was none of these things. The poppet who stared at me from her stool next to the hearth was female and left me feeling confused and mildly distraught. I didn't know why, but I could sense she had a story to tell — a story that I didn't want to hear.

The unusual little poppet continued to stare at me blankly. I should throw it into the fireplace. I thought impatiently. Why was I reacting in such a way? I should burn it once and for all and hope my haunted heart will fully heal. But alas, I could not. Something about her reminded me of my mother No, let it stay.

"Mother, mother! Where are you?" shouted Thomas, gently shaking my left shoulder. "Mother!"

Finally, I looked into his face. So grown, my Thomas, my fourth son.

"Mother, where have you been?" he asked me lovingly.

My children have been prone to my brief absences since they were born. Some say it was the shock of losing my mother so young that caused me to go vacant, to travel elsewhere in my head so deeply into another world that when I come to, I forget where I am and where I was.

But those that say this are wrong. I've always gone away from this world from time to time. In Windsor, when I was a child, the ministers said it was the Devil trying to pry me away from the church and admonished my mother to adhere more closely to scripture and set a better example.

In the privacy of our little wooden home, when the ministers had gone and tended to their personal business again instead of the business of saving souls, my mother would whisper in my ear.

"Pay them no mind child for they know not that you visit with angels. I know this because you are my angel."

She smiled gently and soothed any fears that I had about having a dark stain on my spirit, marks of demons who could have painted their evil symbols upon my soul in my lack of wakefulness. I liked my mother's stories about angels much better.

As I came to, I recognized that the little poppet by the fireplace had stirred the memory of something deeply unpleasant within my soul. 'Twas something suppressed, like a riverbed settled in with its secrets buried and stirred with a crashing boat or falling rock. My inner turmoil had come alive again.

"Mother, did you have one of your spells? Another falling out of this world?" asked Thomas quite concerned.

Thomas, the most sensitive of my male children was always worried about me. He was seventeen, a young man ready to make his mark on the world, yet he stayed to make sure I was well enough to care for the younger children in the family.

Little Ruth overheard the conversation and jumped up from her sewing. Grabbing a wet cloth, she placed it on my head. Her twin sister Mary dropped her stitching as well and stood nearby in support.

"I will be alright," I said. "This is different. I am starting to remember more of my childhood, glimpses of what happened… before."

Ruth gently took my hand. "Mother you don't have to. We understand. If something happened to you, I should not want to speak of it ever again to my own children," she said and then caught the knowing glance of her brother.

"It will be fine, Ruth," I reassured her, squeezing her hand. "It's time to face the past."

"Mother, you don't have to look there. Stay with us here in the present." Ruth urged me, biting her lip and conveying a lack of confidence in that possibility.

"Ruth dear, where did the poppet by the fireplace come from? I do not recall it being here before? It is the poppet that shakes loose memories from my childhood. Still, they are so foggy. Please tell me. Where did you find that poppet?" I asked her again quite intently.

"Oh Mother! I'm so sorry. I wanted to occupy my little sisters while you were at the market with Thomas and Josiah the other day. We found your wooden dowry box in the attic. Father thought to save it in a cold cellar so it would not burn during the Indian attack in Springfield."

I understood finally how Simon rescued the chest.

"He had told us once it was a small dowry you had brought with you from Windsor when you married. Before his death, he told the boys where it was and to bring it to our next home, hiding it out of the way. He said you would find it again when you were ready. After father's death, Daniel remembered it was there, retrieved it, stored it, and brought it here after our new house was built. He placed it in the attic as Father had done in our old cottage," she finished.

I paused, remembering how important it was for Simon to tell me he'd saved the dowry chest on his deathbed. I had been more focused on savoring our last moments together before losing him than of the small dowry box safely hidden away.

"Aye, the little chest I've never had the courage to look in. I would have forgotten it in Springfield. 'Tis true that Aunt Rhody gathered its contents before your father and I married as a dowry of sorts. I had so little, and she wanted to do something for me as surely as my own mother would have done. In it, she gathered a few of my mother's items that she kept in hiding from the authorities — hidden away for me and my offspring. There were just a few precious contents in the chest, but I'd shunned even looking at it all these years. It was too emotional to ever go through my mother's things. Nonetheless, Aunt Rhody insisted that with time, I'd want to have these items, the only remnants of my mother from her time on this Earth."

I stopped thinking of Simon's insistence, like Aunt Rhody's, that I would want to see its contents in the future.

"So, your father took them dutifully from her after our marriage in Windsor. But when we arrived in Springfield, he said he'd hide them, those personal things that caused such pain. He said they would no longer have any power over me."

"Aye, Mother," said Ruth softly. "It was important to Father to save it for you. He thought that one day we would want to have our grandmother's belongings and that perhaps you would have forgotten all about them. Our curiosity got the best of us, and we looked inside. It was wrong of us. Abigail saw the doll and wanted to play with it. She dropped it there on the stool. You were already back when I noticed it. Since it did not seem to bother you, I thought it was truly forgotten."

I stared again at the hearth with the little poppet on a stool near it.

"Please forgive me Mother."

I smiled feebly. "Bring me the poppet, my child."

Gingerly, Ruth placed it in my lap. The other children in the room gathered around me.

I stared at the little linen image of a full woman. Her eyes were stitched into the shape of little crosses. Her mouth was embroidered full and red.

Most curiously, she had extra stuffing in her belly and a strip of fine Flanders lace lined the inside of her skirts as though she were hiding it. Her dress was blue to match her eyes and heavy brown wool thread had been stitched and wound in such a way as to make it slightly curl.

"Was this your doll when you were a child?" asked little Mary. "She is so pretty. Is she with child?"

"No child. It was my mother's, but I played with it. She made it for herself, but she said she would share it with me, especially after it had served its purpose. Something tells me I should have left it be. I should have kept it hidden from the other children on Backer Row."

And with that thought, the incomprehensible wave of anxiety surrounded me again. What was below the surface?

"What was its purpose? Why would Grandma have needed a poppet?" Mary quizzed me. "Right now, I'm not sure, but I wish I knew."

Ruth held my hand.

"It doesn't matter now," she said.

After I had composed myself, little Alice came up to me.

"Mother, I hope you are past ill will for the doll. Can we please keep it and play with it? It amuses Abigail when you are away, and she needs something to divert her attention. Please, will you let us keep it? If you do, I promise to put it back in the chest after each time we are done playing with her."

I had so little to offer my children since Simon died, and I felt guilty because of it. Despite my inner turmoil, I consented to let them play with it in my absence only if they returned the doll to its place in the carved chest.

"Thank you Mummy," she smiled with glee.

Ruth and Mary also assured me that they would make sure it was put away. Even if they forgot, maybe seeing it would make me realize that it was only a harmless little doll, I reasoned.

Chapter 28

Skipmuck (Chicopee) & Hadley, Massachusetts, 1677: Witch Slander.

I was pleased to share the day with Thomas in Hadley to vend our goods from the farm. We had gone to the market together a couple weeks earlier and had done very well. I needed the money for my family and was more than glad to sell again with him. We had milk, honey, soaps and early greens. I looked forward to more good fortune and well-spent time with my fourth son. He, like his father, possessed the ability to assess the reality hidden in the nuances of any given situation.

The market day bustled, and the weather was pleasant. Plenty of coins reached my hands and I bartered for my family's needs too. I enjoyed the time away from home to meet old acquaintances and stock up on supplies. Thomas and I had done so well that my honey was sold out and the milk was close to gone. It was a bountiful and blessed day until things suddenly turned rancid late in the afternoon.

What happened was a shock for both Thomas and me. John Fisher, a disgruntled and repugnant man in his forties, ambushed us at our farm stall.

"Your milk's no good!" he shouted.

His speech was slightly slurred, and it appeared that he'd had too much to drink in the local tavern adjacent to the square where we sold our wares.

"We take good care of our cows and taste their milk the morning we come to market. Why do ye have a complaint with us?" asked Thomas.

"Market before last, I bought your milk, and it was sour as a witch's teat!" He winked and laughed menacingly.

I didn't remember him buying any of our milk and we weren't at the market the week before last. He knows who we are. I thought to myself with alarm. He's heard people gossiping and telling cruel stories from the past in the tavern.

"Nothing's wrong with our milk," I retorted. "You should have said something straight away if there was a problem."

"I know who ye are," John Fisher seethed at me in a threatening manner. "The daughter of that witch from Windsor. No wonder the milk turned sour! What else could ye expect from a witch family." He glared at me as I sat paralyzed with fear. He turned toward Thomas.

"Aye, the apple never falls far from the tree," he mumbled in a course, sloppy voice.

"Don't you ever talk to my mother in that way again!" Thomas had flown out from behind our goods in a rage. A crowd was starting to gather around us.

"I'd like to see ye try and stop me!" Fisher sneered before continuing, "Thomas Beamon, you're the son of a witch because your mother is a witch, just like her mother before her. You and your mother even look like witches!" He elongated the word witch every time he said it for emphasis.

Thomas bit his lip. His face deepened to bright red. Unable to hold back, he unleashed a torrent of anger which slammed John Fisher to the ground. Once there, Thomas let his rage take control and punched John Fisher with abandon. He beat the man into a bloody mess.

"Stop now, Thomas, lest ye kill him," I pleaded with my son.

Thomas came to and was present again as he surveyed the damage he had done. As John Fisher moved in an effort to stand up, Thomas pushed him down again.

"There now, I believe I did stop you. Now get out of here and never stop by our wares again. This won't be the last of it, John Fisher. I'll make sure you pay for your ignorance!" he screamed.

John Fisher was pulled up by an onlooker and scurried away as fast as his injured body could take him.

"Go on now! It's done. Get back to your own affairs!" Thomas yelled at the wide-eyed crowd to disperse.

After the altercation was over, I could barely move. My hands were unsteady and shaking as we packed up to leave the market. I touched Thomas' arm, but he was stone cold from the shock of the exchange as well, saying nothing. Silence overtook us on the ride home. Sitting next to my son, I appreciated his valor in standing up for me, a luxury my mother did not have. He knew the talk of witches could endanger all our lives and he was instinctive in taking the only action that he thought could stop John Fisher in that moment. If only my mother had had such a protector.

Thomas was rattled as he came in upon our return from the farmer's market. And, I must have looked pale and distraught. At first no one else in the family knew what was wrong even though it was obvious that something had occurred to unsettle him and made him quick to temper. His siblings could also observe that I was unusually quiet, going inward to escape the cruel world.

Thomas and I were close. Some boys are especially close to their mother, a special bond that is envied by others. But I pitied him that day to be so strongly connected to me that he let his emotions get the better of him. I admit, I was relieved to have a son, a strong young man who loved me so much that he'd defend me against a crass carcass of a man like John Fisher.

"Why so sour brother?" asked one of my oldest daughters, Ruth. Mary, her twin chimed in. "Aye, why are you so gruff, brother?" she questioned, shocked that he was not his usual cheerful self.

Thomas didn't answer the question.

I put my hand on Ruth's shoulder. "Please leave your brother to be for now."

Thomas knew that to be inside the house was pointless. All he could do was pace the floor. Why spend his time on something fruitless he realized.

"There's more to do outside. I'll finish unloading the wagon, Mother," I nodded knowingly. It was best that he stayed busy to help burn off his anger. I hoped the light breezes of the approaching night would soothe his soul.

Once Thomas had left the house, Ruth and Mary badgered me to tell them what happened.

"So why was our even-keeled Thomas so disturbed? You look upset too. What happened?" Ruth asked with concern.

"Aye, why did our brother stomp about, not speaking a word to us about his troubles? Tell us what happened, Mummy," added Mary.

Josiah and Samuel looked on, slightly older than the girls. They didn't say much but were curious too, enough to linger before going outside to help Thomas unload everything into the barn.

"I'll not say much about it," I responded. "'Twas an encounter with an ignorant man who started a fight with Thomas for no good reason."

I stood straight and stiff, trying to hide my deep emotions. Surely, this type of altercation would have been rare for other families. I did what I usually did with my children — habitual avoidance of a conversation about the dark family history we hoped would disappear from community memory.

"Thomas threatened to take the man to court for the lies and deplorable behavior he displayed. Please, let's stop talking about it. I have a headache now and need to take my leave as well. When and if Thomas is ready to speak, he will," I added.

I left the girls after gathering the little ones to get them some supper and then ready for bed. I was determined to try and forget what happened. It was daily routines that allowed me to draw from my inner strength and muster the will to go on. I would get lost in them until I finally fell asleep from exhaustion.

But thoughts of the fight did not escape me before I fell into a fitful sleep. I repeated the same thoughts. I had what my mother did not, a loyal son who would fight for me, a good young man who would clear my name with every bit of fight within him. He knew what happened to his grandmother. He understood why he could never meet her. I had faith that I would not share my mother's same fate as long as my strong and devoted sons cared for me and continued to believe in me.

Indeed, my son Thomas loved me. The thought of losing me by an undeserved and unjust witchcraft conviction in the same way his grandmother died enraged him. He'd observed my frailties and insecurities, the scars of me having to endure the loss of my own mother and was determined to protect his family even further.

My Thomas took his retaliation against Fisher a step further and sued him for slander. Thomas knew that it was important to stop it quickly before it evolved into something much more deadly. Just weeks later, we went to court.

Chapter 29

Skipmuck (Chicopee), Massachusetts, 1677 &
Windsor, Connecticut, 1647: Menacing Doll

It was mid-afternoon when Thomas dropped me off after our day in court. The magistrates were understanding of Thomas' position and Fisher was ordered to pay twenty shillings to the court and forty shillings to Thomas. John Fisher countersued on account of his injuries from the physical fight. As a result of the countersuit, the court ordered Thomas to pay ten shillings to the court and 10 shillings to Fisher for beating him up. The court realized that witchcraft slander was a lot more serious than injury from a provoked fight through unjust words.

"Rest early tonight, son," I pleaded with Thomas. His eyes were baggy, and he had clearly not slept in anticipation of the trial.

"Aye, Mum," he said without argument. Relieved that he'd received vindication from the cruel witch taunts of John Fisher, yet weary from being reprimanded for attacking the ignorant man, he needed time to stew it over and rest in a place that would always be home.

His many siblings were eager to hear how the trial had turned out for they were not separate from its results. What if they too would be taunted one day? It wasn't mere curiosity in their needing to know the results of the trial, it was the need to learn what to do should it ever happen to them. My name and family history could affect them too in jolting and unexpected ways. It was better to be prepared for anything that might come their way.

As they piled in the room, greedy to hear everything, I cautioned them, "Give Thomas the time he needs before you pressure him too much. It's been an exhausting day."

They nodded in understanding.

"I don't think I can bear to hear the story again. I'll be in the next room attending to the hearth and preparing our supper," I explained.

"Do ye need any help mother?" asked Ruth.

"Nay, child. A little time for myself to think a little about the day might be a good thing," I said.

So, with most of my other children gathered around Thomas, I went about my cooking, first to the garden to snip some herbs and then back to the hearth.

Inside the hearth, I noticed the embers were starting to die down, I instinctively rose to load more wood to prepare for our supper. It was then that I spotted from the corner of my eye the poppet who was sitting on a stool again. Had one of my younger daughters taken it out of the keepsake box to play with it again? She was menacing with her stitched-on smile and her eyes in the shape of tilted crosses. My desire to get rid of her only strengthened. I should have ignored the pleading of my children to keep her. I didn't understand. Such a simple thing made of linen with a little bit of stitching and cornhusk stuffing. Why did I hate the little poppet so?

The wind was swift as it circled from the northwest and through all the little home lots on Backer Row, shaking our little cottages awake. John Young predicted another snowstorm, perhaps the last one of winter before life fully transitioned to spring. We had come through the worst of winter and the ground was beginning to thaw, a promise of the rich beauty and bounty that lay ahead. We had even had several days of mild weather with the first wildflowers of spring peeking through the ground.

Mother slowly arose from her featherbed with a wool blanket over her shoulders to keep warm and carefully rekindled the fire in the central chimney. She didn't try to wake me and was unaware as I spied on her from my own place under blankets in the trundle bed. She put a large pot on a hook and pulled it in toward the fire to boil. Few of her herbs were hanging from the rafters now. She had used most of them over the winter. Yet, she made do with what she had and threw in branches and roots from a basket once the water came to a boil, carefully moving the pot away from the fire again so that the herbs could steep.

She did this diligently every morning to prepare for the day. It was a season of illness and that winter and early spring of 1647 had been especially cruel. Many in town had died in unusually high numbers. We were all tired of grieving but no more than Mother who had had to be absent from her own home often to care for those who fell ill. For that reason, she was making her special tea that she could use generously to nurse the sick. The house was filled with the aromatic scent of conifers, the roots and bark of hemlock and pine decocting into strong medicine.

Finally, I shifted in my bed and Mother noticed me peeping out from my covers to observe her at her work.

She turned and looked at me with her hands on her hips. "Alissa, how long have you been awake my child?" she whispered since John Young was still asleep.

Barely disturbed, he murmured, turning to the outside wall and resumed his snoring.

"Alissa, get dressed and come help me prepare breakfast. Let's talk about the day," she said.

"Yes, Mother." I got up as instructed, placed my woolen clothes over my shift and went to relieve myself. I was at her side for further instruction in minutes.

"Look at you amidst that tangled mess of hair! One would think you wrestled a black bear in your sleep," Mother said and smiled teasingly.

"Alissa, please find the boxwood comb and sit near me. We will see how much I can make order of it."

She combed through my unruly mane lovingly and carefully. I could feel her caresses and the gentle tugging of my hair as she pulled the wooden comb through it. Then, she carefully placed my coif over my head to maintain the newly ordered strands of hair. How loving she was. I've never missed her so much as I did in that moment of remembrance. It hurt so much to allow myself to fully see her kindness and her gentle soul.

I could not escape the prevalent death around me. My dear cousin Sarah had just succumbed to the fever. I felt a bit lost without her.

"What will you do today if I get called to sit with the ill again?" Mother had normally let me be her helper, but she'd seen too much illness among the children of Windsor and wanted me to stay away from anyone who was sick.

I peeped out from my coif and turned my gaze away from the rekindled fire. Mother, I can't bear to be alone. I miss Sarah even more when I am alone. Please, let me go with you," I pleaded.

Mother clasped my hand.

"Nothing is as hard as losing a best friend and close family member, dear daughter. It's too fresh in your mind to be near another who might suffer the same fate, nor should I allow such a risk. You must stay here. Do your chores. More spinning needs to be done and the cottage swept clean.

"I wish I could be with Sarah today, Mother. She was a good spinner, was she not?"

"Of course, you miss her, my love, as do I. Our hearts are heavy with grief. No one more than your Aunt Mary," she reminded me.

The Sensions were the first household on Backer Row to lose a child from the fever. I'd been at Sarah's bedstead dutifully with her mother and my mother in hopes of helping to save my best friend and cousin.

She threw some cornmeal into a metal pot of boiling water.

"God takes as He wills it," she stated as fact, then mashed in some butter.

No quantity of herbs or prayers would do for the god who had besieged us with this punishment. The ministers always rationalized to say that these tragedies in life were caused by not following God's commands perfectly. I didn't understand. Sarah was so good, so sweet. Why were she, her parents, and all who loved her objects of cruel punishment for the sins of the Windsor community? I could not understand. I do know that God's wrath was so extreme that she would not be the only one to die with the pestilence.

"What God has taken he will continue to take until a thirst for vengeance and correction is done. It is right to mourn Sarah. Her parents have just placed her in the ground."

Her tone changed. "I agree it is best that you are not left to your sorrow alone. Priscilla and young Annie must have their own spinning to do. It will console your tender heart to spend time with others who are also in grief."

Mother was angry. In public, she outwardly submitted to God's cruel choices but in private, her tone left no doubt that she thought the world was unjust and God too mean and overbearing.

Remembering those around her who she loved, she switched her tone to one of compassion.

"Aunt Anne is exhausted from her pregnancy. It will be a welcome change for her own daughters to spend time near another hearth. Your father will have his own work to do in his workshop."

She pushed the corn mush back above the fire to keep it warm for our breakfast, adding salt to it for more flavor.

I looked into her kind blue eyes and nodded.

"Yes, Mother. "T'will do us all a bit of good to be together in our sadness. Priscilla and Annie were close to Sarah too."

I remembered happier times on Backer Row with friends and cousins before anyone got sick or died: Rhody's girls, Anne and Hannah Taylor, Sarah Sension, Annie and Priscilla Thornton, and sometimes others and I, all working together in our gardens, gathering berries or herbs in the woods, laughing together at Uncle John's stories and spending time at each other's homes, often sleeping over at night. I knew I'd still feel hollow inside without all of us together, but I was looking forward to having some company, grateful not to be alone.

As was expected, Mother was called again to another bedstead and did the best she could with her few remaining herbs. The tea she'd been preparing in the morning had steeped for a good hour and was brimming with hope for those taken with the fever. The strong aroma of hemlock and pine saplings and roots lingered in our small cottage long after mother had gone.

After I'd fed our animals, a small cow and a hog, I returned to our cozy cottage. It was still too early to see my cousins, so I pulled out my secret playthings to make the time pass.

The poppet was our secret. I'd privately pulled Mother's doll out when no one was looking and gently placed it back into its hiding place when I was done. I liked to play with it and pretended she was my own little baby girl despite her huge pregnant belly. Mother caught me looking at it and promised she would make me one of my own. She cautioned me to be careful to keep it hidden because some people would think the little poppet was more than a plaything.

That spring mother never did get around to making a little play child in the form of a doll for me. She was too busy. The illness had invaded our town and was relentless.

Since I knew mother was so occupied, I decided to try to make my own little doll. I worked on tying pieces of wood together to form legs and arms. The body was scrap cloth and leather I'd sewn together and stuffed with more tiny pieces of cloth that couldn't be used for anything else. I put my little poppet in a place along the eaves where there was storage. I'd hid it there and hoped that when it was finished, I could proudly show it to my mother. I'd been creating it when I was bored or alone. I'd even pulled out Mother's doll and pretended they were having a conversation.

"I want to give you a baby brother," the one lady poppet with child said to the little crude little girl poppet I was almost finished making with twigs and roughly sewn together pieces of leather and linen. She looked like something a Native child would make. I kept the conversation between them going, first speaking for one and then the other.

After some time, I stopped playing with the dolls and made my way through the melting patches of snow and mud until I reached the cottage next door. The sun was hiding in the clouds, and nothing seemed to bring me cheer.

I knocked on the thick wooden door which opened only a small slit to keep out the cold. Aunt Ann peered out.

"Ah, Alissa. Good morning to you. You have come to be with Priscilla and Annie?"

I nodded my head in affirmation.

"It is a lovely idea, child. It is better to be in good company than alone. Samuel is feeling poorly this day."

She was short and very round as a babe pushed outward from the middle of her body. Mother said her time would come slightly later this spring season or near the beginning of summer and I'd soon meet another cousin.

By this time, Priscilla and Annie had also come to the door and were shouting their greetings for me to hear. She turned to them.

"We must not let Alissa be all alone today while her mother is away. You could both benefit to be elsewhere since Samuel is not himself."

"Yes, Mama." The dutiful voices replied in harmony.

"What is the matter with Samuel?" I asked as I looked through the opening into the next room and saw the little boy lying in his trundle bed without much movement. Normally Samuel, an active two-year-old, would have come to greet me, bouncing all around me several times.

"I know not what he suffers from, but I pray it is not the illness responsible for so many recent deaths. Normally, he is blessed with much energy. Hopefully, it still lies underneath the surface, and it will come bursting forth again. But these things need not concern any of you now. Be good girls and help with the carding and spinning of all the wool in the basket. You should go to Alissa's house so as not to disturb Samuel," she commanded.

"You girls can also help me by watching little Mary. Go before you catch your cold. The air is quite chilled for April. The late snow was ominous, but I think it's about to rain. The snow will be washed away very soon. Go along home, Alissa, and all the girls will be there in a few minutes."

Normally, she'd let me stay, embracing me as she welcomed me into her fold. It was unusual that she preferred us to be at my home. I hoped nothing serious was wrong with little Samuel, their toddler boy with the crimson curls that hung in between his eyes. Always snotty-nosed and a little terror ready to wreak havoc on whatever we were doing, he was prone to bouts of tummy aches. Hopefully, it was no more than that.

I did what I was told and fed the fire again upon my return to the little cottage. It was only a brief time before I heard tapping at the door. Opening it, the Thornton girls stood at the other side, eager to come in.

Seeing them, I realized that I had been neglectful. In my need for companionship, I had gone to the Thorntons forgetting to put the dolls away. Maybe part of me secretly wanted to show them off to my friends. As I let them in my house, Mary hopped around excited to be in a new place and Annie and Priscilla put down their baskets of wool. Mary hopped straight over to the little dolls on a side table next to a large chest.

"What is this?" she asked with amazement.

"Aye, what are they?" questioned Priscilla with some trepidation in her voice. Not waiting for a response, she answered her own question. "They are poppets!"

She and Annie stared at them stunned. I didn't know what to say. For me, they were just some playthings to pass the time when I was bored and had no one else to be with. Mother's warning loomed in my head.

Annie gingerly tried to pick one up. "Look. This one is a mommy just like our mama," she said innocently.

Priscilla was pale. She asked me slowly and precisely, "Why do you have poppets here?"

"I don't know," I said. "But I think my mother made one for herself in hopes of bringing me a baby brother one day. She lost a child and has been grieving."

"How does it help her to hurt my mother with this kind of magic?" she asked as Annie and Mary stood looking on.

"Do you think the doll is your mother?" I asked in disbelief. "She is not. My mother only wanted the doll to bring good luck to become with child again. She is afraid she is barren because she has not had more children," I tried to explain in vain.

"Poppets are evil, Alissa! She should be praying to God to forgive her for her sins. Maybe then, He would allow her to have another child. Only the Devil listens to prayers with poppets! And no one makes themselves their own poppet! They are only made to do evil witchcrafts on others."

She looked again intently at the poppets, having terror in her eyes.

"Your mother must be jealous of mine because my mother is pious and devoted and God blesses her time and time again with more children. This doll is to curse my mother because she is fruitful while your own mother is barren."

"Don't you say those things about my mother!" I pushed her to the ground. "The poppet has nothing to do with your mother!" I was aflame with anger.

Priscilla didn't care. She kept pushing me back with her words.

"And the other little poppet looks like a Native made it. They too ask the Devil for his help!"

She had started to get up from the floor and I pushed her down again.

"I made it to play with. It's not for the Devil or anyone else. It's just for me when I am lonely and have no one, no brother or sister here with me like you have with you. I do hate you, Priscilla!" I seethed.

We both started crying confused by the meaning of the poppets and what would happen next.

Was I in trouble for more than pushing Priscilla down? Would she tattle on me? I still didn't understand why the poppets had to be evil. Why couldn't they be for good?

"What you say is not true, Priscilla! Both my mother and I love your mother and there is no jealousy. With each child she has, we are blessed with a new cousin," I explained. Please don't say lies about us. It may seem strange to you, but I am telling the truth. Mother is just desperate to have another child. If you say anything, you will hurt her."

Priscilla gave it some thought, still not wanting to recognize what I said. She was sobbing from the shock of me pushing her to the floor. I held out my hand to her.

"Please let us forget all this and keep each other company with our chores. I will ask mother to get rid of the dolls since they scare you so much. I am sorry I pushed you," I said.

Priscilla's sobs slowed down, but she still wasn't ready to relent. "Prove to me that you will tell your mother. Throw your own doll into the fire now. I won't believe you until you do it!"

Heartbroken to throw my creation into the fire, I knew it was the first of many things I would need to do to change her mind.

"Fine, I throw my little doll into the fire to show, Priscilla, Annie and Mary that there is no evil or jealousy in this house," I declared.

"Good" approved Priscilla. "You'd best be sure that your mother's doll disappears too."

I nodded and tried to act remorsefully but inside, I was seething in anger again. How dare Priscilla dictate what my mother should do? It should not have been of any concern to her. I hid mother's poppet away once they were immersed in carding the wool and Mary had distracted them. I didn't want them to see its hiding place.

"I won't tell for now," said Priscilla "but that poppet must go away, or it will bring evil to our village," she commanded. We spent the rest of the day together in mostly silence and we worked on our spinning and sewing. Mary entertained and diverted us.

Eventually, Priscilla and Annie told me that they were starting to feel ill like their brother and were going to go home. It was just as well. Our exchange had been awkward, and I was sullen about losing my little doll that I worked so hard to create. Most importantly, I was afraid of what Priscilla would do next. I didn't know how I would talk to my mother about it. She had warned me that no good would come in sharing information about the poppets, but I was careless and was just beginning to pay the price for it.

The next night Mrs. Tinker came over in alarm. She said that Priscilla had developed a fever and Annie didn't feel well either. It was clear that they were suffering from the great illness that had already affected so many others. She begged Mother to bring her healing remedies with her, the few she had left.

My mother dutifully went as asked. She sat in vigil with the Thorntons for many hours giving of herself in hopes to prevent the pestilence from taking over their home. I waited for her, lonely and fearful. It was not good for me to have time to think of the latest exchange I had with Priscilla over the poppets. The more I thought about it, the more a gripping tightness pushed into my chest. My body was ignited with a justified sense of alarm.

It was after sitting at Priscilla's bedside that my mother became concerned about her own safety. I still do not know the words that she said, but in her confusion with the fever, Priscilla's words were untrue and damning to my mother. Mother was upset but believed her family and those around her would understand the child was sick with fever.

"Priscilla is addled and confused," my mother said in shock. "Her words are dark and accusatory against me. She mumbles in her sickbed."

The next day Mother lamented that Priscilla was getting worse. She not only had concern for the girl but also for herself. Priscilla's stories became more blaming and accusatory towards her. Mother could no longer go there for fear of upsetting her.

Although she had stopped holding vigil at her bed side, Priscilla still insisted Mother's specter came to see her. I was not privy to what she said in detail, but it was enough to frighten them both and cause an irreparable split in the family after Priscilla's death. 'Tis a horrible feeling indeed to be accused of evil when one is innocent.

I was convinced that Priscilla had tattled about the poppets. I have since come to understand that many believe childless or less fruitful women are jealous of those who have children. People say that they are prone to making pacts with the Devil out of jealousy or desperation. This belief did not describe my mother, but how can fearful people be convinced otherwise?

First little Samuel died, having no more fight to survive in his little body. It was not long after that when Priscilla perished after having fever and fits for three days, finally becoming more peaceful on the day of her death. Her siblings Annie and Thomas followed her to the grave. Priscilla's fevered gibberish had sealed my mother's fate. It was then that the accusations started and the estrangement from Priscilla's parents began. I was certain they viewed my mother with suspicion because of me. The pain was powerful, as were the accusations. I found myself a few short weeks later without my beloved mother. I suppose I had no choice but to forget the details of what happened, or it would have killed me right then. But in remembering it, I sensed my own life was on the precipice of existing no more.

Chapter 30

Skipmuck (Chicopee), Massachusetts, 1677: Falls of Reckoning

I froze in anguish. I knew why the poppet threatened me. The dam blocking my memory that had been steady and strong for decades became demolished suddenly with a heavy storm of brutal and unforgiving recollections forced into view by the poppet. I could no longer hold back the deluge of my heart.

The fortress that blocked me from my past crumbled suddenly and unforgivingly. A torrent of tears overflowed as I remembered and understood why I would want to hide from my own past. It was my personal reckoning. In all honesty, I'd begged God to help me and show me the truth so that my heart might rest from it in the later part of my life. The disdainful truth was my mother's death was caused by my own sinfulness. IT WAS MY FAULT she was dead. I'd finally seen it all.

Such a sinner I was! How could my own family ever forgive me if they knew. I panicked and suddenly dropped the ceramic bowl I was holding, causing it to shatter into pieces. In truth, I had only wanted to be nothing more than loyal to my beautiful mother over the years. The fear that I had done something to cause her death forced me to forget her in ways that fed my guilt. She should have been remembered for her kindness, beauty and generosity. The conflict within my own being became too much to bear.

"No!" I screamed. My heart steeped in guilt, I jolted for the door and threw it open.

The children followed the sounds of unrest and Thomas called after me. "Mother, what is the matter?"

"I should not be here. Get rid of the doll she is cursed!" I screamed. I will atone for my sins, I thought. I would not let my mother be alone in the dark waters. She always called to me from that deep foreboding place. She cannot be in such a dismal place by herself. It was I who put her there. I owe her this!

As I ran from the house, the steady cascading hum of the waterfall became closer. I was compelled to go there. I passed the wide-open fields of corn and wheat and finally slipped into the forest next to the river. My heart pounded loudly, and my body was aflame with panic. I darted toward the falls, barely slowing down to catch my breath and wipe the sweat off my brow.

My older children ran after me, but I was oblivious to them. It was hard for them to keep up with my frantic and irrational pace. The force within me that coerced me to find the dark waters below the falls penetrated my being and propelled me forward rapidly. I should be with my mother after what I did to her!

Moving swiftly through strands of birch, cedar, hemlock and pine, I navigated the steepness of the hill leading me down toward the rocky side of the falls. Once, I tripped in mud and cut my knees on the craggy roots of a formidable hemlock tree. I felt nothing and kept going before anyone could find me and stop me from what I was about to do.

I was only forced to slow down when the jagged rocks at the outer edges of the falls impeded my path. Their mossy edges glistened with the mist from the spraying waters and made their surfaces slippery and difficult to tread upon. All around me the world vibrated and the violently dropping waters pounded forcefully on the rocks encircling the dark pool barely visible below. Slowly, I traversed across the flattest stones along the path to the edge of the shelf leading closest to the falls.

Torrents of water from the falls cascaded steadily onto boulders and the noise in my head urging me to join my mother in the black pool of water below drowned out any other sounds. My sole purpose was to reach the edge of the falls. From there I was able to see the dark waters below that I'd seen in repetitive nightmares.

"Alissa!" I heard once and then again.

"Alissa!"

Where was she? Where was my mother's voice coming from?

Despite my dark and foreboding mood, the sun managed to pour in through the slit of the open sky above the river. It was the one thing I noted that caused me to turn my head and glance toward the fern-covered bank of the river from where I had come. Several yards away, my children and my best friend Sarah were yelling, barely heard above the din of the raging falls. They had locked arms to form a chain with Sarah at the lead. She had insisted on reaching me.

Still obsessed with joining my mother in the deep murky depths of watery hell, I stared forward into the abyss of death itself. I don't know how long I stood there in my trance of other-worldly delusions, but eventually Sarah overcame her own fears of the water.

Her hand was gripped firmly in her son's, and his was gripped in my own son's. They tied a rope to a sturdy white oak not far from the shore. They hoped to reach me with it before the length ran out.

"Alissa, do not go there! Come back! Come this way and grab my hand!" she commanded.

Teetering on the precipice of life and death, I shouted, "My mother should not be alone. I cannot leave her! It is my fault she is there in the deep swirling waters!" I poured out the guilt of my heart as I spoke.

"Oh no, Alissa, you were not the cause of your mother's death! It was not your fault! You are innocent!" she tried to coax me back.

Still, I hesitated. What she told me made no sense. I looked back toward the deep murky pool.

"No! Alissa! Your mum is not there in the dark waters. She is alive in the faces and souls of your children. Do not leave them!" Sarah shouted desperately at me, trying to pierce through the steady noise of the falls. I was still out of her reach.

I paused for a moment thinking of the doll and the ruin I thought it had brought to my family. Did Sarah speak the truth? How could she? She didn't know. Maybe she lied to pull me back.

"Alissa, come back now! Your children need you. I need you! Please come back. We've been through so much together. You are my sister. We are twins in life, and I cannot live without you. Your mother is not in the dark waters below! Please, I will show you where she is! Come see her here on the bank in the faces of the children who love you. She is alive in all that they do. She is a part of them," Sarah consoled me as she continued to make her way out to me.

It was then that I came to my senses, seeing Sarah wading further into the water in her struggle to reach me. Water came splashing over my shoes in a gush and I had to hold fast to a jagged bolder to keep myself from slipping over a ledge on the precipice of the falls.

I wanted to come back but was afraid I couldn't. I looked around focused on finding any possible path back to my family, back to my dear friend, and back to life itself. In the corner of my eye, growing just a foot or two from where I clung to the boulder, was a small tree growing in a crag. If I gradually moved to the other side of the boulder, I could reach out my leg and then my right arm to grab the little life-saving tree.

Inch by inch, I maneuvered my body carefully across the width of the boulder that allowed me to reach the small but sturdy tree. Sarah and our sons had almost caught up to me.

In my eagerness to reach her, I lost my footing trying to step to the other side of the crag as well as my grasp of the little tree on it. I trembled with fear as sharp stones and jagged branches pierced into my back. Had it not been for a large dead branch behind me, the current would have surely pushed me forward and down the falls. Sarah also slipped in her haste to reach me with our sons.

For her, for the children, and even for myself, I began to pray and ask for help so that we would all be safely delivered from the treacherous waters. For the first time, I heard my mother's voice not in the deep waters below, but right there with me.

My death was not your fault, my dear Alissa. Now gather your strength and go to your family. Cease to punish yourself. My wish for you is to have a peaceful life with my grandchildren. Go and be strong. From this day forth, you should be blessed to live in love and peace and not cursed to live in despair. I love you forever.

I needed her and she came. From my dangerous perch, hope was not lost. It had just been found.

Sarah and the boys continued to plod their way toward me, and I found the force and calm to stand again using the fallen trunk as a guide. I imagined my mother propping me up and helping me to be steady and upright. Finally close enough to throw me a loop of rope, I put it around my waist as they directed me to do. The details of Sarah's dear face came closer, and our boys encouraged me to keep taking slow careful steps toward the shore.

Sarah stretched her hand out to me from the rocks.

"Almost there, dear sister!"

I reached out to her until our grips were locked tightly and followed the line of my rescuers while they led me back to shore. Sarah and I were without words as we reached the shore. We cried as we hugged each other tightly.

"Thank you, my sister," I said, humbled to have such a brave and devoted woman to be my sister and friend.

Then, looking around at the tearful faces of my children, I did see my mother in them. For the first time, seeing her among them brought me peace and not fear. I extended my arms out to them all and humbly thanked them and Sarah's sons for bringing me to the shore.

I started to explain, but Thomas stopped me.

"No, Mummy. Not now. We'll take ye home first. You needn't worry. You need to dry off and get some warm drink in ye first. They'll be time for talking about it later. But it doesn't matter. You're with us now." He sighed in relief.

"Thank you," I whispered, grateful to be given another chance at life.

That fateful day, it was Sarah, my dear sister of the heart, and our boys who saved my life. Both sets of our daughters were waiting at the house and helped to clean and dress my wounds, put me into warm clothes and filled my belly with warm food and drink.

My life changed forever on that day. The burdens that damaged my heart were mostly lifted and life moved forward in miraculous ways.

Chapter 31

Skipmuck (Chicopee), Massachusetts, 1677: Forgiveness

The days following my near death at the falls, Sarah came to keep watch over me, still worried that I would slip out of my senses again.

"What was it you were thinking of as you went to the falls?" she asked me with only kindness in her voice.

I hesitated. How would Sarah still be my friend? How could she love me if she knew how much at fault I was for my mother's death? I was still not convinced of my total innocence. I thought of how she had waded into treacherous waters and saved my life with no hesitation.

"I'm so sorry that I endangered you, Sarah. You should not have risked your own life for mine. In truth, I was confused, only thinking of my mother's voice calling for me when she left on the shallop to Hartford, forever taken from me."

"My dear, Alissa. There is nothing I wouldn't do for you and there's nothing you need to withhold from me. What happened to make you want to jump into the dangerous falls? Why did you lose your will to go on?" she asked, gently cradling an arm around me as we sat in front of the fire.

"You promise that there is nothing I could say to you that would push you away?" I asked shyly.

"Of course I promise, Alissa! We have been close friends for many years. Aye, more like sisters! You know this much by now!" she chided me softly.

"As I ran to the sharp rocks near the fall preparing to plunge into the deep waters, 'twas as if I was back in time. I finally understood I was guilty for my sweet mother being sent away from me. All these many years, I've had nightmares of her calling me in alarm from the dark turbulent waters. I had betrayed her, and I couldn't leave her alone. I know it makes little sense," I admitted.

"Go on, Alissa. Free yourself in telling your story," she urged me.

"It was only your sweet voice and imagining my mother's that brought me back to my children and present times. What happened is awful, Sarah. My children will hate me for it if you don't," I said, unconvinced of my innocence.

"Let your worries rest here on the table," she continued. "Please, tell me. What do you fear you did to bring your mother to the gallows? I cannot believe she died because of you; you were just a child. That would be impossible! You loved her and she loved you. Out with it, Alissa!" she smiled holding onto my right shoulder.

Sarah Miller had a reassuring attitude and was often able to get me to confide in her. It had always been to my benefit and my relief. So why would it be any different now?

I took a deep breath. "I'll tell you, but I'm still not sure it is best to recount it to the children."

She nodded in agreement. "It's always up to you what you tell them or don't tell them."

"Right before my mother's accusations, I played with her fertility doll…" I began. I tried to tell the story in as much detail as I could remember, only pausing for sips of cider on the table. Sarah listened silently and never took her compassionate eyes off me as I spoke my truth intermingled with sobbing at times.

"Do you see now?" I asked her when I was done. "Surely, Priscilla told our secret even after I threw my own poppet into the fire. Priscilla got sick that very day and that night my mother was upset by what she had said in her sickness. I'm sure that after becoming sick, it only confirmed Priscilla's suspicions that the doll was evil — something that was used to curse and wish ill will, not something that blessed," I cried.

Sarah comforted me and hugged me letting me know she still loved me and was still at my side. When I stopped sobbing, she made it clear that she had something to say.

"I know these times have been trying with the loss of both our husbands. As if it were not enough for you to handle already, John Fisher awakened old wounds with his slander against you and Thomas. 'Tis no wonder that seeing the poppet and the memories attached to it was a weight way too much for you to bear."

"Aye," I answered.

Sarah gently squeezed my hand.

"There's something I never told you," she said, lowering her head. "I was at the meeting house as a child when your mum was being blamed for killing off folk through witchcraft. My mother took me there and I heard the testimonies. We hadn't moved to Springfield yet. I was already twelve, so I remember it. I never told you before because I didn't want to bring it up and hurt you."

I nodded, taking in her admission.

"Alissa, you will never be at peace unless you hear the truth. Please, may I tell you what I remember, dear sister? I know it will be painful, but you must not continue to think that your mother's death was your fault. I still recall some of those testimonies with chilling detail," she declared.

"Go on. I am ready," I said shaking. "But only what is necessary for me to understand."

Sarah shook her head.

"Dear sister, all you need to know is the main complaint voiced against your mother. Some of those who had lost a child during the epidemic including the doctor, minister, and magistrates blamed your mother. They saw her coming to homes with her Native remedies after she ran out of her usual simples. The doctor thought it was peculiar and suspicious that she would use the potions of Indians — wild people seen to be devil worshippers. That's the crux of it. The doll you speak of was never mentioned. Not once dear Alissa!"

"But I tell ye, I know that Annie and Priscilla, especially Priscilla, talked about it with their father!" I protested.

"Perhaps they did but Thomas Thornton may have wished to bring no further attention to his family. As it was, he hurried to leave town with the remaining family members that same year. And perhaps too, knowing you and loving you for many years, the Thorntons did not wish to drag you into this tragedy."

Sarah clasped both my hands.

"I assure you, Alissa, the poppet had nothing to do with your mother's death, but if it still haunts you, get rid of it! Purify the past by throwing it into the fire! Free your spirit from it! It's time, Alissa."

I looked her in the eyes. "I am ready to be free. I am ready to feel happy again," already feeling much lighter from what she had told me about the poppet. Yet, there was still something hanging on.

I climbed up the ladder to the loft and found the little dowry chest. I had ordered my daughters to place the doll there. I grabbed it from deep within the carved wooden box and stared at the strange little thing with regret and sorrow for the havoc people's perceptions of it might have caused. It was supposed to bring healing to my mother in the form of another child, but instead it might have contributed to the end of her life even though it wasn't mentioned when they gathered evidence against her. I was sure it was still in the forefront of Thomas Thornton's thoughts as he testified against her. For this, I still maintained some guilt. The little poppet had to go.

"Here she is," I brought the poppet to Sarah to see.

"Good. Now throw it in the fire! Say you banish all evil and only welcome good into your home from this day forth." She nodded at me to go on. "Forgive yourself, Alissa. Let it go. You were innocent. Others took your mother from you. You are not to blame."

I shook my head to acknowledge that I was ready. I teared up to think of how much I had suffered as a little girl — so devastated to lose my mother.

"I cast thee into the fire for purification of my soul and deliverance from evil! May only blessings come into this house from this day forth!"

"That's it! Only blessings will enter this house from this day hence!" Sarah repeated. She hugged me and we stared into the fire as the rest of the poppet burned into ash. When it was done, we brought the ashes into the woods far from the yard and buried them.

After that day, Sarah and I became closer than ever. Our deep loving friendship and sisterhood continued throughout the rest of our lives. Even twins could not have had a better understanding of each other.

My disappointed daughters eventually understood why I had to get rid of the doll. In an effort to leave them with a connection to their grandmother, I went through the little chest with them and passed on some of her things to them that I knew would never be considered as evil — pieces of clothing, her linens, a comb — ordinary little things of a life extinguished too soon.

My mother still came to me in my dreams. She always told me she loved me and there was nothing that I had to be forgiven for. Instead, she saw her grandchildren there and remarked how lovely they were and how she could see herself being carried on through them. And I never went so close to the waterfall again. I only looked at it from a distance. But when I did, I imagined the time I was there, the water washing away some of my guilt and fears as my mother held my hand.

Chapter 32

Norwalk, Connecticut, 1678: A Visit

Thomas pulled the reins and directed the horse to veer off from the main highway and down the narrow dirt road toward a brightly painted saltbox in the distance. The air stirred with earthy breezes. We were close to the sound with gulls swooping in and out of our sight, screeching their remarks that indeed we had traveled to another world. Inhaling the fresh salty air brought me a sense of peace and evoked memories of my mother's stories of her journey across the ocean to New England.

The marsh framed the land coated in medleys of greens and yellows as we rolled closer to Aunt Rhody's door. I took in the life pulsing all around me, breathing it in deeply, ready for everything that would connect me with kin missed so dearly over the years. Aunt Rhody had seen us coming in the distance and opened her door. Her silhouette was the same diminutive figure only slightly more hunched over. Her white hair blended with her cap.

"Alissa!" she shouted, looking as bright as the sun. "I'm so grateful to see you again before I die. I've longed for this reunion for many years."

She cradled my face in her hands and peered into my eyes to find the child who was still inhabiting the depths of my soul. The lines of old age had done nothing to diminish her natural beauty.

"The joy is all mine Aunt Rhody," I managed to say. She had meant so much to me before my mother's demise and even more after. She had been my strength and also my soft place to find comfort in times of turbulence. Without her, I wasn't sure how I would have survived.

"There now," she said, wiping away the tears of elation and gratitude. "You're here now and we will resume as we once were. Except now, I get to see some of your beautiful children. They will soon realize how much their aunt has loved them from afar."

She looked at the traveling cart with my handsome Thomas lifting my youngest children, Alice, Benjie and Abby to the ground.

As Aunt Rhody and I stood in front of her threshold, we stared at each other in awe. The sea roses bloomed in ecstasy. I imagined all of nature celebrating with us. Still as if in a dream, I managed to introduce my children to Aunt Rhody with great pleasure, the fruits of my labor with Simon, the better parts of myself incarnate.

It wasn't long before the sun began to set and men from the fields came forth. The chiseled young men were very familiar, but Rhody had to remind me who some of them were.

Baby Zub, now a man in his thirties approached me. We had become strangers yet held a common bond from the past. Mary Sension's sons were with him. I remembered them more clearly as they were slightly older than I when the family had split apart. Finally, Walter Hoyt emerged, much older and greyer, but his eyes still conveyed kindness and clarity. I was happy Aunt Rhody and he still had each other in their elder years.

My children and I visited for over a month and enjoyed the town of Norwalk, our sojourn by the sound with our kin. We benefitted from being there, basking in the kind-hearted hospitality of Aunt Rhody and her family. I regretted not being able to come sooner. My heart was heavy at first to know I had missed another meeting with Aunt Mary and her husband Matthew. They'd died together during an illness a few years before the attack on Springfield. But, as Aunt Rhody and I rekindled memories of the past, I could sense Aunt Mary and my mother's spirits there with us.

One fine evening, Aunt Rhody and I sat close together after dinner outside under the stars and a full vibrant moon. I started to hum something familiar, a song I'd always remembered Aunt Rhody singing to me and her girls. I'd forgotten the words but as I hummed it, Aunt Rhody looked at me in surprise.

"Alissa, do you remember that song?" she asked.

"I remember very little of it, Aunt Rhody — only the feeling of it, but not the words or the meaning. I only know that it's connected to you, my mother, and your daughters, my long-lost cousins. It was from a happier time, and we sang it on our farm lot in Windsor."

"That is all exactly so, Alissa. We were growing the three sisters as the local Natives had taught us: beans, squash and corn. We were singing the ballad of The Three Ravens. It is still one of my favorites. We sang it in the fields because we had freedom to do so there. I've thought of it often."

She began to sing. Her voice, melancholier than I had remembered it, was still so beautiful.

"   *There were three ravens sat on a tree.*"
"*Down a down hey down hey down.*" I hadn't forgotten the refrain.

> *"They were as black as they might be,*
> *With a down.*
> *Then one of them said to his mate:*
> *Where shall we our breakfast take?"*

"*With a down derry derry derry down down.*" I joined in, singing softly in reverence to my lost family members.

> *"Down in yonder greenfield."*

"*Down a down hey down hey down.*" I continued to sing and imagined the hidden garden next to the river and my giggling cousins.

> *"There lies a knight slain under his shield;*
> *With a down.*
> *His hounds they lie down at his feet,*
> *So well they do their master keep."*
>
> *"With a down derry derry derry down down."*

I held my hands out to my aunt and the spirits of my dead relations. The memory of my mother's gentle hands in mine, bringing me to a place of closeness with her.

> *"His hawks they fly so eagerly,*
> *Down a down hey down hey down.*

There is no fowl dare him come nigh
With a down."
"But down there comes a fallow doe,
As great with young as she might go."
"With a down, derry derry derry down down."

"She lifted up his bloody head,
Down a down hey down, hey down.
And kissed his wounds that were so red.
With a down.

She got him up upon her back
And carried him to an earthen lake."
"With a down derry derry derry down down."

"She buried him before the prime.
Down a down hey down hey down.
She was dead herself ere evensong time.
With a down.
Now God send to every gentleman,
Such hounds, such hawks and such a loved one,"
"With a down derry derry derry down, down."

Rhody and I smiled at each other, with a hint of tears in our eyes.

"Aunt Rhody, I must tell you of a recent experience," I bared my soul to her about the incident at the waterfall.

"I've always felt guilty about my mother's death, but I never knew why, now I do. I realize I was so conflicted about her death because my sentiments of ongoing loyalty to her seemed upended by anything I had done to contribute to her death."

"You were just a child, Alissa. Your mother's death was not your fault. It is I who deserve to feel that guilt until my dying day. I wish I could have stood up for her. I was too afraid for my own life," she explained. "But you, Alissa, like the loyal hawks and hounds in the song, honor your mother when you speak of her to your children to keep her memory alive. When you show them the same kindness and love that she gave you, you honor her memory. What's more Alissa, you must know, she was like the slain knight. She battled a terrible illness with her herbal cures until they ran out. In the end, she was killed by those who didn't understand everything she had done for her community to battle and fight the disease that took over. My brother John, your true father, knew the truth."

"Aye, he did Aunt Rhody. I have wondered since his death if he was my true father. So, it is true!

"Aye." She nodded and smiled.

" I remember near the confluence of a beautiful stream and the Rivulet, he took me to a place covered in wildflowers. Some of them were the most exquisite ones I've ever seen called Lady Slippers. He told me he'd retrieved Mother's body and buried her there. It was our secret place for her. I was never to tell anyone about it," I said.

Aunt Rhody began to sing again.

> *"He lifted up her bloody head,*
> *Down a down hey down ,hey down.*
> *And kissed her wounds that were so red.*
> *With a down.*
> *He got her up upon her back*
> *And carried her to an earthen grave."*
> *"With a down derry derry derry down down."*

She paused. "In the end, he died after burying her, years not hours later, but in service of trying to prevent others from meeting the same fate as his beloved. Our family has always found it peculiar that he died in the middle of the witch panic in Hartford after he'd secured the release of the Dutch woman indicted for witchcraft. It was his final act of devotion to your mother, Alissa."

We were silent after that, looking at the stars, absorbing their beauty. For me, I hoped somewhere, somehow, my parents' spirits would meet again. As for me, I decided that my love and devotion to both of them would never die. I would do my part to assure it lingered well beyond my own death and that my own children would be touched by their stories.

Chapter 33: Epilogue

Skipmuck (Chicopee) and Springfield, Massachusetts, 1685: Families Intertwined

I ran my hands gently along the dowry chest. No longer in a hidden place in the attic, it enjoyed a prominent place near my featherbed. The white oak of its face was as sturdy as ever, not weakened by time, a reflection of myself, stronger and more whole with age. Its wood was singed only slightly at a corner in the back, giving it character. Its engravings of simple flowers reminded me of my mother's sweetness and her connection to nature.

After overcoming my travails and deciding what I wanted to keep and what I wanted burned out of my life forever, the chest only contained those family objects which allowed my heart to overflow with joy and appreciation. That the chest survived fire and ember at a time that I would have wished the whole thing had burned away was a testament to miraculous forces at work in the world.

With time, I'd added to the little chest. Inside were drawers of the embroidered linens sewn with great care by my own daughters, folded neatly next to the ones of my own creation as a child. Common motifs of leaves and intricate flowers carried on through each generation as adornments. The tiny needlepoint that was the most striking was a tiny image of a Lady's Slipper that I'd stitched after seeing my mother's grave. It brought me joy to find it again and remember that I had honored my mother in little ways.

Mary and Ruth sat next to each other beaming on the bed, both beautiful and excited as I pulled out and unfolded two shawls, one for each young woman that Sarah and I had made together for this momentous family day. We'd also fashioned new caps for them and adorned them with the fine lace from Brugge that my mother had kept hidden in the bottom of the chest.

"Dear daughters, you make me so proud, and your father joins me in spirit with the same sentiment," I said as I helped them with the last adjustments to their attire.

"Are you ready?" I asked, "Your men are waiting in anticipation. Of this, I am certain," I said and winked at both of them. They giggled and squeezed each other's hands.

Ruth smiled at her sister and then me. "We're ready," she said nodding.

"Aye. Take us to our future husbands, Mummy," said Mary.

"Come, my loves," I reached out my hands for each of them to clasp and usher into the main hall where Millers and Beamons of all ages and descriptions stood waiting. At the far end of the room, the two groomsmen, John and Samuel Miller, stood calm and confident with their mother, dear Sarah, buzzing with excitement at their sides.

Just two years apart, they were close to each other not just in looks but also shared experiences. No longer unruly little boys racing around Sarah's home while we sewed and attended to our little babes, the young men looked proudly on as my daughters joined them near the magistrate.

The Beamon and Miller families had gathered countless times before for grief, work, and play. Shared life in almost every form had brought us together, but nothing so definitive and sweet as the joining of two of Sarah's sons with two of my daughters. With their unions, the sisterhood between Sarah and me would solidify even more.

Our local magistrate read the words that bound the young couples and our families together. Words of brevity outlining basic obligations and responsibilities that he garbled and muttered until they fell out of his aged mouth. They could not begin to convey the essence of the lives our families had already shared together, nor did they reflect adequately the anticipation of the great experiences yet to come — babies, more weddings, more love. It wasn't until the magistrate's last perfunctory words did the elation of the event come to fruition with 'Hoozahs', hugs, and kisses, followed by shared toasts to the young couples.

Two couples. Two families. Two dear friends who had been sisters of the heart joined in blood through their future grandchildren for time immemorial. A bond that would never be broken.

"Sister, my dear sister!" I embraced Sarah with all my might.

"Aye. Sisters to the end!" shouted Sarah with tears in her eyes.

We gave each other comfort and our intertwined families gave us great joy. In the end, the marriages of our children to each other were only a formality to make us officially recognized kin. We'd already had a connection from the first day we'd met.

Both couples, Ruth and Samuel, Mary and John, and many of their siblings stayed in Springfield over the years. My daughters Alice and Abigail also married two brothers, the Baldwins, from Milford — Alice married Nathaniel and Abigail wed Obadiah. They settled near related family, Miles Merwin, the Sensions and the Hoyts. Many of the boys married too — Simon to Hannah with whom he went with to Deerfield and John married Abigail Eggleston. Benjamin married Hannah Higgins and Josiah was taken in with Lydia Warner, eventually wedding her too. One son, Samuel, married Margaret Chapman and moved to Windsor. Many grandchildren followed who kept me busy and content. Daniel and Thomas remained single and were always there for me.

I never remarried in my later years. No one could compare to Simon. And I wondered if my family history made me an outcast to some. It didn't matter. What mattered was the family I had and the family who shaped me. I could finally embrace the beautiful memories I had of my mother as well as Simon and share those with my many children and grandchildren — my cloak of protection as well as a source of pure joy to me throughout my later years.

Author's Note

This book is the last in a series of stories pertaining to Alice 'Alse' Young and those closest to her. She became an ever-present influence on me for over a decade. In ways I still don't understand, the absence of a story about her prior to 2015 influenced me to create something to hold the memory of her existence and to do legitimate research. I hope that she has deemed my job finished. It was my intention to bring her to life in a way that people would understand the brutality of her death and those of others in Connecticut from witch-hunting. And in the aftermath of that brutality, I struggled to understand how much suffering those who loved her must have gone through, no one more so than the only daughter we know of as Alice Young Beamon ("Alissa" in these stories).

Unlike her mother, Alice Young Beamon had many children. Was she driven to do so in an act to protect herself and fit in? In Puritan religious view, women's worth was tied to their fecundity and motherhood. Fruitful women were often seen as "good" and those that had no children or few were often labeled as "bad" jealous witches. Indeed, Malcolm Gaskill states this in his book, *The Ruin of All Witches*, about witch trials in Springfield and the mentality of the time, "Witches were active in the community and were known to be envious of fertile women, who became victims of their murderous magic. Every mother's worry found substance in the person of the witch." Was Alice Young's infertility a strike against her in an already fearful atmosphere of an influenza epidemic in which many children in Windsor died while her child lived? These ideas could have been imposed easily on her daughter, Alice Young Beamon, if she were unable to bear many children.

Thankfully, Alice Young Beamon did have at least a dozen children, a protection to her survival in many ways. The final way took form in an incident in which a man named John Fisher in Hadley, Massachusetts called her son, Thomas, a witch and said Thomas and his mother looked like witches. Thomas beat up the man and brought him to court for slander reflecting the fact that being called a witch could be deadly business.

Through research, I discovered with my co-researcher Dr. Katherine Hermes that Alice Young Beamon Jr. was living in Windsor at the time she married Simon Beamon. Without any evidence, I had to decide with whom she was living. Who would have been the best candidate for this role? It wasn't hard to imagine who that might be. Rhoda (Rhody) Tinker Hobbs Taylor Hoyt, Alice's neighbor on Backer Row and possible family member, stayed there longer than her other Tinker siblings who moved away after Alice Young's hanging in 1647. Rhoda did not leave after Alice's death so that she could wed Walter Hoyt before moving to Norwalk with him. Her husband John Taylor had gone missing in a shipwreck, and she was not free to marry until several years had passed. Rhoda left Windsor around the same time that Alice Young Beamon married.

One of the most interesting facts of all was that Lydia Gilbert, Windsor's second witch trial victim, was convicted to death for witchcraft just days before Alice Young Jr.'s marriage. Did that conviction have any influence on its timing? It is certainly plausible understanding the risks for Alice Jr. Women were often targeted for accusations based on connections to a family member who was already a convicted or accused witch.

As far as Lydia Gilbert's identity, I have taken the opinion along with other historians that Lydia Gilbert was the wife of John Gilbert Jr, the son and not John Gilbert Sr., the father. Furthermore, many historians think that her maiden name was Lydia Bliss. No one is sure how she is related to the one Bliss family that was in Connecticut and later moved to Springfield, Massachusetts at the time. I chose to make her a stepdaughter to Margaret Bliss. The novel reflects the latest historical theories.

There is no historical evidence of Alice Young Beamon going to Stratford with John Young, her possible father. Strangely enough, when John Young died in Stratford on April 7th of 1661, he did not leave a will and Alice Young Beamon was not named as an heir. It is peculiar because we know from his probate records that he was sick for several months and would have certainly had time to draw up a last will and testament. Alice Young Jr. was married at the time and already had four sons. John Young's property remained unclaimed in Stratford for seven years after his death until the town finally sold it.

Dr. Katherine Hermes and I discovered this information through further research after I published One of Windsor in 2015. More about the possible factors that played a part in the death and hanging of Alice Young can be found in the research article "Between God and Satan: Thomas Thornton, Witch-hunting, and Religious Mission in English Atlantic World, 1647-1693" in Connecticut History Review, Fall 2022 edition. Much of that newer research is reflected in this novel about Alice Young Beamon's life.

The Ruin of All Witches by Malcolm Gaskill, previously mentioned above, was an important source of information in learning about early life in Springfield, Massachusetts, especially in relation to witch trials that took place there before Alice Young Beamon became part of the community. People close to Alice Jr., namely her husband Simon Beamon and her best friend, Sarah Miller, were both affected by and active participants in the witch trials of Hugh and Mary Parsons. Simon Beamon defended another Mary Parsons, also accused of witchcraft and the wife of Joseph Parsons in a defamation trial. In the novel, I changed Hugh and Mary Parsons' names to Hugh Percy and Molly Percy to avoid confusion with the historical character of Mary Bliss Parsons. Her name remained unchanged in the novel. It was fascinating to see how two people who had previously bought into the idea of the harm of "witches" also embraced a young woman whose mother had been the first to hang for witchcraft in New England. These interesting historical intersections were a true part of the novel.

We're not sure of the date of Simon Beamon's death but he is listed in death records between two people that died during the raid on Springfield in 1675. In records, four people were listed as dying from their injuries days after the Springfield attack. Two were named but two others were not. He could have possibly been one of them.

This latest story is not meant to be a genealogy in any way but rather a study of the trauma young Alice (Alissa in the story) would have had to go through before trauma or post-traumatic stress disorder even had names. It is impossible for me to know how she personally went through the trauma of losing her mother so that part of the story is purely a creative invention. Her friend Sarah Miller was very real, and Alice Jr. did move toward the waterfall in Chicopee after Springfield was burned to the ground in October of 1675. It was remarkable to me how much Alice Young Jr. and Sarah Miller had in common in real life. They were next door neighbors, both from Windsor, and both of their mothers had been accused of witchcraft. Fortunately, Sarah's mother, Mercy Marshfield, did not die because her accusation did not lead to an indictment.

I did not do an inordinate amount of research on the Beamon children since that was not my focus. However, the details of the children's lives in the epilogue are true to the best of my knowledge. I was unable to find specific vital records for all the children. I do not know if Mary and Ruth were twins, but they did marry Sarah Miller's two sons. I'm not sure if it happened at different or the same times. Eventually, Thomas Beamon did marry Phebe Park and had many children with her in Preston, Connecticut after his mother's death. That is why it is not mentioned in the story.

The waterfall has changed in Chicopee. What was once wild became utilized and reshaped for industry. It is probably unrecognizable from the mid seventeenth century.

Alice Young Beamon died in Springfield on Oct 5, 1708. Thousands of great grandchildren are her legacy, as was her longevity and her strength.

The idea of respectful memory of the dead as a way to keep them alive was an important part of this story. As a way to illustrate that, I incorporated the beautiful ballad of *The Three Ravens* that was published in the early seventeenth century, the year Rhoda Tinker was born, 1611, but it may have existed from centuries earlier. You can find many lovely versions of this ballad in videos on YouTube.

On May 25th on the eve of the 376th anniversary of Alice Young's hanging, the state of Connecticut finally acknowledged its witch trial victims. I was part of the groups (CT WITCH Memorial and Connecticut Witch Trial Exoneration Project) that helped pass the resolution, but I speak here as an individual and not for the groups.

It was both a joyful and momentous occasion that involved a lot of goodwill from both parties in the Connecticut state legislature — the Connecticut General Assembly. Resolution HJ 34: A Resolution Concerning Certain Witchcraft Convictions in Colonial Connecticut, names all victims — both those convicted and those indicted. The resolution apologizes to victims and their families and acknowledges their suffering. At the beginning of the resolution, it states that historians as a profession and society in general accept that these witch trial victims were innocent and it also states the real root causes for the witch hunts, specifically fear, community panic, and misogyny. It was a victory for advocates like me, descendants, and those who care about justice. We all owe a debt of gratitude to legislators Representative Jane Garibay and Senator Saud Anwar for championing it and everyone else in the legislature that co-sponsored it and overwhelmingly voted for it.

But as far as we've come, the forces that led to the witch hangings are still among us. On the day of Judiciary testimony for this resolution, a representative asked a woman testifying on behalf of her grandmother to pass the resolution if she had proof that her grandmother wasn't actually a witch. Apparently, he didn't understand that spectral evidence and identification of witch's teats (moles, skin tags, or other skin irregularities) was the evidence used to convict someone of witchcraft in the cases referred to in our resolution. Nor did he understand the consensus of historians that there were no actual supernatural contracts with demonic forces involved, the Puritan definition of a witch. He and another representative insisted that changes be made to the resolution in the House of Representatives in order for it to pass. "The state of Connecticut declares their innocence" was taken out of the bill and "convicted of witchcraft and familiarity of the devil" were placed into the resolution several times despite the title of the resolution clearly stating it pertained to colonial witchcraft convictions. The media did not pick up on all these changes. The word "exoneration" was replaced with "absolve" under cover of saying "exoneration" was a legal term that needed to be replaced by another less legal one. In doing so, the meaning changed. It is strange indeed, that the word used to replace "exoneration", a term implying wrongful conviction and innocence, was "absolve", a religious term which implied the victims were guilty to begin with and needed to be forgiven. Why was that word "absolve" chosen instead of several other possibilities? Why was it the one that passage of the bill hedged on?

I illustrate this story and these details to show that forces of ignorance and fear have always been around and will continue to be around in varying degrees. We cannot forget that and pretend these forces don't exist. Around the world, people are still dying from witch hunts. In broader terms, people are being discriminated against in many ways or even being killed because of how they see themselves, who they love, or how they express their spirituality. I hope that in my novels about the witch trials in Connecticut, that people will be better able to identify these forces and stand up against them in a stance of common humanity and love for all. Let's celebrate House Joint Resolution 34 as well as unity and goodwill when it's present, but also use awareness of darker forces such as fear, to help guide us to a better place through education and action.

Author Bio

Award-winning author, Beth M. Caruso, has been involved in efforts to educate the public about the Connecticut witch trials through her written work and exoneration efforts.

Beth's first historical novel is *One of Windsor: The Untold Story of America's First Witch Hanging* (2015) which tells the tale of Alice 'Alse' Young and the beginnings of New England's colonial witch trials. *The Salty Rose: Alchemists, Witches & A Tapper In New Amsterdam* (2019) won the literary prize in Genre Fiction (2020) from IPNE (Independent Publishers of New England). It explores John Winthrop the Younger's influence on stopping the witch trials in Connecticut and gives an insider's view of the takeover of the Dutch colony of New Netherland and the Hartford Witch Panic. Her latest novel, *Between Good & Evil: Curse of the Windsor Witch's Daughter* (2024) is a sequel to *One of Windsor*. Beth also co-authored the research article "Between God and Satan: Thomas Thornton, Witch-Hunting, and Religious Mission in the English Atlantic World, 1647-1693." which appeared in the Fall 2022 edition of *Connecticut History Review* (61:2) with historian, Dr. Katherine Hermes.

Since 2015, Beth has been educating the public about the Connecticut witch trials through lectures, articles, and social media. She has been advocating for exoneration through websites and collaborations. In 2016, she co-founded CT WITCH Memorial with Tony Griego to raise awareness about the witch trials before obtaining exoneration for trial victims Alice Young and Lydia Gilbert in Windsor in 2017. She is also a co-founder of the

Connecticut Witch Trial Exoneration Project that helped to pass Resolution HJ 34 in the Connecticut General Assembly in May 2023 to acknowledge Connecticut's witch trial victims.

Beth lives in New England where she enjoys spending time with her family and many pets. She frequently kayaks, gardens, and travels. Her next novel will take readers outside of New England in an early twentieth century immigrant story. Stay tuned!

Website: *www.oneofwindsor.com*
Email: *oneofwindsor@yahoo.com*
Facebook: *https://www.facebook.com/bethmcaruso/*
Linkedin: *https://www.linkedin.com/in/beth-m-caruso-2122324b/*
Instagram: *https://www.instagram.com/one_of_windsor/*

Acknowledgments "Team Alice Jr."

I would like to acknowledge the skilled team that made Between Good & Evil come to life. Copy-editor Christina Carmon approached the task of perfecting this novel with enthusiasm, attention to detail, and rock-solid support. Accomplished artist Sue Tait Porcaro was in tune with the vibe of Alice Jr.'s story from the first time I described it and quickly created a beautifully detailed cover that captured the essence of the story. Book designer and typographer Patrick Schreiber brought an amazing array of expertise, flexibility, and graciousness which allowed for just the right end result. I owe a huge debt of gratitude to them for their talents and assistance with this project.

Beta Readers serve a crucial purpose in the development of any novel through their comments regarding an author's first drafts of their novel. Susanne Aspley, a writer herself, has helped me with all three books in the series and has given crucial advice and always provided the encouragement that only a good friend can give. Steve Watton, a reader for both this novel and The Salty Rose, is able to both conceptualize the big picture and give valuable advice. Liz McAuliffe cheered me on during all three novels and caught the things I originally missed as well as offered valuable suggestions. Brianna Dunlap's critiques and understanding of this time period have helped me to think in more detailed and balanced ways. I appreciate Mary Hotaling's intelligent contributions and generosity to all three novels. Sadly, Mary passed on during this process. She is greatly missed. Lastly, Josh Hutchinson and Sarah Jack, the dream team at the *Witch Hunt* podcast were able to provide an even broader perspective through their wide understanding of witch hunts.

Special thanks to the hundreds of Alice Young descendants who have reached out to me over the years and were insistent that I would find it within me to write about Alice Jr. one day. Your support, appreciation and belief in me has kept me going and enabled me to find a deep place of empathy to be able to tell this latest story.

And last but not least, thank you to my family and friends for their interest and support in this decade-long project. This has been a journey full of both tears and laughter which has brought me profound satisfaction in building awareness about the history of the Connecticut witch trials.

Modern Witch Hunts

I'd like to recommend the organization End Witch Hunts which I am a member of to all my readers. This is a message from the organization:

Today in the twenty-first century, the world is still not free from witch hunts. In addition to the metaphorical witch hunts in which groups are labeled as the "Other", real witchcraft accusations with violent ends remain a problem today. With recent cases in more than sixty nations spread across the globe, harmful practices related to accusations of witchcraft affect thousands of innocent people every year. Victims are subjected to stigmatization, banishment, torture, and even death.

End Witch Hunts employs a three-pronged approach to the problem, focusing on knowledge, memory, and advocacy. Through traditional media, social media, web sites, blogs, literature, and a podcast, the organization shares lessons from past witch-hunts and raises awareness of modern-day witchcraft accusations and the associated violence. The organization also works with groups to exonerate and memorialize past victims and amplifies messages from local advocacy groups and encourages leaders to make the necessary changes to end witch hunts.

To learn more, visit https://www.endwitchhunts.org and listen to the organization's official podcast Witch Hunt, formerly known as Thou Shalt Not Suffer: The Witch Trial Podcast. You can help by sharing what you learn with the people in your life, volunteering, or donating. No contribution is too small.

Written Works by Beth M. Caruso

Connecticut Witch Trials Trilogy by Beth M. Caruso:
1: *One of Windsor: The Untold Story of America's First Witch Hanging* (2015)
2: *The Salty Rose: Alchemists, Witches & A Tapper in New Amsterdam* (2019)
3: *Between Good and Evil: Curse of the Windsor Witch's Daughter* (2024)

Original Research

Katherine A. Hermes and Beth M. Caruso, "Between God and Satan:
Thomas Thornton, Witch-Hunting, and Religious Mission in the English
Atlantic World, 1647-1693," *Connecticut History Review* 61, no. 2
(Fall 2022): 42-82.

www.ingramcontent.com/pod-product-compliance
Lightning Source LLC
Chambersburg PA
CBHW060704190726
48289CB00002B/532